"Mmmmmm, Sean," I moaned, but I wasn't ready to give in so soon.

I wanted to see how much Sean wanted me, so I made him wait.

"Slow down, baby, and let's dance."

He was disappointed; I saw it in his eyes. He was ready to get into me, but I needed to see how much control he was willing to let me have. I kissed him and slid off the dresser.

He grabbed my hand as I tried to get past him. "Uh-uh, baby, come here," he whispered in my ear.

I turned to him, kissed him on his lips, and with puppy eyes I said, "I want to dance, Sean."

He pulled me close and we slow danced. When the song ended, I pulled smoothly away from him and headed back to the leather settee and my Moscato.

Sean walked into the room with his shirt off.

I couldn't keep my eyes off him as he walked to the bar and picked up his drink. I tried not to stare, but I couldn't help myself. I wanted Sean to want me, but he'd flipped the script.

Also by Karyn Grice

What Happens in Vegas, Stays in Vegas

No Strings Attached

KARYN GRICE

Pocket Books   Karen Hunter Publishing

New York   London   Toronto   Sydney   New Delhi

Pocket Books
A Division of Simon & Schuster, Inc.
1230 Avenue of the Americas
New York, NY 10020

Karen Hunter Publishing
A Division of Suitt-Hunter Enterprises, LLC
P.O. Box 692
South Orange, NJ 07079

This book is a work of fiction. Names, characters, places, and incidents either are products of the author's imagination or are used fictitiously. Any resemblance to actual events or locales or persons, living or dead, is entirely coincidental.

First Karen Hunter Publishing/Pocket Books paperback edition July 2012

POCKET and colophon are registered trademarks of Simon & Schuster, Inc.

For information about special discounts for bulk purchases, please contact Simon & Schuster Special Sales at 1-866-506-1949 or business@simonandschuster.com.

The Simon & Schuster Speakers Bureau can bring authors to your live event. For more information or to book an event contact the Simon & Schuster Speakers Bureau at 1-866-248-3049 or visit our website at www.simonspeakers.com.

Manufactured in the United States of America

10 9 8 7 6 5 4 3 2 1

ISBN 978-1-4516-7257-2
ISBN 978-1-4391-6709-0 (ebook)

Dedicated to

Ivory and Mattye Truly, my loving parents

I wish you were here

Acknowledgments

I thank God for the gift he has given me to share with you.

My journey as a writer has been interesting, so far. It didn't begin the day I started writing; it began many years earlier. I never would have guessed in a billion years that writing would be a part of my life, but it is and I love it!

I wish my parents were here so I could thank them for giving me the right blend of freedom and supervision, which has created some very memorable experiences for me. I'm happy to have my sister, Eva Robinson, and my brother, Kevin Truly, in my life and I want to thank you for your support.

I owe my husband, Stan, more date nights than we've had. Thank you for standing beside me during this journey; thankfully you sometimes understand how time-consuming writing can be.

Eric, thank you for your support. I hope you decide to do something with your gift. Thank you Kristyn for being my cheerleader, encouraging and believing in me every step of the way. Crystal, you've suffered through my rattling on and on about nothing. Thank you for listening and believing in me.

Deanna Cowart, thank you for doing everything

you could to see my first book published. I must also thank all of my readers: (the originals) Eva Robinson, Tina Noble, Deanna Cowart, Kim Grice (IL), and Patricia Smith; (second crew) Kim Grice (IL), Kim Grice (TN), Alethea Funk, Monica Macklin, Lisa Briscoe, and Amy Peterson for taking the time to read my stories and for giving me honest feedback.

Kim Grice (IL). You have read everything I've written and you have enthusiastically given me rave reviews. Your encouragement and support means a lot to me.

Rene Williamson, Letric Watson, Angel Elliott, and Annette Harrison, thank you for being a part of my inner circle. Our email conversations keep me sane and we sure do have a great time when we get together. Marla DeLoach, thanks for reading for me and we miss you in warm, balmy Chicago. Well, it probably seems warm and balmy to you now since you've moved to Fargo. Thank goodness for email and Facebook, huh?

Deniera Burks . . . I'm so lucky to have you on my side. You are a graphics, marketing, social-networking dynamo and that's secondary to your other talents. You've created so many beautiful items that bling . . . you're the Bling Queen! Luxe Candles, Diva Dana's, Crystal Tee's, jewelry, furniture. It seems as though everything you touch turns to BLING. Thank you for believing in me and helping me with all of the things that I've been clueless about.

Zondra Hughes. Mz. Multitalent herself. You are one of the best editors and writers around. I'm so excited to take this journey with you. Thanks for being the friend that I need and the guiding light to push me forward.

Von Kauwaceon—I'm gonna need a new outfit for my close up, LOL! Hook me up, Rico!

Kim Grice (TN). I know you're not a regular reader so that makes your support extra special. Thanks for our weekly talks; you keep me encouraged.

Claudette Wilson. You're so sweet. I couldn't ask for a nicer sister-in-law. Thank you for your encouragement; it means a lot to me.

LeJoye Wilson. You crack me up. South Coast Plaza, here we come. Let me know when, Joye.

Al Wilson. Thanks for your support and for making the trip to New York with us. The next time I drag you across the country, we'll have more to talk about afterward.

Stacey Rodgers, thank you for your support. Our love of writing has brought us closer and I'm thankful for that. Shouldn't you be writing something?

My editor, John Paine. Thank you for teaching me character development. You've created a monster! I liked writing before, but now I love it. Thanks for your guidance and encouragement.

Last, but not least, Ms. Karen Hunter. Thank you, Karen, for believing in me. I'm not sure where I'd be right now if you hadn't taken me under your wing.

I'm thankful for the opportunity you've presented me with, and I'm very happy to be able to say that Karen Hunter is my publisher!

Thanks to everyone who has been with me during this journey!

No Strings Attached

1

Jasmine

I was steaming as I paced back and forth behind the sliding cell door. I was waiting to be released. I couldn't believe the mess I was in, and over a damn man. I had been charged with assault and then thrown in a cage at the Second District police station in Chicago.

The holding cell was overcrowded and the caged women were on edge. Ashley, my business partner, needed to hurry up and bail me out. There was an argument between two women about a jailhouse problem breaking out, but that didn't matter to me. I had my own issues to deal with. As I continued to pace impatiently, I tuned out their cussing and the wretched smell in the cell, and reflected on how the hell I got put in there.

I had gotten up early that morning. I had lots of errands to run, plus I wanted to clean my house. I hadn't had a chance to do a deep cleaning in weeks. My four-bedroom, two-bath home had a lot of space for one person, but I enjoyed every foot. I planned to remake my bed in the bright red, nine-hundred-thread-count sheet set I had recently purchased. I thought it would bring some sizzle to my bedroom.

After slipping on a pair of sweatpants and a T-shirt and pulling my hair into a ponytail, I had pulled the linens off my bed and headed to the basement to get the washer started. Before going to sleep last night, I had made a to-do list.

Since I owned a Lexus dealership, my car was important to me. I couldn't be seen in a dirty car. Oh no. So as soon as I put a load in, I was going to get my car detailed. While climbing the stairs from the basement, I heard my doorbell ring. I wasn't expecting anyone, and I wasn't in the mood for company. I was hoping it wasn't the Jehovah Witnesses. I was usually pretty nice to them, but today I had too much work to do.

I was surprised when I opened the door and saw Tyrone standing on my front porch. Tyrone was one of a few men that I dated on occasion. We didn't have a serious relationship, but he was fun to hang out with.

He was fidgety and seemed frightened. That didn't improve my mood any. I opened the screen door to hear what he had to say. He leaned in and whispered, "Jasmine, I told my wife that I was coming over here to tell you that it's over. If you can just go along with what I'm saying, I can get this done and then we can continue to see each other."

I almost laughed but was able to contain it. This was the first I'd heard of any wife. Plus, Tyrone wasn't all that for me to act a fool over in front of my neighbors. I figured he'd had a moment of temporary insanity if he thought that was going to happen.

He stood there with a stupid grin on his face as he waited for my response. I looked past him and saw his wife standing at the curb with her head wrapped in a bandanna. Her outfit told me that she was ready for battle: tattered jeans, gym shoes, and a T-shirt tied at the waist. She stood staring at me with her hand on her hip. Was that Vaseline on her face? I wondered.

Tyrone had brought his problem to my house. How was that right? I glared at him for a few seconds before reaching behind the door for the aluminum bat that I kept for emergency purposes.

"Can I see you tonight?" he mouthed.

With another look at his wife standing at the curb, something inside me snapped. I took the bat from behind the door and stepped out onto the porch. My first swing hit Tyrone on his left arm as he threw it up in a defensive position.

"What are you doing, Jasmine?" he said, as he retreated down the stairs.

I quickly followed and swung the bat at him again.

"You played me," I said as the second blow hit him in the back.

I saw his wife on her cell phone, but she didn't come near us. After the third swing, Tyrone ran to his wife, screaming.

"What is wrong with you, Jasmine?" he shouted back at me.

I stopped on the bottom step and yelled, "Nothing is wrong with me! But you'd better get away from my house before something seriously wrong happens to you!"

I was turning to go back inside when I saw a squad car roll around the corner. One of my neighbors must have called, because the officers arrived so fast.

After closing the door, I watched out my living-room window as Tyrone and his wife had an animated conversation with the officers. "Shit," I said quietly. If he could lie to his wife like that, there was no telling what he would say to the police. When I saw the officers sternly marching to my door, I knew I was in trouble. I could see the evil look on Tyrone's wife's face. They were pressing charges. I waited for the bell to ring.

As I expected, I was arrested.

That was how my day began.

I heard the guard walking toward the holding pen. He stopped in front of the cell door and called, "Jasmine Taylor."

I quickly approached, waiting to be set free. Officer Wilson was his name, according to his tag. I was usually turned on by a man in uniform, but not today. Standing behind bars had drained every sexy emotion out of me.

Officer Wilson opened the door. "Jasmine Taylor?"

"Yes."

I walked down a long, dimly lit hallway with Officer Wilson following close behind. We stopped at another set of cell doors.

"It will be a few minutes," he said.

"Do you have the time?" I asked politely.

He looked at his walkie-talkie. "It's three forty-five."

"Thank you."

We waited for a few minutes before the doors were unlocked and we had clearance to pass through. After retrieving my sack of personal belongings, I was released. This was my first visit to a police station, and I hoped it would be my last.

I was very happy to see Ashley. She had been waiting for more than two hours for my release in the crowded station lobby with lots of angry people. The entire incident was a nightmare that I never wanted to live again.

I saw Ashley from a distance. Her height made her look out of place. She was five-ten, slender, and always dressed well. When I approached her, she hugged me and said, "What happened?"

A flash of my former anger at Tyrone came back to me.

"We can talk about it when we get in the car," I said.

Ashley's silver RX350 was parked a few blocks from the station. Once inside the car, I said, "Thank you for coming down here to get me. I can't believe I was arrested."

"What happened?"

I fastened my seat belt, cracked the window, and told her how everything had played out.

Ashley looked like she wanted to laugh, but instead she asked with concern, "Is he crazy?"

By this time I was seeing the humor in the situation myself.

"I may have beaten the crazy out of him. His punk-ass wife showed up dressed for battle, but instead of stepping to me, she pulled out her cell and called the police. This man was trespassing on my property and I get charged with assault!"

Ashley laughed with me. She knew just about all my secrets. She didn't judge me and was a good listener. When we arrived at my house, I reimbursed her for the bail money. After making sure that I was okay, she headed home.

Ashley was my partner in Taylor & Daniels, a successful Lexus car dealership in Chicago. Like me, she was single, going on thirty. As I entered my home, I eyed the bat posted up behind the front door and shook my head. I needed some stability with the men in my life. My last long-term relationship had ended in disaster two years ago, and I had been running wild ever since, dating multiple men and not making a commitment to any of them.

After closing the door behind Ashley, I leaned against it and closed my eyes. My original plan had been to clean the house, but that was the last thing I wanted to do with the remainder of my day. First and foremost, a hot bubble bath.

My home, located in Hyde Park, a historic

neighborhood in Chicago, was built in the late 1800s. The area was culturally diverse and I enjoyed the short walks to my favorite shops. A huge selling point was the stone fireplace in the master bath.

When I bought the house, it needed a lot of work. I hired an architect to redesign the floor plan. There were originally five bedrooms, but I knew it would be just as fabulous with four, and I wanted to increase the square footage of the master suite.

I decided to restore instead of replace. I hired a friend from high school whom I'd kept in touch with over the years to head the project. He was able to preserve most of the original woodwork and fixtures. The hardwood floors were restored and stained. The fireplace was the focal point of my dream bathroom, and I also loved the depth of the vintage claw-foot bathtub. The Carrera marble tiles on the floor were heated and the same tiles were used on the walls, which were laid in a subway fashion. The space was perfect for me to unwind and relax.

Once the tub was full with warm bubbly water, I lit four scented candles, trying to get the smell of jail urine out of my mind before climbing into the bath. My body relaxed as I slid to the bottom of the tub, head and all. When I came up for air, I dried my face and hands, turned on the CD player, and listened to Jill Scott's latest. I put the bath pillow under my head and relaxed. I had been seeking comfort, and I had found it.

After my bath, I headed for the kitchen to fix a salad. I had all my ingredients on the counter when my phone rang.

"Hello?"

"Hey, Jasmine," said a familiar voice. "This is Sean. How are you?"

Instantly, I was in a better mood. Spending time with Sean always helped me forget my troubles.

"I'm doing all right. I haven't talked to you in a while. Where have you been?"

"You know me, I've got a lot going on," he said. "But you also know I'm only a phone call away and always thinking about you. I need to see you. Do you have time for me this evening?"

"I've always got time for you, Sean."

"Great! Ray Cash is in town and he wants us to join him and his date for dinner at the Signature Room. Are you up to it or did you want to keep me to yourself?"

I giggled at the sly tone in his voice. "I finally get to meet Ray."

"Have you wanted to meet him before now?"

I didn't want him to think that I was starstruck, so I said, "I knew that you were friends and I just wondered why we had never met. I've met most of your friends from Detroit except him."

"I guess you two have never been at the same place at the same time with me, but you both are here now, so we'll do the introductions tonight. All right, baby?"

"Yes, all right." Still, I wasn't willing to give up the

other option. "I guess I can share you for a little while, but after dinner, you're all mine, right?"

"Yes, all yours." His voice was as smooth as a purr. "I'll pick you up. Eight o'clock okay?"

"Yes. Sounds good."

I put my salad fixings away, grabbed a few Wheat Thins, and darted to my bedroom to look for something sexy to wear.

I hadn't told Sean about my earlier incarceration because I didn't want him to know anything about my life with the other men I saw. When I was with him, it was just us, no one else.

Of all the men I dated, Sean was the only one who had my heart. I was in love with him, though I didn't dare say anything. I didn't want to drive him away.

Sean was a very successful music producer. We saw each other often, although Sean lived out in Malibu. He wined and dined me when he came to town. I'd visited him at his home in California and his condo in New York on many occasions. We'd spend a week together or sometimes we'd just be together for a night. I knew he had other women and he knew I saw other guys. Our arrangement worked for both of us—or at least it had until lately. Now I wanted more.

Sean and I had met a little more than two years ago, when he walked into my dealership to buy a car for his aunt Frances. He was in town, working at one of the local studios. I was sitting in my office with

Ashley, going over the inventory, when I saw him on the showroom floor with Martin, one of our salesmen. I couldn't concentrate because I couldn't keep my eyes off him. Ashley turned to see what was distracting me.

"Girl, why don't you just go out there and introduce yourself?"

"Am I that obvious?"

"Uh, yeah," she said. "Go on. I'll finish this up."

"How does my hair look?" I asked, trying to fluff it up. "I knew I should have gone to the shop yesterday like I planned."

"Jasmine, you look fine."

Although my hair wasn't exactly how I wanted it, my dress was perfect. I wore a charcoal Chanel pencil dress. I quickly changed into my leather pumps to complete the outfit.

"It's time to get over Nicco and move forward."

"I'm over Nicco, Ashley," I said, annoyed. I stood and straightened my dress. "Is this dress too tight?"

"Yes, but what's new about that?" She chuckled.

I tugged down the hem, getting it just so. "All right. Wish me luck."

Sean was sitting inside one of the floor models when I walked up to the car.

"Good afternoon," I said in my sexiest voice. "Are you finding everything to your satisfaction?"

Sean looked up at me. He didn't show any interest as he said, "Yeah, I want to test-drive this car."

I turned to Martin, who was standing nearby, and asked, "Can you have one of the porters bring around a demo?"

"Sure, Jasmine." Martin moved closer and made the introduction. "Sean, this is my supervisor, and the owner, Jasmine Taylor. She'll take good care of you."

"All right, thanks," he said.

Sean remained in the car, messing with the controls on the dashboard. I was a little surprised that he hadn't gotten out of the car to get a better look at me.

I took the opportunity to check him out from head to toe. He wore a pair of Lucky Brand indigo jeans, a striped button-down shirt, and a nice pair of leather shoes. I think they were Prada. His jewelry was expensive but not too showy.

"So, Sean, right?" I said, breaking the trance the Lexus had on him.

"Yeah," he said. "Hey, do you have this car in black and in stock?"

"I'll check my inventory. Please excuse me."

As I headed to my office, I saw Sean staring at me through the glass. That was a little more like it.

When I walked into my office, Ashley said, "Well?"

"Nothing so far," I said happily. "I may have to work to get this one's attention."

"You need to work for it for a change," she said, smiling.

Checking my computer, I saw that we did have a black LS430 in stock. When I stepped back onto the showroom floor, Sean was leaning against the car, waiting for me.

As I walked to him, my low-cut, form-fitting dress clung to my hips, and this time I had Sean's full attention.

"Okay, Sean. It's your lucky day. We have a black LS430 in stock, fully loaded. Would you like to see it?"

"Yes. Thank you. Jasmine, right?"

"Yes, Jasmine."

"Nice to meet you," he said, shaking my hand. His touch was electric, tingling all the way up my arm. It was lust at first touch.

Besides being well dressed, Sean was handsome. He was slightly over six feet tall, his complexion was medium to dark brown, and he had brown eyes and a beautiful smile.

I saw the shiny new LS430 waiting at the front door. Martin handed Sean the keys and Sean looked at me. "After you."

I smiled and headed for the door.

He walked around the car, getting a better look at all the great features. We climbed inside at the same time. Sean continued to examine the controls on the dash and check out the luxury features that came standard in this model.

"This is a nice car," he said.

"It's one of our bestsellers." We closed the doors, fastened our seat belts, and I directed Sean to Lake Shore Drive so that he could try out the car on an open road.

After we were on the road for a few minutes, I said, "So how do you like the ride so far?"

"It's beautiful. It accelerates in what?"

"Zero to sixty in 5.4 seconds, and even better, a quarter mile in 13.9 seconds. Top speed hits one hundred thirty miles per hour, but I'm sure you'd never have a need to drive that fast."

He looked at me and smiled in amusement.

"The 4.6-liter V8 generates three hundred eighty horsepower, and three hundred sixty-seven pound-feet of torque contributes to its impressive acceleration. You see how fast we took off."

"Yeah, it's pretty fast."

"The performance improvement is almost entirely a result of the six-speed automatic. First gear is lower, and second, third, and fourth gears are closer together, all of which makes for a quicker launch and quicker acceleration."

I touched the gearshift and added, "You can manually control shifting, though we found it usually best to put it in Drive and let it do its job. The V8 and six-speed automatic deliver strong acceleration for quick passing and highway merging."

He was shaking his head, acknowledging how impressed he was with the car. "Plenty of leg room and ceiling room, too. I see you know your business. I'm impressed," he said. "I was hoping to have the car delivered to my aunt. Is that something that you can do?"

"It certainly is, Mr. Williams. When we finish your paperwork, we'll include delivery instructions."

"Thank you, Jasmine." He looked extremely pleased. "Thank you very much."

Sean took me to dinner that night, and we have been seeing each other ever since.

We met while I was transitioning out of a long-term relationship that had ended in disaster, and I was on a serious anti-man campaign. Sean softened my heart toward men in general and offered me a relationship that I could handle at that time. I was extremely attracted to him from the beginning, but my heart was too fragile to handle any more disappointment from a man. I proposed a relationship where we didn't answer to each other and saw each other when we could. He readily agreed. I guess that plan backfired—because he seems to be very happy with our arrangement and by now I'm in love with him.

Still, Sean's phone call put me in a good mood. Spending time with him tonight would give me an opportunity to wear a new dress that a local designer made exclusively for me.

No matter what we were to each other, I wanted his eyes to light up when he saw me.

2

My name is Sean Anthony Williams. I'm thirty-four years old and one of the most sought-after music producers in the business. I was in Chicago, working with one of the top R&B artists in the industry, an old friend named Raymond Cash. I'd known Ray since we were kids in Detroit. Ray was a natural ladies' man. He had girls chasing him and fighting over him even as far back as seventh grade. The reason girls would ever talk to me and Jimmy was to get close to Ray. We knew that and took advantage of it.

Once we entered high school, though, I started pulling just as many women as Ray did on my own. The ladies were drawn to my creativity. I was DJing at a party somewhere in Detroit every weekend.

Not only was I a great DJ, I produced Ray's first CD when he was seventeen. His career and mine took off once that CD hit the charts.

Ray had called me a while back to insist that I produce his next CD. We hadn't worked together in years, and I found myself looking forward to hanging out. The last time I saw him was at a party in South Beach last year. He almost got us arrested, just like every time we hung out. Jimmy vowed never to go out with Ray again, but I thought he was harmless.

I hadn't introduced him to Jasmine yet, but since he'd invited me and a date to dinner with him and his latest tomorrow night, I guess I'd get it over with. I couldn't tell Jasmine I was in town and had dinner with Ray and not invite her. It wouldn't be right because she's a fan of his. I'm not worried about him getting too much of Jasmine's attention, but I get tired of telling him to step off when he's around a beautiful woman. It's almost like he can't control himself.

He brought one of his girlfriends to town with him, but we're having dinner and a drink without the women tonight. I'm staying at the Sheraton and he's staying at the Peninsula. We agreed to meet at the restaurant at six o'clock. I had become very familiar with the city and suggested we eat at Monk's, on Lake. I was in the mood for a burger and I knew Ray would feel the same.

I was waiting in a booth when he came in. He started talking to the hostess and she was smiling in his face, letting him get close. I'm sure she had no idea who he was, but Ray had that effect on people—they were drawn to him. I rose and greeted him when he approached the table.

"Ray! Man, what's up?" I said as we hugged.

"Sean. It's good to see you, brother."

We sat down, ignoring the menus on the table.

"What's been going on, Sean? I haven't seen you at all this year. When was the last time you were in Detroit?"

"About a month ago. I go home a lot. I'm looking for a house in the area."

"Yeah. I have a condo not too far from my mom's. I like to have my own space when I go home." He winked at me, and I could fill in the rest of the story.

"Sometimes I stay at a hotel," I said, "but my own space would be better. I've seen a few spots and will have something soon. So anyway, tell me about this album. What is it about? Did you write the songs?"

"Yeah, man, you know I write my own shit." He'd come with a question in mind, though, and switched right to it. "When are you gonna get your own studio here? You do a lot of work out here. Why don't you have them come to your studio in Malibu instead?"

"Sometimes it's easier for us to work in our client's environment. Me and Jimmy are building a studio here in about three months."

Ray couldn't see where that made any sense. "What's with you and Chicago? You spend a lot of time here. Is there some chick?"

"I have friends," I said smoothly.

He wasn't fooled, though. "There must be someone you really like here because you spend as much time in Chicago as you do in Malibu. What's her name, man?"

I chuckled. I wish I hadn't, because Ray took it and ran with it.

"Ah, so it is a woman. What's her name, Sean? Are you bringing her to dinner tomorrow?"

"Damn, Ray." I held up my hands, to show I was busted. "Yeah, I'm bringing a friend to dinner tomorrow. Her name is Jasmine."

"Is Jasmine the reason you spend so much time in Chicago?"

"I have a lot of business here, you know that, but I enjoy spending time with Jasmine, too."

He laughed loudly. "Ah, shit. All right, Sean. I'm looking forward to meeting Jasmine."

I just shook my head. *Damn, I hope he doesn't make a mess tomorrow.*

3

Jasmine

When Sean arrived, I wasn't fully dressed. I slipped on a robe and made my way downstairs to greet him. When we came face-to-face, I was instantly reminded of why I was in love with him. I didn't show it, though. I didn't quite know how he felt about me, nor was I ready to find out.

I opened the screen door to let him inside. "Damn."

"What's up, baby, you're not happy to see me?"

"You know I'm happy to see you, Sean."

He opened his arms wide. "So what's up, give me some love."

As I slid into his embrace, I inhaled Giorgio Armani's Acqua Di Gio. Sean had all the qualities that I wanted in my man. He treated me with respect, had plenty of money, great looks, a wonderful personality, and sex with him was off the chain. He made me feel like I was the only woman in the world when we were together, but I knew better than that.

He hugged me tight around my waist and held me for a while. "I've missed you, baby. I've missed you more than you know."

I snuggled in a little tighter. "I've missed you too, Sean."

We stared at each other for a few seconds before he broke the silence. In a very soft voice he said, "You are absolutely beautiful."

That was so nice. I was still wearing my robe, so he meant just me, without the gift wrapping.

He quickly changed to a playful tone and held up a bag. "Hey, I thought you would be ready to go."

I kissed his cheek and said, "I'm sorry. Give me ten minutes and I'll be ready." I grabbed him by the wrist, the one holding my gift. "But first let's see what you brought me."

I carried the bag into the living room and sat on the sofa. Sean sat next to me and crossed his legs. He liked to watch me open his gifts. I looked at him, smiled, and dug inside.

"Ooh, Sean, Amy Peterson Chocolates!" He knew how much I loved those Heavenly Clusters. I was excited that he'd remembered where to find them, since they were a specialty item. That was one of the many things that attracted me to him. Sean made small things special because he took time to find the brands he knew I loved the most. I also found a jewelry box inside the bag. I opened the box and was speechless. Inside was a beautiful multicarat black-and-white-diamond tennis bracelet.

I threw my arms around his neck and said, "I love

it, Sean. Thank you so much. You know you don't have to shower me with gifts, don't you?"

He tapped my nose with his forefinger. "I know. I just like to see a smile on your beautiful face, and if diamonds and chocolate make you happy, then I want to be the one to make you happy."

I gave him a juicy kiss filled with lots of promise. "Thank you, Sean." I hopped off the sofa and said, "I'll be dressed shortly."

"All right. You got any beer?" he said as he headed to the kitchen.

"In the fridge," I replied.

I took the bag of goodies upstairs with me. As I put on my jewelry, I decided to wear the bracelet tonight. I ate a piece of candy while I finished dressing. At last I stood in the mirror and stared at myself. *This dress is sexy*, I told myself. It was black and white with a plunging neckline that accentuated my full C cups. I wore a sash around my waist and a pair of Gucci platform sandals with a peep toe. My feet were soft and smooth, ready to play footsie with Sean. I grabbed my purse and headed downstairs. Sean stood at the bottom of the stairs and stared as I walked to him.

He smiled broadly and said, "Sexy."

"Yeah?"

"Yes. You look great, baby."

He took my hand as I reached the bottom stair and I kissed him on his lips. "You look great, too."

When we went outside, I saw that Sean was driving a dark blue Audi A8 with a beautiful beige leather interior. "Hey, you're supposed to take me out in the Lexus," I joked.

"I'm not going to be a billboard for you," he joked back.

Once we were on the road, he asked, "So, are you getting serious with anyone?"

"No."

"Why not?" he said. "Look at you, why aren't you married?"

"If I were married, I wouldn't be able to spend time with you."

He feigned surprise. "You would let something like a husband come between us?"

I laughed and said, "If I ever get married, I'll have to learn to be in a monogamous relationship, wouldn't you agree?"

"Yeah, I guess so." He was quiet for a minute before saying, "Hey, I don't want Ray to be under the impression that you're available, Jasmine. Off-limits."

Something in his voice grabbed my attention. "Sean, I would never date a friend of yours."

"He's aggressive. If he thought there was a chance, he would take it."

A controlling edge had entered his voice, and I smoothed things over. "Don't worry about me and Ray. It's you who I want to spend my time with, okay?"

"Yeah, okay."

I didn't know what to make of that flare of temper. Was he threatened by Ray?

Neither of us said anything after that. We listened to the radio for the remainder of our ride. I kept glancing over at him. The streetlights kept playing off his chiseled features. He didn't give anything away.

When we arrived at the Hancock Center, the valet opened my door, but Sean rushed to my side of the car and extended his hand to help me out.

We walked hand in hand to the bank of elevators, heading for the Signature Room. The restaurant was located on the ninety-fifth floor, and we were lucky to get an elevator to ourselves. When the doors closed, Sean pulled me close and planted soft kisses on my face and lips without saying a word.

When the doors opened, we were greeted by a hostess who recognized Sean. "Your table is waiting, Mr. Williams. Did you want to wait at the bar for the rest of your party?"

"No, I don't expect them for a half an hour or so."

"Okay, please follow me." She ushered us to a private area. Pointing at the ice bucket, she said, "Your bottle of Krug Grande Cuvee, as requested."

"Thank you."

Once we were seated, Sean said, "I hope you're in the champagne mood, Jasmine."

I smiled and said, "We'll see what happens."

Sean poured a glass for each of us. "I wanted to spend a few minutes with you before Ray arrived, since I haven't seen you in a while." He leaned toward me. "I think about you too much and I couldn't wait to be with you tonight. Do you miss me when I'm away?"

He was being so romantic that I had to bite my tongue and look away. "Of course I miss you." I didn't want him to see my love for him shining in my eyes.

A waiter appeared to take our order, and I was happy for the interruption. Sean had never been so forthcoming about his feelings for me. I was afraid I would get caught up.

As the waiter loomed over us, he sat back in his seat. He told the waiter that we were expecting another couple soon and would place our orders once they arrived.

That interruption seemed to have broken the spell I had on him.

After the waiter left, Sean said, "So, what's been up? How's the business?"

I answered crisply. "Business is great. I think we'll have a record-breaking month. You know how it gets when spring rolls around. People are looking for the latest and hottest car, and since Lexus made some changes to the models this year, sales are off the charts!"

"Not to mention that you are the best saleswoman in the business."

I lifted my glass of bubbly. "Well, yeah, you're right about that."

We saw people at other tables stretching their necks, and a murmur of excitement filled the restaurant.

Sean sighed. "Ray must be here."

"Why do you say that?"

"He causes a commotion everywhere he goes."

I turned as Ray and his date approached the table. He walked ahead of her, but when she came into view, the first thing I noticed was how tight her red satin dress was. When Ray and I made eye contact, he winked at me. I smiled as Sean stood and said, "It's about time you got here!"

He turned to me and said, "Ray, this is Jasmine, a very close friend of mine. Jasmine, Ray and . . . ?" He waited for Ray to introduce his date.

Ray finally stopped staring at me. "Tammi, Sean and Jasmine. Have a seat, baby."

Tammi took a seat and Ray sat next to me. He turned to me and smiled shrewdly.

"Jasmine. So how do you know Sean? You know we go way back."

His appeal was electric, but it wasn't the first time I'd met a handsome man. "Yes, I know. Sean has told me that he's known you since you were children."

"Yeah, me and Sean share lots of secrets, ain't that right, Sean?"

"Whatever, man," Sean said, watching me. "Me and Jasmine were drinking champagne. What are y'all drinking?"

"I'm not in the mood for that." Ray summoned the

waitress to our table and ordered drinks for him and Tammi. "What about you, Jasmine? Is your drink okay?"

"Yes, thank you. There's still champagne in the bottle."

He pulled the bottle out of the bucket and said, "Krug! What's the occasion?"

Sean took the bottle and neatly put it back in the bucket. "It's always a special occasion when I'm with Jasmine."

"Oh!" Ray said, clearly understanding that Sean was serious about my being off-limits.

When the waitress returned with their drinks, Sean scanned the menu and ordered for both him and me. That was something he liked to do, so I always let him. He liked to be in control, and he handled everything so well that I felt comfortable and secure with whatever decisions he made for us. If he suggested something that I didn't have a taste for, which was rare, I'd just tell him what I wanted.

After Ray and Tammi placed their orders, I listened while Sean and Ray talked about what they were working on. When Sean saw that I was growing bored, he changed the subject.

Our meals arrived a short time later. We ate and talked about our businesses, families, and friends.

I quickly noticed that Ray seemed to think he was superior to Sean. I could only guess that it was because his role in the business was as a front man and Sean worked behind the scenes.

Sean didn't play into it, though. When Ray bragged about one thing or another he owned, Sean let him have the floor, knowing that he also had whatever toy Ray talked about.

As the plates were cleared, Sean moved closer to me. Like a stolen kiss, his hand crept under my dress and up my thigh. He whispered in my ear, "Are you staying with me tonight?"

He slid his hand between my legs and slipped his finger under my thong.

"Mmmmm, yes," I purred in his ear.

Oblivious to the heat being generated, Ray and Tammi were talking about an event they planned to attend once they returned to Detroit.

Feeling a new urgency to leave, Sean looked around in search of our waitress. He pulled out his credit card. "I'll see you in L.A. next week, right, Ray?"

"Yeah, I'll be there. I'm heading to Detroit in the morning." He turned to me and said, "Jasmine, it was a pleasure meeting you. I hope to see you again soon."

"It was nice meeting you, too, Ray. I'm sure we'll see each other again."

He smiled and said, "All right, beautiful, I look forward to it."

After he signed the check, Sean and I headed for the elevator. A large crowd had gathered, waiting to be seated.

"Would you like to go upstairs to the Signature Lounge and have a few drinks?"

"I've shared you enough." My words were laced with lust. "Let's go where we can be alone."

He paused ever so slightly. "Okay."

The elevator doors opened in front of us. Sean pulled me inside and pulled me into a corner. While kissing my neck, he whispered in my ear, "Mmmm, I miss you too much, Jasmine. Why don't you move to L.A.?"

The way Sean held me, feeling his warm lips on my neck, made me lose my train of thought. I just wanted to stay like that.

He stopped and said, "Did you hear me, Jasmine?"

I looked into his eyes. "You know I'm not moving, Sean, but I'll visit more often, okay?"

He kissed me on my forehead, and said, "Okay."

When the valet arrived with the car, Sean waited to open my door and help me inside before tipping the valet and getting in himself. He was the perfect gentleman, and I loved that about him.

His hotel wasn't far from the restaurant and that was good, because I couldn't wait. During dinner, I had fantasized about the last time we were together. I could still feel the warmth of his tongue as he teased my nipples and the way he caressed me, making me feel special, like our being together was more than sex to him. We held hands again as we headed to Sean's suite.

Once inside, Sean grabbed me, kicked the door closed with his foot, and pulled me into his arms. "I couldn't wait to be alone with you," he whispered.

"I've been thinking about making love to you again ever since the last time we were together."

"Then why did we go out?"

I stepped back and put my hand on my hip. "Excuse me! I'm worth more than sex, Sean."

He chuckled. "I know, baby, I'm sorry. Would you like a drink?"

"Yes, thank you."

I was drawn to the leather settee with oversized throw pillows at the bay window. The cushions were soft and seemed to suck me in as I sank into the corner and stared out at the lights from nearby Navy Pier. A few minutes later, Sean handed me a glass of wine. I took a sip of the Moscato and savored its sweetness. As I continued to admire the beautiful view, I could see Sean's reflection as he stood at the marble-topped wet bar, preparing a drink for himself.

I wondered if Sean ever thought about more than sex with me. As I sipped the wine, I shrugged. That didn't matter right now. If he did, he was good at hiding it. I headed to the bedroom, and within seconds Sean molded his body to mine as we walked in together.

"I love this dress. Did you wear it for me?" he said as he brushed his fingers across my hard nipples, showing through the fabric.

"Yes, just for you," I said as the Moscato helped lighten my mood.

He took my hand and said, "Dance with me."

He used the remote to start the stereo and soft jazz began to play. Sean pulled me close and planted warm kisses on my neck as he caressed my body. I was lost in the moment and had to stop myself from telling Sean that I was in love with him.

As we continued slow grinding, I bumped into the dresser and felt Sean's erection as he pushed himself between my legs. He lifted me up onto the dresser, and I opened my legs wider to give Sean the access he wanted. With one hand he pulled me close, and with the other, he moved the crotch of my thong to the side and slide his fingers inside me.

"Mmmmmm, Sean," I moaned, but I wasn't ready to give in so soon. I wanted to see how much Sean wanted me, so I made him wait.

"Slow down, baby, and let's dance."

He was disappointed; I saw it in his eyes. He was ready to get into me, but I needed to see how much control he was willing to let me have. I kissed him and slid off the dresser.

He grabbed my hand as I tried to get past him. "Uh-uh, baby, come here," he whispered in my ear.

I turned to him, kissed him on his lips, and with puppy eyes I said, "I want to dance, Sean."

He pulled me close and we slow danced. When the song ended, I pulled smoothly away from him and headed back to the leather settee and my Moscato.

Sean walked into the room with his shirt off.

I couldn't keep my eyes off him as he walked to the

bar and picked up his drink. I tried not to stare, but I couldn't help myself. I wanted Sean to want me, but he'd flipped the script.

I turned away, toward the window, but saw his reflection as he walked slowly to me. As he sat next to me he said, "What's up, Jasmine? You're not feeling me tonight?"

I smiled warmly. "Yes, I'm always feeling you, Sean." I climbed onto his lap, traced his lips with my finger, and said, "I just wanted to slow things down a little bit."

He kissed me long and hard and said, "Is this slow enough?"

"You're doing great." I stood and kicked my shoes off and walked to the bar to refill my wine.

I felt Sean come up behind me. He pulled me into his arms, and with one quick move he unhooked my dress at the neck and watched the top fall down to my waist. As Sean's mouth covered my breast, my knees buckled.

He caught me and said, "Come here." Sean took my hand and guided me into the bedroom. After helping me out of my dress and undressing himself, he pulled me down onto his lap and began kissing my face, down my neck, and with his tongue he teased my nipples. Each time his tongue touched me, I got wetter.

"Mmmm, Sean, that feels so good. Why are you teasing me?"

"I wouldn't tease you. Tell me what you need," he

said, though it sounded like he already knew the answer.

"I need you inside me."

"I can do that."

He laid me on the bed and planted warm, wet kisses all over my body. I scooted farther back onto the bed and said playfully, "Come here, baby."

Instead of coming to me, Sean stayed at the end of the bed and grabbed my right foot and pulled me to him.

"Baby," he said between kisses, "what are you up to? Why are you stalling?"

I couldn't stall any longer and he couldn't get any more passionate than he already was. I climbed onto his lap. "What do you need, Sean?"

He grabbed my butt with both hands and glided my wet pussy over his hard dick. His black silk boxer shorts kept him contained. He slipped his fingers inside me instead.

"Ahh," I moaned as I tightened my pussy around Sean's fingers in anticipation of his hard dick.

"Why are you teasing me, Sean?"

"Teasing you? I'm trying to please you, baby."

He turned me onto my back and we stared at each other without saying a word.

I didn't know what he was thinking, but I was happy because I was with the man I loved, giving myself to him, and his focus was on me. *That's enough for now*, I told myself.

Sean climbed above me and continued to plant kisses on my face and neck.

"Mmmm, that's good," I said.

He looked into my eyes and smiled as he kissed his way down my chest. I was getting excited as he moved closer to my now-throbbing vagina.

"Open your legs and let me in, baby."

I looked at the top of his head and parted my legs. I began to arch my back, wanting to feel Sean's tongue inside me, but he wasn't in a hurry. He kissed my inner thigh and I felt his finger as he traced the edges of my tattoo.

I opened my legs wider as Sean began to kiss my pussy like he'd been kissing my mouth. He darted his tongue in and out of me and he sucked my clitoris like it was my tongue. I didn't mean to, but I screamed as I reached an explosive climax.

"Is that what you need, baby?"

As I panted, trying to catch my breath, Sean pushed his hard dick inside me.

"Mmmmmm," I moaned loudly.

"Are you all right?" He paused.

"Don't stop, baby. That was the sound of pleasure."

He looked me in the eyes. "Have you missed me, Jasmine?"

"Yes, I've missed everything about you." I wrapped my arms around his neck as we kissed. "Let me do you."

He rolled onto his back and I climbed on top of him.

We kissed deeply for a few minutes before I reached between my legs and held Sean's dick until I felt him slide inside me. This time he was the one who groaned.

"Damn, Jasmine, you know your pussy is good, don't you?"

"That's what you tell me."

"I'm telling you the truth, too. Work that pussy, baby . . . ride that dick."

After I rocked him for a while, he tapped me on the leg and said, "Let me see that ass."

I rolled off Sean and got on my knees, and Sean crawled up behind me.

He pushed into me with a little force and I loved it. I pushed up against him as he began slapping my butt every now and then. Then he leaned over my back, grabbed on to the headboard, and started stroking hard and fast.

I closed my eyes, moving my body along with his until we both reached a desperate, gasping climax.

We collapsed in each other's arms, both of us sweaty, trying to catch our breath.

He kissed me and said, "Good job, baby."

I was a little hurt. His comment reminded me of how he felt about our relationship. I'd agreed to the original terms, but I was still offended that he still hadn't seen me as anything more than sex.

I turned away from him and closed my eyes. Sean snuggled close behind me and within minutes he was asleep.

4

Jasmine

I was a little distant the next morning. I told myself to stop trying to make something out of nothing. I didn't want him to leave, but I couldn't ask him to stay, either, because he would think I was getting too clingy.

I knew he had to get back to L.A., and I was running late for a staff meeting scheduled for eleven o'clock.

When I arrived at the dealership, I stopped in my office and grabbed my notepad. I rushed to the conference room, where everyone was waiting. I didn't want to waste any more of my staff's time, so I jumped right in.

I began by saying, "First, I want to congratulate Richard on his outstanding sales record this month. Everyone, please be sure to check out the new plaque on the showroom floor for Richard. He's our Salesman of the Month for the second month in a row."

Everyone clapped and congratulated Richard. The department heads then talked about what was going on in their areas. Kevin, our used-car manager, gave us an update, and Ashley discussed the numbers. Our meeting lasted a little over thirty minutes and all issues were addressed. That's the way I liked meetings to run.

After that, Ashley and I went into my office to talk. "What happened to you this morning? You're never late."

I sat behind my desk and turned on my computer. "Sean was in town and I was with him last night."

"You're so happy when you're with him. When are you going to settle down?"

I sighed and said honestly, "Sometimes I want to settle down, but then something will happen and I just . . . I don't know why I'm like this, Ashley. Maybe I need therapy."

She didn't buy that. "You don't need any therapy. You need to tell Sean how you feel about him and work on having a committed relationship with him."

I opened a file cabinet and started searching for a file. Ashley was queen of the committed relationship, because that's the type of person she was.

"He's not interested in me like that. Plus, things are great the way they are."

"You're not happy with things the way they are," she countered, "and he's probably just going along with it because he thinks that's what you want." She was warming to her argument. "Things change, Jasmine, and the only way you'll know how he feels is if you ask him. So why don't you just ask him?"

I turned to Ashley and said, "Because it would mess things up. We get along fine with things the way they are. He's good to me and we have a really good time together." I located the customer file at last. "Plus, if I start pushing him for more, he may back away."

"But you're in love with him. Why can't you tell him?"

My words were laced with sadness. "Because he's not in love with me and we agreed that there would be no strings attached, no questions asked."

Ashley wasn't satisfied with my answer. I knew that I would have to face my feelings and be honest with her. That was the reason why I confided in her so often. She made me be real about everything, and I loved that about her.

"What do you think his reaction would be if you told him how you felt?"

I returned to my desk. "I don't know and I don't want to find out right now."

"Is Sean still in town?"

"No, he left this morning." That idea put an extra edge in my voice. He was always leaving for someplace else. "And for the record, I don't think Sean will ever get serious with me. I'm just his girl in Chicago."

"And what is he to you?"

"Come on, Ashley," I said. She could be like a dog with a bone. Suddenly a thought came to me, to get her off this subject. "Guess who I met last night?"

"Who?"

"Ray Cash."

"What!"

"He and Sean grew up together, and they are here working on Ray's new CD."

She planted both elbows on the desk and put her head between her hands. "What was he like?"

"He looked as good as his pictures, if not better, but I found him to be a little full of himself." That reminded me of something, and I added, "Sean was acting funny, though."

"Funny how?"

"Kind of protective. I'd never seen him act like that before, so I don't know what to make of it."

Her face lit with a knowing smile. "He probably wanted his friend to know that you were special to him."

"He told me that Ray was off-limits to me. I would never talk to his friend." By now I had decided that Sean's jealousy might be a sign that he really cared for me. I wasn't going to think about that anymore, though. "On another note, did Tiffany get settled in?"

"Yes. She is in orientation with Marie. We are still taking her to lunch today, aren't we?"

"Yes, of course. Noon at Giordano's, right?"

"Yes. I made reservations."

I tried to think back. "I haven't seen Tiffany in three or four years, since high-school graduation. She's all grown-up now."

Ashley looked worried and said, "Yeah, well, she is that. Wait until you see how she's dressed."

I sat up and said, "Yeah, like what?"

Before she could respond, I saw Tiffany walking toward my office. Two of the porters in the distance were hawking her every move. She was dressed a bit sexy for the dealership, especially for the accounting department. Tiffany was lean and fit, large-breasted for such a small waist, with long runner's legs.

Tiffany was Ashley's younger half sister. Ashley's parents had divorced while Ashley was very young, and her father had remarried shortly afterward.

I stood as Tiffany walked into my office, beaming. "Jasmine!" she said. "It's been years since I last saw you."

I walked around my desk with outstretched arms. "Tiffany! Wow, girl, you have really grown up." We hugged. "Have a seat, and let's catch up a little bit. You know Ashley and I are taking you to lunch today, right?"

Her makeup was flawless, although a little heavy for daytime hours. Her eye shadow and lipstick, I noticed, were a perfect match for her burgundy blouse and skintight black skirt.

"Yes, I've been looking forward to it."

We talked about her duties at the dealership and promised to get caught up on personal stuff at lunchtime.

After Tiffany left my office, Ashley turned to me. "I hope this works out, Jasmine. My dad has been pushing for us to bond." She seemed doubtful about the idea. "You know I want this to work, Jasmine, and I want to give Tiffany a chance to grow with us, but, I don't know . . . she's different."

"She's young, Ashley. Let's just give her a chance, and I'm sure you two will have the relationship your dad has always hoped for."

She turned businesslike again. After all, we were hiring Tiffany. "All right. We should leave at eleven forty-five to make it to our reservation on time. We can walk."

"Okay. I'll be ready." I glanced out the window at the showroom. "The floor is crowded. Let's get out there and make some sales!"

My cell phone had been ringing off the hook while I was on the showroom floor with customers. I didn't recognize the number and they didn't leave a voice-mail message, so I turned my phone off.

I had been working with a return customer for the last hour, trying to close the deal on the new GS350 that he was interested in. Mr. Martin had bought his previous two Lexuses from us. His credit was A-1, so the transaction ran smoothly, and I was able to send Mr. Martin on his way.

I went into my office to return calls. While I dialed the number, my phone rang from that same number.

"Who is this?" she said.

I hate when people do that. "Who are you calling?" I said in an irritated voice.

"I'm trying to see who my man is calling."

Uh-oh, that didn't sound good. I closed my office door. "And your man is?"

"Dave Montgomery."

"Dave Montgomery? The fireman?" I asked. "He's never mentioned having a woman."

She responded hotly, "Yeah, well, Dave and I have been together for the past six years, we have two kids, and we are supposed to get married. I would appreciate it if you would stay away from my man."

This was news to me. "Girl, please. Why are you calling me? You need to talk to Dave about that. When he stops calling me, I'll stop talking to him."

She was furious. "Damn, bitch, what's up with you? I'm telling you that he's my fiancé and we have kids together, but as long as he wants to keep fucking you, you're game?"

Her tone had me riled up, and I wasn't backing down. "Look, sweetie, I've got some things to take care of, so I hope you can work things out with Dave." I hung up. My phone rang a couple of times after that, but I ignored it. I felt bad for Dave's girl and decided that I would cut him off. Still, why was she so spineless that she would confront me and not him?

At lunch I learned that Tiffany was extremely book smart but lacked plain common sense. Her future plans, she announced flatly, were to have a man support her. When I tried to tell her that she would better serve herself by being self-sufficient and making her own money, I saw her mood change.

"Well, Jasmine," she said, "I never had a problem getting what I want from a man, and if I can get what I need and don't have to work for it, why should I?"

I checked with Ashley because I wanted to see her response. Ashley seemed surprised to hear her sister speak this way.

"I'm just saying, Tiffany, that it's not smart to rely on someone else to take care of your needs. Man, woman, parent, or whomever. When you reach a certain age, you should be able to take care of yourself. If you happen to meet a wealthy guy and he wants to take care of you, fine, but don't make him being wealthy a reason not to have your own source of income."

"Um," she said, sizing up my glamorous looks. "I'm sure that you didn't get everything you have on your own. I'm sure a man was there to help you. If I recall correctly, you were dating that guy with all the money . . . uh, what's his name? Nicco! You were dating Nicco. I'm sure he has given you lots of expensive things."

The mention of his name was incredibly annoying. "I date lots of men who give me expensive things," I informed her, "but I don't depend on them or what they give me. Whatever gifts I get from my friends are just that, gifts!"

"O-kay." She turned completely away from me and said to Ashley, "So, are we still going shopping this evening? I need new clothes if I'm going to be working for a living."

I raised my eyebrows and thought, *Who is she to dismiss me like that?* I didn't like her already, but she was Ashley's baby sister. *I need to play nice,* I told myself. Once she started working for a living, she'd see what I meant.

I'd gotten settled back in the office when my phone rang again. It was Dave Montgomery. I laughed when I saw his name on my screen. The dog had been caught. "David, why am I not surprised to hear from you?"

"Jasmine, I'm sorry about the phone calls you received from my girl." He was a slick talker, one of the reasons I liked him. "She started going through my phone, calling every number she didn't recognize. I was hoping that she didn't scare you away because I still want to get with you when you have time."

I thought about how these men are no good. First, Tyrone trying to run a game on his wife, and now Dave. Was the man upstairs trying to tell me something?

"It's cool, Dave, but I can't have that kind of drama in my life. Why don't we take a break and see how things look for us in a couple of months?"

He didn't sound so slick when he replied, "It's like that, huh? All right, Jasmine. I'll check in with you later."

I was relieved when he conceded. I just wanted it over. "Thanks for understanding, Dave."

After that conversation, my thoughts returned to Sean. He wasn't like those brothers. He wasn't trying to run a game on me. The only problem was, he was honest about how many women were chasing him.

5

My pilot was on standby at Midway Airport for my flight home. I was actually surprised that I didn't get into any trouble while hanging out with Ray. Ray would be coming to Los Angeles to finish laying his tracks. He'd be sure to find trouble here, he always did.

During my flight, I thought a lot about Jasmine. After that romantic evening with her, she was consuming my thoughts. Her scent was in my skin, on my clothes. I could see her when I closed my eyes. I had to get out of Chicago before I asked her for more than I was ready for.

When we first got together, she told me how badly her relationship ended with her ex-boyfriend, Nicco, and how she wasn't interested in a relationship again. She just wanted to be friends. I was really cool with that because that's all I wanted, too. I began spending lots of time in Chicago working with artists, and I liked having a beautiful and smart woman on my arm when I needed a date for an event or to spend a quiet evening with.

To me, Jasmine was supersexy. That's the first thing I

noticed about her. But, although her fine-looking body got my attention, I quickly discovered how intelligent she was. We often joked about things, but I had a lot of respect for her opinion on many subjects. The more I checked her out, the more impressed I became. She ran her business professionally and was at the top of her game. She was a match for me in every key area of my life.

I had never before encountered a woman who intrigued me the way she did. I'd never met a woman that I wanted more than she wanted me. When I met a woman and she saw what I could do for her, she was mine. I didn't have to do anything. With Jasmine, she told me up front that I couldn't have any more of her than what she decided to give. That was a first for me, but I was cool with it.

The more time I spent with her, the more my thoughts about settling down began to change. I had never met anyone that I wanted to settle down with until I met her. Now, the fact that she could see other men was starting to bother me.

On impulse I called Jasmine to let her know how much I'd enjoyed spending time with her. I guess you could call it a moment of weakness, but during our conversation I invited her to spend time with me at my condo in New York.

After two years of being the friend, I'm ready to be her man. I need to see what's up with her. Sometimes I think she wants something more with me, but she rarely calls and doesn't seem to care about me when I'm not around. I'll soon see what's up. I'm going to bring it real with her and see where we stand.

Business usually helped keep my mind off her, so I went to the studio after dropping my bags off at home. Jimmy was in his office, listening to new music. He stopped the CD with the remote when he saw me.

"Welcome back, Sean."

"Thanks, man. How's everything?"

"Good. Everything is good."

Jimmy had been my best friend since first grade. We didn't meet Ray until we were in fifth grade, when he moved to Detroit from Flint.

Jimmy and I came to Los Angeles from Detroit together. We also ran a couple of businesses together.

"Did you get the itinerary for the New York thing that's coming up?" I asked him.

"Yeah, my assistant is taking care of my arrangements. How long do you think we'll be there?"

"I was thinking three weeks to a month, maybe longer. You'll have time to come home before the project is done. I know Lola will not be happy about you being gone and by yourself for three whole weeks."

"Yeah, thanks to Ray, but she knows what's up." He shook his head, thinking about how Lola would respond to the news. "She still be trippin' when I have to travel."

"Man, she knows how it is. This is a single man's lifestyle."

We'd talked about this before, and he came back at me. "Yeah, I guess it is, but I'd rather come home to a good woman who cares about me. You should think about that."

I immediately ran for cover. "Man, I ain't trying to be tied down to no one woman."

"Not even Jasmine?"

I pretended like his comment didn't bother me. Instead I went on offense. "Man, what happened to you? Why are you always trying to put me in the same predicament as you?"

"What you talking about, Sean?"

"You wish you could get pussy from a different beautiful woman every day of the week like I do. But instead of being happy for me, you trying to put my dick on lockdown like yours." I waved away the thought. "Let me do this, man. I'll give it up when I'm ready."

"All right, man. I'm just saying you talk about her all the time. If you love her, you love her. Why you got to fight it?" He looked me in the eye. "She's gonna make you turn in your playa card, man. I can see it coming."

Jimmy was smart. He'd known me for years and he knew when I was attracted to a woman. He'd never seen me at this level, though. He gave me an assessing look. "How long do you think she'll wait for you to grow up?"

"She's happy with our arrangement, Jimmy. I'm sure she's dating. I'm not stupid."

"Just remember what I said. She won't be available forever."

"Yeah, I know." Getting tired of the conversation, I headed out the door and went to my office.

I had numerous voice-mail messages. Six were from Brenda, an intimate friend. She made herself available when I needed her. She was beautiful, and I was definitely attracted to her, but she wanted more than I wanted to give. She knew that I wasn't interested in being tied down, but she kept trying anyway.

She had been calling relentlessly, wanting to work things out since I'd put the brakes on our arrangement a few days ago. I took care of Brenda in many ways, and I was really disappointed in her behavior. I'd bought her a BMW for her last birthday, among other things, and I made sure she had nice things. But that wasn't enough for her.

I called her at home. "What's up, Brenda? I saw that you called. What you need?"

"I hadn't heard from you. Don't you miss me?"

"Come on now, Brenda. I told you up front that I wasn't looking to get serious. But you started following me and questioning me, and I can't have that kind of drama in my life."

"But I love you, Sean."

I was composing an e-mail to a client while we talked. I really didn't want to hear her whining, but I wouldn't disrespect her. "Come on, Brenda, don't do this to yourself."

"Is it because of Jasmine?"

I stopped typing and said carefully, "What do you know about Jasmine?"

"I've been at your house when she calls, and you seem to forget that I'm even in the room when you're talking to her. What has she got that I don't have, Sean?"

That was a door I was not going to open. "It's not Jasmine. You've become too possessive, Brenda. You're a beautiful woman, and you deserve more than what I'm willing to give. I really need to concentrate on my career."

In a somber voice she said, "I did everything for you, Sean. I was always there when you wanted me. Anything you asked of me, I did, so that we could be together."

My voice rose a notch. "Brenda, I can't do this."

"Can we still get together sometimes?"

"You mean get together sexually with no strings attached, the arrangement we originally agreed on?"

She was crushed. "Yeah, Sean," she said quietly. "That's what I'm saying. I just want to be with you."

"All right, Brenda, I'll holla."

Ray called when he arrived in L.A. He wanted to hang out. I told Jimmy about our last outing in Chicago and how it had been drama-free.

"Why don't you join us for a drink later? Ray was cool the last time I saw him."

Jimmy thought about it for a few seconds and said, "All right, I haven't seen him in a while anyway. It might be good to see him." He had known Ray forever, too. "I'm still pissed, though, about getting arrested at that strip club. You know, he never apologized. Nothing!"

"Let it go, Jimmy. The charges were dropped."

"Yeah, but you didn't have to explain to your wife why you were arrested on an attempted-rape charge."

I almost laughed because I remembered that Jimmy had made me go home with him while he explained everything to Lola after I bailed him out. I'd had other plans that night and wasn't able to go out with them.

Ray was all ready at Bar Copa in Santa Monica when we arrived with some other guys from the studio. I didn't plan to stay long because I had a few tracks I wanted to remaster. He was talking to a couple of pretty girls, but Jimmy and I took seats on the other end. Jimmy was being really cautious.

Ray came over as soon as he saw us. "Jimmy! Man, what's up?"

"Ray."

He noticed how dry Jimmy was and said, "I know you ain't still mad about what happened last time."

"Hell yeah, I'm still mad. I got arrested," Jimmy said.

"The charges were dropped, right?"

Jimmy looked at Ray like he wanted to kick his ass.

To defuse the situation, Jimmy turned to the bartender and ordered a drink. Ray put his hand to his mouth in an attempt to cover a laugh. I was glad that Jimmy didn't see it, because he might have snapped. Jimmy went through hell with Lola after that incident.

I wasn't feeling up to partying, and I left the bar after an hour or so. Jimmy left with me because he didn't want to be there alone with Ray. It would be a while before Jimmy could get past that. Ray had the crowd hanging on his every word, especially the women. I could sense trouble brewing and I didn't want to be a part of it.

When I got home, I saw that Brenda had called my house eight times. I'd turned my cell phone off a couple of hours earlier because of her. I knew I had to let her go altogether.

The next morning, I started packing for my trip to New York. I knew it would take me some time to get it done since I would be gone for a while. I liked to keep the suitcase open in my closet so that I could put things inside when I remembered them.

Just as I headed out of the house, my cell phone rang. The caller ID said, L.A. COUNTY JAIL. I had a sinking feeling in the pit of my stomach.

"Hello."

"Sean, man, it's me, Ray."

"Ray! Why are you calling from the county?"

"Man, those two tricks I was talking to last night set me up on a prostitution charge. I need you to pick me up. They had me in here all night."

I was glad I'd gotten out in time. "Is there any media there?" I said quietly.

"Naw, not yet. If you hurry, maybe I can get out of here before they get wind of it."

"All right. I'm on my way."

I called Jimmy at the studio to let him know that I was running late. I didn't tell him about Ray because I didn't want to hear "I told you so" from him. I shook my head. I liked it better when Ray was home in Detroit. He was someone else's problem then.

When I got to the police station, camera crews were already there, hunting for a story. I saw Carla Daniels, a reporter that I've known for years.

"Sean!" she shouted when she saw me. She came rushing over. "What are you doing here? What's going on?"

"I'm here to pick up a friend."

"Oh yeah? Who?"

I said, "Seriously, Carla. It's a private matter. You'll have to work this one out on your own."

"Okay, Sean. It's like that, huh? Why haven't you called me?"

I wasn't falling for that trick. "One has nothing to do with the other. I haven't called you because I've been out of town. I just got back. We should get together for dinner one day soon."

She smiled seductively and said, "I'll wait to hear from you."

The deputies let me take Ray out through the back entrance. I was driving a Suburban with dark-tinted windows, so once Ray was inside the car, he was safe. I was driving him to where he had left his car when I said, "So, Ray, what happened this time?"

He was outraged. "Like I said, those chicks hanging all over me at the bar were cops. They set me up, man. Now I have a solicitation charge. Plus, I had a small amount of weed on me."

"What did your attorney say?"

He rubbed his head wearily. "It doesn't matter. It's gonna cost a fortune. I'm tried of paying all of these legal fees for all of this bullshit. It's something different every day. My attorneys get more of my money than me."

I turned partway toward him. "Well, stop fucking up, then. It's that simple."

"Fuck you, Sean. Shit happens."

"Yeah, but more to you than anyone else."

"Whatever."

The websites were stirring with gossip about Ray's arrest the following day, but the story didn't take off and I was very happy about that. But, over the next few days, Ray had a string of media following him, and he brought a lot of chaos to the studio. Finally, we agreed to finish in New York. He had to go in front of a judge and get permission to leave the state. I'm sure he was used to doing it, so I didn't see any problem with his getting the okay to travel.

I just wished we were going to Detroit.

6

Jasmine

Tiffany was getting to know everyone at the dealership. She proved to be very good with numbers and had a good working relationship with the other employees. I could sense that she didn't care for me since the comment I made to her at lunch, but it is what it is. I think I gave her some good advice.

She dressed too promiscuously for the office, and I was concerned about that because of all the attention she received from the porters and mechanics. She caused a stir whenever she entered a room. Not totally because of the way she looked, but because of her attire and personality. She openly flirted and took the guys' attention away from their work. If she wanted to be a slut on her own time, that was her business, but when it interrupted the flow of my business, then we needed to make some changes. I decided to talk to Ashley about it at Sisqo's this evening. It was Friday and we were going out.

After work, I headed home to slip into my "tiny" black dress. Ashley and I met at Sisqo's on Cottage Grove most Fridays to mingle with the other after-work people. Most were regulars, but lots of new faces showed up every week.

When I pulled into the parking lot, I saw Ashley's truck and a few other cars that I recognized. I knew it would be an interesting night when I saw NICCO 1 on the license plate of a black Escalade. Nicco was the man who broke my heart into tiny pieces and stomped all over it.

Nicco had been the love of my life, and for a few brief years my whole world had revolved around him. He helped me get the dealership off the ground, he advised me in my business, helped me purchase my house, and took me on vacations. Nicco took care of me—and mistreated me at the same time.

I was completely blindsided when he told me he was marrying another woman. I fell apart. I was home in bed for a week, distraught. I promised myself never to let another man get that close to me again.

For the first month or more after Nicco and I broke up, I struggled to function. It was the darkest time in my life. Even now the memory was bitter. Seeing him was the last thing I needed.

I was tempted to turn around and head back home, but I wouldn't allow that. He wasn't driving me out of one of my spots. Besides, my curiosity got the best of me.

What kind of drama was Nicco trying to bring by coming in here?

When I walked through the door and adjusted to

the dimness inside, the first face I saw was Nicco's. He was leaning against the wall in a corner of the small bar, facing the door with a drink in his hand. I knew what he was drinking, because he always drank the same thing: Absolut and cranberry juice. He was looking even better than I'd remembered. "Damn, why does he have to look so good?" I mumbled under my breath.

I wasn't giving away a thing, though. I adjusted my dress and found Ashley and a few other friends at the opposite end of the bar. I turned my back to him, shutting him out.

Ashley looked up and said in a nervous voice, "Jasmine, guess who's here?"

"I know," I replied calmly. "I saw his car in the parking lot. I wonder what he wants."

She was watching over my shoulder. "Well, you will get the opportunity to find out. He's on his way over."

He wasn't getting to me that easily. "I'll be back."

I sauntered over to another part of the bar and started a conversation with another friend. I soon felt Nicco's body heat as he stood behind me. I felt his breath on my neck when he whispered in my ear, "Jazz, baby, how are you?"

I slowly turned to face him. I kept my voice friendly. "Hello, Nicco. What a surprise."

"I've been missing you. Come and go for a ride with me. I need to talk to you."

Old habits die hard. I couldn't believe it myself

when I followed Nicco out of Sisqo's. I must be the stupidest woman on earth, I thought. He cheated on me, left me for that ugly heifer, I haven't seen him in years, and all he had to say was, "I need to talk to you," and I followed him like a puppy.

"You're looking even better than I remember," Nicco said as he walked behind me.

My tone stiffened up considerably. "Thank you."

He opened the passenger door and helped me inside. As he walked around the front of the truck to the driver's side, he kept his eyes on me. *What am I getting myself into?*

After climbing in, starting the engine, and getting situated, he grabbed my hand and said, "I've missed you, Jazz."

I yanked back my hand. "What did you need to talk to me about?"

He had big dreamy eyes and he used them on me full-force. "How stupid I was and how much I've missed you, and to ask you what I need to do to get you back."

I looked at him like he was crazy. "No, Nicco, we won't be getting back together!" I said, outraged. "Where is your wife? How do you think she would feel if she knew you were here with me right now?"

He put the truck in Drive and headed north on Cottage Grove.

"Pat and I are not together anymore," he told me, shaking his head. "I knew that I had made a huge mistake when I married her, and I asked her for a divorce. I've been out of the house for over a month." He paused. "You see, I wanted to get my situation in order before I came to you. I was planning to wait until my divorce was final, but I couldn't wait to see you any longer. It should be final in about two weeks. Is there any way you can forgive me and give us another chance?"

Oh, so I was the rebound choice. "Nicco, I've moved on from what we had. I'll never forget how awful you made me feel. I won't pretend that it didn't happen."

"That's not what I'm asking, Jazz," he said earnestly. "I'm asking you to give us another chance. I don't need your answer tonight. I'm asking if you could please give me a chance to show you how much I want to be with you."

My wall was up completely. I kept my eyes trained on the street ahead. "It's been two years, Nicco. You don't know me anymore."

"I know you very well, Jasmine. Let's talk and get to know each other again, okay?"

I didn't respond. Not a word. We rode in silence for a short distance until we reached a club called Jazzy. It was obvious that Nicco was a regular because everyone knew him.

The atmosphere was very relaxed, the DJ played soft jazz, and the decor was modern/contemporary. I was impressed, as I always was by Nicco's good taste. We walked to the bar. As I sat down, he went behind the bar and began to fix me a drink, rum and Coke on ice. They would allow him to do that? I was puzzled before he smiled and said, "This is my place, baby. Didn't you recognize the name?"

"You named this place after me?" I asked in disbelief. "I'm sure that didn't go over well with your wife."

The bartender came over and finished preparing my drink.

Nicco came from behind the bar and sat next to me. "Give me a break, baby. She won't be my wife too much longer. I thought 'Jazzy' said it all. This place is classy, just like you, and every time I pull up to the door, I think about you. I never considered any other name."

I was flattered, but I remained wary. "How long have you been in business?"

"Three months. It's been rough, but I'm confident that things will look up soon."

I followed his gaze around the place. "I like the atmosphere. It's a very nice club, Nicco."

He stood, extended his hand, and said, "Come on, let's grab a table."

I didn't take his hand, but I followed him to a table. We sat near the entrance, where we had a good view of the club. Shortly after we were seated, one of Nicco's employees came over and said that she needed to talk to him.

"Excuse me, Jazz, I need to take care of something."

When Nicco left the table, I took another look at the decor. I had already fallen in love with the huge mahogany bar with its beautiful marble top. Nicco had an eye for the finer things, and I knew the materials he used were top of the line.

While admiring the bar, through the mirror, I saw a nice-looking guy walk in the door. I turned to face him and we made eye contact. The handsome stranger smiled at me and took a seat at the bar.

I watched as the barmaid took his drink order. I didn't want to be obvious, so I turned away. A few minutes later, the barmaid set a fresh drink in front of me and said, "The good-looking guy at the bar said good evening." I smiled.

I saw the stranger stand as if he was coming to talk to me, but Nicco returned before the stranger took his first step.

Nicco looked slightly bothered by whatever drama he'd gone to oversee. "I see you got a fresh drink."

"Yeah."

He sat next to me and started in again. "Jazz, I'm sorry about everything that happened between us. I just want to start over with you." I was as still as a statue. "I realized early that I made a huge mistake, but Pat was pregnant and I didn't think it would be right to leave. I knew I couldn't come to you while I was still with her." He put his hand on top of mine.

I pulled my hand away once again and sat back in the seat, out of reach. "So you have a child?"

"Yes, a daughter. Her name is Maria." A father's proud smile came over his face. "She's one year old, and if it wasn't for her, I wouldn't have stayed as long as I did. I miss seeing her every day, but I do spend as much time as possible with her."

Out of the corner of my eye I saw the gorgeous stranger coming to our table. Nicco turned to see who I was looking at, and a huge smile spread across his face. He jumped up and they hugged.

"Man, when did you get here?"

"About fifteen minutes ago."

"Why didn't you say anything? Where were you?"

"At the bar. I didn't want to interrupt your conversation. It looked pretty serious."

"Man, I'm sorry. Michael, this is Jasmine. I know you remember me talking about her all the time," he said with a glance at me. "Jasmine, this is my friend Michael from New York. I know you remember me talking about him, too."

I looked him over quickly; I didn't want my stare to linger. He stood at least six feet tall, medium-brown complexion, low-cut fade, and nicely trimmed facial hair. From where I sat, he looked to be in excellent physical condition.

"So this is mystery Michael. I thought you were a myth."

"No, I'm real." His voice was silky, caressing me. "It's nice to finally meet you, Jasmine. I've heard so many wonderful things about you."

"It's nice to meet you, too, Michael."

"Come on, man, and join us." Nicco clapped his back and half shoved him into a seat.

As I watched Michael and Nicco interact, a touch of anger crept under my skin. *I bet he has heard so many wonderful things about me,* I fumed, *like how I sat by and let Nicco treat me like dirt.*

"You know what, Nicco?" I said. "I need to get back to my car. You two need the rest of the evening to get caught up."

"Jasmine, don't leave on my account," Michael offered. "I'll be here for five days. I'm sure I'll be tired of him by tomorrow."

I could tell by the way Michael looked me over that he knew quite a bit about me. "No, really, I need to get back." I turned around and said, "Nicco . . ."

"Yeah, baby," Nicco said unhappily. "Give me a minute, I need to take care of something. Y'all excuse me for a minute."

Once he was gone, Michael promptly sat across from me. "Are you and Nicco getting back together?"

"No."

"You sound sure."

"I am sure. I bet you know what went down with us. Tonight is the first time I've seen Nicco in two years." I waved toward the door. "He showed up at my spot and asked me to take a ride with him, and we ended up here." I wanted to emphasize where I stood, so that Michael wouldn't report anything back to Nicco. "I will always care about him, but I can't go back there."

"Does he know that you're not interested?"

"I told him that, but you know how Nicco is. He won't give up easily."

"Maybe persistence will pay off."

"No, it won't." Changing the subject, I said, "So, last I heard you were in a long-term relationship. Are you married, too?"

He smiled. "No, I'm not married. As a matter of fact, I'm very single. You?"

The sexual energy built between us instantly. "Yes, I'm solo all the way." We smiled at each other, and an idea popped into my mind. "Will you be with Nicco for the duration of your stay?"

"I can get away. What did you have in mind?"

I knew that what I was about to propose was wrong, but I was still hurt by the way Nicco had treated me. I had revenge on my mind. "Would you like to have lunch with me tomorrow?"

"Yes, I would."

I handed him my business card. "Call me and let's set something up."

When Nicco returned, he said, "Are you ready, baby?"

I cringed at hearing that. "Yeah," I said flatly.

"Come on, Michael, I need you to take a ride with me."

We climbed into Nicco's truck and headed back to

Sisqo's. On the way, Nicco and Michael talked about business. I just listened. When we arrived at Sisqo's, Nicco helped me out of the truck. Michael climbed out of the backseat to go up front. His shoulder brushed mine lightly.

"It was a pleasure to finally meet you, Jasmine."

"You too, Michael. Enjoy your visit."

Nicco walked me to the door and tried to kiss me, but I turned away.

"Jazz, please think about what I've asked you. Know that I never stopped loving you."

"I'm not that same naïve person you used to know."

He looked puzzled. "What does that mean?"

I backed up a step, preparing to leave. "It means that you don't know me, Nicco. I'm gonna go inside now."

He watched me open the door and said, "I'll talk to you tomorrow."

I looked around for Ashley when I entered the bar. I spotted her engrossed in a conversation with Ed Tisdale, a guy she dated off and on.

I sat at the bar and ordered a drink. When Ashley saw me, she hurried over and sat next to me, her eyes full of curiosity. "Girl, where have you been and what's going on?"

I gave her a general synopsis of what had happened with Nicco and expressed how stupid I felt about jumping in the car and riding off with him.

"You shouldn't feel stupid," she said, very sympathetic. "He was your one, Jasmine. Every woman I know has been weak for at least one man, and Nicco was yours. So he's doing well, huh?"

I had always wondered if Ashley had a thing for him. "Yeah, he looks good, healthy and successful. He named his club Jazzy."

She loved that idea. "Damn, he is really trying to impress you. Do you think you'll get back with him?"

I looked at Ashley like she was crazy. "Girl, you know what I went through with Nicco. There is nothing he can say or do. No."

She didn't say anything, and I went on. "I can never trust him again. He had me believing that he was in love with me and that he was interested in marrying me. He told me about Pat one week before his wedding. Come on, Ashley, I could never be with Nicco again."

The queen of commitment wasn't giving up yet. "I know how much he hurt you, but you were so in love with him. . . ."

"Girl, never again. He doesn't respect me. I'm sure that he was planning his wedding to Pat while he was fucking me daily, and I mean daily. His sex drive is superhigh." The excitement I'd felt then was burned to ashes now. "I mean, how could he? He was staying with me at night, I had a key to his place, he wined and dined me—and all the while he was living a double life."

"So what's up with his friend Michael? I saw him get out of Nicco's truck."

The anger on my face melted away. "I heard about him for years while Nicco and I were together. They were roommates in college. I talked to Michael on the phone, on occasion, but I never had the opportunity to meet him in person. So when he came in the club, I had no idea who he was. I'm sure he had no idea who I was, or he would not have sent me a drink."

Her eyebrows rose at that news. "Do you think he will call?"

I took a sip of my drink. "Yes, he'll call."

"But now that he knows who you are, don't you think he may back off?"

I stirred the thin straw in my glass, trying to mix the Coke. "I remember Nicco saying how he had trouble being faithful. He'll call."

Ashley loved how bold I was. "What if Nicco finds out about you getting with Michael?"

"If Nicco finds out, I'll deal with it, but the connection is going to happen," I said with a chuckle. Paying Nicco back seemed more appealing every time I thought about it. "Hopefully, we can keep it between us."

"Girl, you scare me sometimes. You've really changed in the last few years."

"I guess we have Nicco to thank for that." I didn't like the brittle edge in my voice and I switched gears. "Hey, can I ask you something?"

"Sure, what's up?"

"It's about Tiffany."

Ashley tensed a little.

"I don't know if you've noticed, but she's not very fond of me anymore, and I think it's because of the comment I made about gold digging."

"Yeah, she said something about you not liking her."

"It's not that I don't like her, Ashley. You know I've always liked Tiffany, but she's young and I was just trying to give her some advice." I moved on to the point I really wanted to make. "I also was wondering if you could say something about the way she dresses."

Her eyes flashed, so I knew she had noticed as well. "You know that won't go over well."

"Probably not, but she's disrupting the work flow with her unprofessional attire. She dresses like she's going to the club, not to work."

"I know, Jasmine," she conceded. "I just didn't want to get her too upset, but I'll talk to her."

I couldn't believe that Ashley was worried about upsetting Tiffany when she was disrupting business.

"I can talk to her with you."

"No, let me do this. I'm sure it will be fine."

During my ride home, I thought about Nicco coming into the bar. I had always known that we'd run into each other again, but I'd never thought he'd come back to Sisqo's.

I wondered how I would feel when I saw him again. I was happy because I didn't have to struggle to resist him. His spell over me was broken. I bet he never dreamed that he'd ever lose the hold he'd once had on me.

7

While at work the next afternoon, I received flowers from Nicco. How typical of him, trying to bully me. "Mr. James would like a response," the delivery guy said.

"Response for what?"

He reached for the bouquet, removed the card, and handed it to me. After reading the card, I wrote, "No. I'm not available." But I had a feeling that would not stop him.

I saw Tiffany as she approached my office, but she waited outside for the delivery guy to leave. He looked her over with a lewd smile on his face.

"Can I talk to you for a minute, Jasmine?" she said.

"Sure, Tiffany. Come on in and close the door."

She wore a short, tight black skirt and matching jacket. I wasn't sure if she was wearing a blouse under her jacket or not, but I could see lots of cleavage.

She sat in the chair directly across from me, with her nose slightly upturned, and said, "Ashley told me that you're uncomfortable with the way I dress."

I didn't blink. "No, I said that your attire was inappropriate for the office; there's a difference. I don't care how you dress in your personal life, Tiffany. As a matter of fact, most of the things you wear are very nice—but for the club, not the office."

Belligerence formed around her lips. "So what am I supposed to wear?"

"Look around at everyone else and see how they're dressed."

"I'm supposed to dress like an old lady like you and Ashley?"

I didn't rise to the bait. She might not be professional, but I was. "Just take a look around, Tiffany, and choose your outfits a little more carefully, that's all I'm saying."

She abruptly stood. "Sure, Jasmine, whatever you want," she said as she walked out of my office.

I sat back in my chair and watched her strut across the showroom floor. I'd have to wait to see if she'd gotten my message.

Then my phone rang.

"Hello?" I said.

"This is Michael." His voice was deep and sexy, and it vibrated through the phone. "I've been thinking about you since the moment I laid eyes on you. I can't believe Nicco let you get away."

I closed my office door and said, "Well, that's in the past. So, what's up, Michael?"

"I was hoping we could get together." He was direct. I liked that in a man. "How about we meet for a drink after work?"

"Where are you staying?"

"I'm at the Hard Rock Hotel on Michigan Avenue."

That worked perfectly into my plan. "Let's take a stroll and get to know each other. Can you find the John Hancock Center?"

"Yes. I'll see you there around eight?"

"Yeah, I'll be there."

So, that business was done. Now for the other part.

I found Ashley in her office. I closed the door and said, "Tiffany came to see me."

Ashley looked surprised and a little afraid. "What did she say?"

"She confronted me about commenting on her attire." I made a calming motion to indicate I'd smoothed it over. "I told her to look around and try to dress like everyone else. She didn't seem too happy about it."

Then I said what was on my mind. "I'm really surprised at her, Ashley. I agreed to bring her in because she was such a wonderful young lady who had a lot going for herself. I don't know what happened in college, but she needs to check her attitude at the door."

"I know," she said, sighing. "She's spoiled. I'll talk to her again."

I didn't want to stress her. "No, don't say anything else. Tiffany's a grown woman, and whatever issues we have, we'll resolve. Don't worry about it."

I smiled at her and added, "I'm going to meet Michael after work for a drink."

"Are you sure you want to do this, Jasmine?"

"We're just meeting for a cocktail," I said. "I'm interested, okay?"

"Yeah, okay, Jasmine."

At eight o'clock, I arrived in front of the John Hancock Center, but I didn't see Michael until he appeared in front of me.

He looked as sexy as the first time I'd seen him. "Michael, I'm so happy you found time for me. Come on, let's walk."

"You look great, Jasmine."

"Thank you. It's really nice out tonight."

He grabbed my hand and said, "It is, isn't it?"

His hand was soft and dry. I took that as a good sign. "It's a good night to walk and talk and get to know each other. How do you like Chicago?"

"I like it a lot. It's a beautiful city."

We began to stroll. I stopped at Salvatore Ferragamo's to admire a pair of shoes in the window display. I'll be back tomorrow, I thought.

"You never told me what you do for a living. I can see you like fine clothes and jewelry."

He looked me over and said, "I do like the finer things, Jasmine. I'm a marketing manager."

He was sounding better and better. "I like your style, Michael. Hey, did you say you were staying at the Hard Rock Hotel?"

"Yes. Would you like to go to the hotel bar and have a drink?"

"That sounds good."

"Let's get my car. I'll bring you back to get your car later."

We drove the short distance to the hotel. Once we were seated at the bar, I noticed how Michael couldn't keep his eyes off me. I wore a low-cut salmon-colored dress that hugged my curves. When I sat on the bar stool, I crossed my legs to show as much leg as possible. Other patrons at the bar noticed, too, but I focused my attention on Michael. I could see his erection and how he kept moving around uncomfortably in his seat.

His voice was as smooth as ever, though. "I feel like I already know you. Over the years, I've heard so many wonderful things about you."

"Really? Like what?" I was intrigued. I wondered what Nicco had told his friends about me.

"Well, Nicco was very descriptive when he talked about you."

"Descriptive how? What did he tell you about me?"

"Let's just say that I know about your tattoo."

This just pissed me off more. "I hope you don't feel the need to tell Nicco everything."

He took my meaning right away. "I know how and when to keep my mouth shut."

"Umm."

The waitress took our orders.

Michael said, "Nicco believes that he has a really good chance at getting you back."

I flatlined that idea. "Not gonna happen."

"So we're both single, then."

"Yes."

I was happy that the conversation didn't linger on Nicco for long. I'm sure Michael just wanted to know how involved we were. He was pleased to know that nothing was going on.

He abruptly asked if I wanted to go up to his room. A man who was direct turned me on. The liquor I had drunk had me mellow and I wanted to get close to him.

"I'm ready when you are."

He took my hand and led me to the elevator. We were alone as we went up, and Michael stood in front of me and leaned his body into mine. "What's up, Ms. Jasmine?"

"You tell me," I said softly.

"I'm trying to get close to you."

"I don't think you can get any closer than you are right now."

"Oh, I can get closer than this, if you let me."

I played right along. "How close are you trying to get?"

"Inside."

I smiled, but didn't have to respond. He bent down and we kissed, long and deep.

We broke our kiss when the elevator doors opened. He didn't give a damn about me, I knew that. All he wanted from me was sex, and I wanted the same. I could feel his excitement.

Michael's suite overlooked North Michigan Avenue. I walked to the window and stared out while Michael turned on a set of recessed lights and headed to the bar.

"Would you like another drink, Jasmine?"

"Yes, juice if you have any."

I watched the cars speed by and pedestrians walking along the crowded streets far below. "This is a beautiful view."

"Not nearly as beautiful as the view I have," Michael said. He approached me from behind and slipped his arms around my waist.

I took the glass of juice out of his hand and took a sip. I turned to face him and said, "Can you excuse me for a minute? I need to use the restroom."

He released me and said, "Of course."

Michael watched me as I strutted down the hallway.

I was attracted to Michael, but a big part of the attraction was because he was a friend of Nicco's. I was turned on by the thought of Nicco finding out about me and his friend. I wanted to hurt Nicco as much as he had hurt me, and this should do it, I thought.

I didn't know what Michael's motivation was to be with me and I didn't care. I was there for my own selfish reasons.

I removed my salmon spandex wrap dress and hung it on the back of the door, then took a comb, lipstick, FDS, and a small bottle of perfume from my purse.

For a fleeting second, I felt guilty. Then my heart grew hard. This was something I had to do. After freshening up and checking myself in the mirror, I smiled and walked into the sitting area wearing a red teddy and black leather pumps. Michael was at the stereo, and a Maxwell song began playing. When he heard me enter the room, he looked at me. His mouth fell open.

"Damn! You look good as hell!"

I spun around and said, "You like?"

"Hell yeah. Come here."

I walked into his arms. He grabbed my ass with both hands, pulled me close, and said, "I know you got some good pussy, don't you?"

"That's what they say."

He chuckled. "Yeah, that is what they say, ain't it?"

"Take your clothes off, Michael, and let's get to it."

"I like your style, Jasmine," he said as he took off his pants. "I'm gonna tear that ass up, but you already know that, don't you?"

"Yeah. That's why I'm here."

Soon he stood in front of me nude, fully erect. "Look at that," he said as he grabbed his dick. "Can you handle all of that?"

I wrapped my hands around his dick and said, "Mmmmm . . . that's a lot of meat, baby, but I'm sure I can handle it." I gave it a slight tug. "Come on and join me in the bedroom."

Unexpectedly, Michael swooped me up in his arms and said, "Let me."

I raised my leg high in invitation and Michael planted kisses all over it. "I can't wait to get inside."

He put me down in front of the bed and smoothly helped me remove my teddy. Something told me he'd had practice. I began to kick my shoes off.

"No. Leave them on."

"Okay."

We sat on the edge of the bed and started kissing again. Michael's warm, wet lips felt good against my skin. He kissed my neck, like he knew it was my weak spot, and I relaxed in his arms. He knew exactly what to do to make me submit to him.

I scooted to the middle of the bed, laid on my back, and let my legs fall open. "Now you can see the tat."

He climbed in between my legs and said, "Ahh, the infamous tattoo. I never dreamed that I would actually see it."

My tattoo was two inches of railroad tracks with a train engine on the tracks. The skirt of the train was a tongue with saliva dripping off it, headed toward my vagina. Nicco had persuaded me to get it, so it was very appropriate right now.

Michael kissed my inner thigh and then buried his face between my legs. When his lips touched mine, I relaxed and gave myself to him.

He lifted his head and said, "You taste as good as you look."

"It couldn't come close to as good as you're making me feel."

When he sat up, I looked at his dick, hard and dripping, and took it in my mouth.

"Oh shit," he said. "Oh shit!"

He pulled out after a few minutes and began fondling my breasts.

"Was it too good for you?"

"Yeah, it was. What else you got?"

"Don't you want to come inside?"

He teased me with the head of his dick for a few seconds before pushing himself inside. I loved his thickness, how he filled me up as he continued to push deeper.

My breath caught in my throat. I closed my eyes and thought about Sean making love to me. I felt him push in and out of me, stroking me. I opened my eyes to stare at Michael, who was looking deep into my eyes as he worked his magic.

"That's it, Michael. That feels good."

"I knew you would like it."

Michael and I had great chemistry. I felt sexy with him, so I gave as much of me as he wanted, and he wanted it all. He kept pushing deeper inside me, and I enjoyed each long and hard stroke. Our first climax came hard.

"Oh shit!" I screamed.

"What's up, baby? You like that?" he said as he stared into my eyes and pushed with his final urgent strokes.

"Mmmmm," I purred as I came down from my high.

Michael rolled off me and lay on his back. "Yeah, that's what I've been dreaming about."

I smiled and turned to my side.

Michael was freaky. He made me feel trashy and I liked it. I dozed off as I lay there. I hadn't planned to stay all night, but Michael wore me out. About an hour after our first sexual marathon, I felt Michael's lips on my neck and his fingers playing with my nipples.

He whispered in my ear, "Can I get some more pussy, Jasmine?"

I rolled onto my back and opened my legs. "You can have all the pussy you want from me tonight."

"Just tonight?"

I kissed his lips and said, "One day at a time."

We had sex off and on for a couple of hours. Every time I drifted off to sleep, I felt him pushing against me. We both finally fell asleep around five o'clock in the morning.

I vaguely heard a cell phone ringing, and when I opened my eyes I saw Michael staring at me, searching for my response to what had happened between us. I gave him a reassuring smile and he smiled back. At least his cell phone stopped ringing.

He pulled me close. "Good morning."

"Good morning."

He kissed me lightly on the mouth and down my neck. He slid his hand across my abs and between my legs.

The man could give me a serious workout. "Mmmm . . . Michael, haven't you had enough of me yet?"

"I'll never get enough of you."

I felt his hard dick pressing against my leg, waiting for more. I was excited about having him inside me again. My pussy throbbed in anticipation. I opened my legs and let Michael have more of me. Just as he entered me, his cell phone rang again.

"Maybe you should get that," I said.

His voice was husky. "They can wait. This is more important."

The phone rang a couple more times. After an hour or more of fooling around, I announced that I had to leave. Before he could respond, the phone rang again.

"Michael, answer your phone while I use the bath-room."

He was irritated when he said, "Hello!"

I could hear bits and pieces of his conversation while I was in the bathroom. A chill ran down my spine when I realized that he was talking to Nicco. Neither of us mentioned the phone call when I came back into the bedroom.

Michael took me to breakfast. We talked about how much we enjoyed each other and when we could get together again. After breakfast, he took me back to my car.

After kissing and saying goodbye, I hopped in my car and headed home. I had turned my phone off last night so that I wouldn't be disturbed. I checked my missed calls and voice-mail messages. I saw that Nicco had called and left a few messages, and Ashley had called to see where I was because I was late for inventory.

I heard my home phone ringing while I was opening the door. I dropped my purse on the kitchen counter and grabbed the phone.

"Hey, Ashley, I was just about to call you back. What's going on?"

"Guess who's here looking at cars?"

"Who?"

"Nicco."

I groaned.

"He said he'll wait for you to get here, so you may as well come on down here and talk to him. By the way, I should tell you that Tiffany has been smiling in his face since he's been here."

I didn't like the sound of that. "She surely does not want to get involved with him."

"He said he had been trying to call you since last night, and then he remembered our inventory day."

I laughed wickedly, knowing I could tell Ashley. "Girl, I'm just getting in from my date with Michael."

"Jasmine, you slept with him already?"

My laughter continued. "We didn't get much sleep."

"I'm sure if you told Nicco about your night, he'd go away."

The idea was tempting, but that wasn't what I had in mind.

When I walked into the dealership, Nicco was sitting inside of one of the cars on the showroom floor. Sure enough, Tiffany was leaning against the door, smiling in his face.

I shook my head as I walked past them and into my office. Dropping my purse on one of the empty chairs, I took my seat behind my desk. Let Nicco come to me.

A few minutes later, he appeared in my doorway and flashed his lady-killer smile. I was totally immune.

"I was wondering when you were coming to work. I've been calling you all night and this morning. Hot date?"

I fanned my hand in front of my face. "I guess you could call it that."

His face instantly filled with jealousy. "I thought you said you weren't seeing anyone."

I was happy to see him suffer. "I'm not seeing anyone in particular."

"Oh, it's like that?"

"Yes, Nicco, it's exactly like that."

He began pacing back and forth in front of my

desk. "I thought we were working things out. I didn't think you would be out fucking some other dude while we're trying to get our thing right."

"Nicco, you already know that I'm not trying to work anything out with you."

My phone rang and the caller ID flashed on my computer screen. It was Sean. Suddenly, what I'd done with Michael didn't seem as fun anymore. "Excuse me, Nicco, I have to take this."

Still angry, he stepped out of my office and into the showroom.

"Hey, baby, what's up?"

"Jasmine, I'm missing you. I wanted to hear your voice."

I saw Tiffany sashay her way back to where Nicco stood. He smiled when she stopped in front of him. I turned my attention back to my phone conversation.

"I miss you, too. I can't wait to see you."

"Me and Jimmy just got in, and I wanted to tell you to look out for the key to the condo. I sent it by FedEx, so you should get it tomorrow."

Tingles of excitement started jumping up and down my arms. "Okay. Hey, I'll be there next Friday morning."

"Make sure you give me your flight information so that I can have a car pick you up from the airport."

Nicco came back into my office and sat in the chair across from me.

I put on a super-cuddly voice. "Okay, I'll text you

the information before the day is out." I looked directly at Nicco and said, "I'm really looking forward to spending time with you."

"Me too, baby, I'll see you next Friday."

Nicco was hanging on every word and couldn't wait to comment when I got off the phone. "Man, whoever that was must have been important. He put the smile on your face that I've been waiting to see. Who was that, Jazz?"

"A friend."

"Is that the friend you spent the night with?"

"No."

His face twisted again. "How many friends do you have?"

I stood up and started walking to the door, hoping Nicco would follow. "That's really none of your business."

"Are you still seeing that dude from L.A.?"

I stopped. "How do you know about him?"

He gave me a sly grin. "You would be surprised at what I know."

I stood in the doorway. "Nicco, I have work to do, so if you don't need anything else . . ."

He leaned forward in the chair. "Jazz, I miss you. I know you can't just cut off all of these dudes at once, but I want you back—in a one-on-one relationship."

I laughed at the absurd idea. "When did we ever have a one-on-one relationship? You forgot about your wife already?" I let that hang in the air for a second before I went on. "Nicco, I said no. Why can't you respect my decision?"

"I respect your decision, Jazz, I just can't accept it. I won't give up."

He stood up to leave, walked past me, and then came back.

"By the way, I'm having a party at my club Wednesday for Mike. He's leaving Thursday, and I was hoping you could come by and have a drink with us. Do you think you can make it?"

I nixed that idea right off. "I feel like I'm already spending too much time around you."

"It's not for me, it's for Mike," he pleaded. "He doesn't have a lot of friends here, and he feels like he's known you for years."

"Why don't you invite Pat? He's known her for years for real."

"Jazz, please." Nicco gave a snort of disgust. "Let's not go through the Pat thing every time we have a conversation."

That was easy for him to say. "Do you see what I'm trying to tell you, Nicco? I can't forget. Every chance I get to bring it up, you know that I will."

I could see the gears turning in his head. "Give me a little time. I know I can push the bad thoughts of the past to the back of your mind. Please come Wednesday. Bring Ashley with you, it should be fun."

Although I knew I shouldn't, I gave in. Besides, seeing Michael and Nicco together sounded like fun. "Okay, I'll see you Wednesday. What time?"

"Anytime after nine should be good. And make sure you tell Ashley."

"I will."

Tiffany stopped him at my office door and they walked out together. I didn't know what type of game she was playing, but I wasn't interested in playing with her.

Ashley came into my office shortly after Nicco had left. "Well?"

"He wants us to come to a get-together at his club Wednesday for Michael. Are you interested?"

Ashley blinked in surprise. "Are you going?"

"Yeah."

"Well, hell yeah, I'm going," she said with a devilish glint in her eyes. "There is no way I'll miss the opportunity to watch you squirm."

I didn't understand why Ashley thought I would be on the hot seat. I said coolly, "I won't be squirming."

"Like hell you won't. Think about it. You'll be in the same room with your past lover and your current lover, and they're friends."

I waved my hand her way. "Girl, please. It won't be the first time."

"Yeah, all right, Jasmine. This is a different situation. These guys know each other and are best friends." She was smiling at the idea of all the drama. "Just let me know what time we're going, because I don't want to miss any of the festivities."

"I'll let you know."

Suddenly she looked a little uneasy. "Tiffany couldn't keep her eyes off Nicco," she said.

"Yeah, I noticed. I don't know what she thinks she's doing, but he's the last person she should be going after." The two of us exchanged knowing glances. "You know I can't say anything, because she'll think I'm jealous."

"You're probably right. Oh, here she comes."

Tiffany was beaming when she walked into my office. "Jasmine, your friend Nicco—what kind of friend is he?"

I said casually, "We dated for a couple of years, and he's having trouble letting go."

"Well, if you're not interested, you wouldn't be upset if I went out with him, would you?"

I opened my arms wide in invitation. "What can I say, Tiffany? I don't have any claims on Nicco."

She smiled and said, "Cool."

Ashley didn't say anything until Tiffany was out of earshot. "She really should not get mixed up with him," she hissed to me.

"I know that and you know that, but I sure can't tell her. Will you?"

That looked like totally the last thing she wanted to do. "Yeah. It looks like we need to have another talk."

8

I finally got all my loose ends tied up before leaving for New York. Derrick was on standby at the Burbank Airport, and Jimmy was also there when I arrived.

"Good morning Mr. Williams," Sonja said. She was one of two flight attendants that flew with us regularly. She was looking sexy as usual, and I thought about our last flight together as I climbed the stairs to the cabin. We almost got intimate, but I didn't want to taint our working relationship, so she's off limits to me. She knew I desired her, though, and she took the extra step to make sure that all of my in-flight requirements were met.

After landing at Teterboro, Samson, the driver I usually requested when I was in town, was waiting on the tarmac. He stood beside a black-and-gray Maybach.

"Mr. Williams, it's good to see you again. Welcome to New York."

"Thank you, Samson."

After helping Jimmy and me get situated in the car, we made the short ride to my condo in midtown Manhattan. I was hungry and I knew there was no food at my place, so we stopped at a nearby deli and picked up some sandwiches. I'd get a friend to get some groceries in the house later today. I needed a new assistant, but I hadn't had the time to interview one.

Jimmy was staying at the condo with me until Jasmine arrived next week. He'd stayed there a couple of months ago, when I first bought the place. He didn't want to be in the way while Jasmine was in town and reserved a room at a hotel near the studio. I'm sure Jasmine wouldn't have minded his being in the condo—it's big enough for all of us—but Jimmy insisted.

Having Ray in New York worked out better. So far, no one knew that he was in town, and I was hoping that we could keep it that way.

When Ray came into the studio that afternoon, he said, "When are we going out on the town, Sean? I'm tired of being all cooped up in here. You won't let me bring any females to the studio and I ain't got nobody here with me. Man, I need some companionship."

I barely looked up from my mixing board. "That's how you always get in trouble, Ray. I'll tell you what, let's finish these last tracks and you can party all you want."

He smacked his lips and said, "Man, I ain't trying to hear that. I need to get out and socialize." He turned to Jimmy and said, "What about you? You want to go to a club or something?"

Jimmy nearly flinched at the suggestion, because he knew that trouble followed Ray. "Naw, man, I'm cool."

"Man, forget you, too!" He flipped his phone open and said, "Let me call somebody who wants to have some fun. Y'all is too damn boring!"

Jimmy said, "Yeah, whatever, man. I ain't interested in getting locked up tonight."

Ray closed his phone abruptly. "Oh, it's like that, Jimmy?"

Jimmy wasn't taking anything from Ray. "Yeah, it's exactly like that. Trouble follows you, man."

In the stare-down, Ray was the first one to look away. He opened his phone again and started dialing. His feelings were hurt. "Yeah, well, I guess you should stay away from me then." He wandered out of the booth as he started talking to someone.

Ray was gone for ten minutes or so. When he returned he announced, "We need to get this done. Let's go, everybody! I've got plans and I want to get this wrapped up today."

People sat up and paid attention. Everyone got back on his job and we were able to finish up our last few tracks two hours later.

"All right, Sean. Perform your magic, man, and get with me when you're ready."

I saw how eager he was to be let loose. "I will, Ray. Have a good night."

"You know I will." He grabbed his jacket, his entourage gathered their things, and they were gone.

Jimmy said, "I didn't think we would ever finish, but I'm so glad that we did." He lay on the sofa and closed his eyes.

I had lots of editing to do on the tracks Ray had laid down, but I had to get out of the studio, too. Ray was right—we had been cooped up in there for too long—and I needed to socialize.

Jimmy said, "I'm gonna take a short nap and then start working on these tracks."

"You don't want to go out?"

"Naw, man, I need to get some of this done. I plan to go to L.A. tomorrow. I'll be here all night."

Back at home, I got dressed, then headed to Donnie's, a spot I've been going to since I first started coming to New York. I had met Donnie at Teterboro while we both were waiting to depart for Los Angeles. He was on a business trip and his plane was having trouble. A high-ranking music executive had chartered a plane for me, and I offered Donnie a spot. We talked throughout the flight and found we had lots in common. We'd hung out often since then.

I was sitting at the bar, talking to Donnie, when a group of ladies came in and took seats at the other end of the bar. They were all nice-looking, but one stood out. I decided to send her a drink and see if I could find some company for the night.

Donnie had other business to tend to, and we promised to get together for dinner soon.

After asking Ken, the bartender, to give the standout whatever she wanted, he came back and said, "Carrie said to thank you."

"Carrie, huh? All right. Thanks, Ken."

I picked up my drink and headed to the other end of the bar. I was dressed casually in dark jeans, a white button-down shirt with a wife beater underneath, and leather shoes, and I was freshly shaven. I didn't want to dress too flashy, but my jewelry was screaming money. I wore the Rolex watch that Jasmine had given me because I wanted it known tonight that I was on top.

Carrie smiled at me as I approached. The other ladies began to look my way, too. Close-up, they were all beautiful.

"Hi, Carrie."

She smiled at me, a nice casual slide of her lips. "Hello. Thank you for the drink."

"You're welcome. Would you like to dance?"

"Sure!" she said.

She slid off the bar stool, just as sexy as I hoped. The other ladies were nice-looking, but Carrie was definitely the star and would fit the bill for what I needed tonight.

I took her hand and led her to the dance floor. We danced, but I didn't try to talk to her because the music was too loud. I watched how Carrie moved her body and imagined her moving the same way in my king-size bed.

As we headed back to the bar, I said, "My name is

Sean, Carrie. I was hoping to have the opportunity to talk to you."

"Okay, Sean. All the seats at the bar are taken."

"Come with me. Let your friends know that you're going with me to VIP and that you'll return in a little while."

She was excited about having access to the VIP section—I saw it in her eyes. She smiled at me and said, "Okay, hold on a minute."

While she talked to her friends, I asked Ken to send a bottle of Cristal to the VIP area for me and Carrie.

After conferring with her friends, she walked up to me. "Okay, Sean, lead the way."

I grabbed her hand and we headed upstairs behind the red velvet rope.

The area was empty because it was still early. I told the bouncer to let Carrie and me have a little privacy, and he promised to keep the area restricted.

"Have a seat, Carrie. What are you drinking?"

"Cosmopolitan."

"Are you in the mood for a little bubbly?"

She leaned back and smiled. "Yes."

One of the waitresses brought an ice bucket, two glasses, and a bottle of Cristal.

I saw her eyes glued to my watch and the diamond-encrusted link bracelet that I wore as I reached for the bottle. I poured a glass for Carrie and one for myself.

I moved close to her and said, "What brings you out tonight?"

"I was looking for some fun, you know."

"Yeah, I know. I'm out doing the same thing. Maybe we can have some fun together."

"I'm sure that we can. What do you do, Sean?"

"I produce music."

She really perked up then. "Anyone we know?"

"Yes, lots of popular people."

We talked about some of the music I produced and Carrie's real estate business. She was cute and smart, but tonight all I wanted was sexy, and she was that, too. Cristal loosened her up good. Pretty soon I needed to get her back to my place before she was drunk.

"You want to get out of here? Go back to my place and listen to some tracks that I'm working on?"

She practically wrapped me in her arms. "Yeah, Sean, I do."

"Why don't you let your friends know that you're leaving with me? Do you have a car here?"

"No, I rode with one of my friends."

"Cool. I'll get you home when you're ready to go."

"Okay. I'll be back."

While she was gone, I called Samson and told him to meet me in front of the club. When Carrie returned, we left together.

She was impressed that I had a driver. Samson was driving a BMW 750li. We climbed in and headed for my condo.

When we pulled up to the building, Samson helped Carrie out of the car and I followed close behind, watching her every move. Yeah, she was exactly what I needed to release a little stress. I hoped she was thinking the same.

I unlocked the elevator and we rode to the penthouse. Carrie said, "This is your place, Sean? I thought you said you lived in Malibu."

"I do, but this is my spot in New York."

When the elevator doors opened, Carrie said, "Wow. This place is beautiful, Sean."

"Thank you. Come on in and have a seat."

"Do you mind if I look around?"

"No, not at all. Make yourself at home."

While Carrie walked around, I turned on some music and opened another bottle of Cristal. It was all I had in the refrigerator. I hoped she wasn't hungry.

When she returned to the living room, I handed her a glass.

She took it with her slim fingers. "Thank you, Sean." She took a sip and added, "Dance with me."

We set our glasses on the table and I pulled her into my arms. We slow danced, and when I wrapped my arms around her waist, she wrapped her arms around my neck. She was warm, soft, and smelled powdery.

After the song stopped, we sat on the sofa and drank and talked. When the bottle was empty, Carrie was almost drunk.

"Sean."

"Yeah."

"I'm feeling you."

"I'm feeling you, too, Carrie. You want to go upstairs and watch the stars from the skylights above my bed?" I knew the line was corny, but I was buzzing. I also knew that all I had to do was ask her and she was mine.

She popped up and headed toward the stairs, then stopped and with one sultry fling pulled her dress over her head. She stood posed at the foot of the stairs in stilettos and a thong. I stopped the music with the remote and watched Carrie as she walked up the stairs.

When she disappeared into my bedroom, I hurried up behind her. Carrie was lying in my bed, naked and waiting, when I saw her from the open doorway. I started removing my clothes.

"Come on, Sean, and get what you want."

"What do you think I want from you?"

"Some pussy, right?" she asked softly.

"Yeah, baby, that's right."

I reached into my nightstand and grabbed a condom. Carrie delicately took it out of my hand and laid it on the bed.

I climbed into the bed and she began kissing me all over. As she kissed her way down my body, I felt totally relaxed.

Sex with Carrie was good. I could tell that this wasn't her first one-night stand. Yes, one-night stand. I had no desire to see her again.

When I woke up the next morning, Carrie was

gone. When I went downstairs, I found a note from Carrie saying that she needed cab fare and had found some money in my pocket. Alarmed, I check my wallet. I'd had about a grand and she'd taken it all.

I was pissed, but it was my own fault. I should have never brought her back to my place, number one; and number two, I should have locked my shit away before falling asleep.

Jimmy found me in the kitchen, drinking a cup of coffee. "What's up, Sean?"

In a sullen voice I said, "Yeah. What's up, Jimmy?"

"What's wrong with you? Did you have a party up in here last night? Your clothes are all over the place."

I cracked a hint of a smile. "Yeah, I know. I had a little company last night."

"Oh yeah? Who?"

"Some trick who jacked me."

He looked immediately concerned. "What did she take?"

"The cash in my pocket. I'm glad I didn't take off my jewelry—she probably would have taken it, too."

"How much did she get?"

"About a grand."

He whistled and then he cracked a smile. "Was it good?"

I thought for a minute and said, "Well yeah, it was good. She earned it." Both of us laughed.

I walked to the sink and put my cup inside. "I need to clean up this mess and get a shower, and then I'll be heading to the studio. Did you get a lot done last night?"

"Yeah, I did. I'll talk to you before I leave for L.A. this evening. I'm going to bed, man."

"All right, Jimmy."

After Jimmy left, I picked my clothes up off the floor, threw out the empty bottle, and put the glasses in the sink.

When I went upstairs, the first thing I did was pull the sheets off my bed. I was still mad, not because Carrie had jacked me but because I'd been careless.

My phone rang when I stepped out of the shower; the screen showed it was Ebonie. I thought about not answering, but I hadn't seen her in a while. I should have called her last night instead of picking up a stranger.

"Hey, Ebonie. How are you?"

"I'm well, Sean. I miss you. When will you be back in New York?"

"Actually, I'm here now."

A touch of gruffness entered her tone. "Really. When were you going to tell me?"

I hated when women did that. She knew I didn't answer to her. "I just got in last night," I lied. "I've got to go in the studio today. Why don't you come by the condo tomorrow and spend the evening with me?"

"Okay, Sean. About nine o'clock?"

"Yeah. I'll see you then."

A thought of Jasmine flashed into my mind as I hung up. I'd made all those promises to myself when I was in Chicago, but now I was drifting back into my old life.

9

Jasmine

Michael called me from Nicco's club the night before his party.

"Jasmine, how are you?"

"I'm doing well, Michael," I said cautiously. "How are you?"

"I'd be a lot better if I could see you before I go back to New York."

"I thought you were feeling guilty about what happened between us."

He was surprised. "Why would you say that?"

"Because I haven't heard from you since I left your room."

"I'm really sorry about that. Nicco had me running around for the past few days. I would have called you before now, but I didn't know if you wanted to see me again. Can I see you?"

I tried to hold him off. "Nicco told me about your get-together. He convinced me to come, so I guess I'll see you tomorrow."

"Can I see you before then? I want to spend some private time with you. You know."

I smiled because I did know. Michael had been a very inventive lover. I wanted more of it.

"Where do you live? I can come to your house right now."

I gave Michael my address.

I put away the romance novel I was reading and went to find something sexy to wear for him. After looking through my walk-in closet, I decided to wear nothing. I slipped on a silk robe, put on some music, and waited for Michael to arrive.

When my doorbell rang, I checked myself in the mirror and pulled my robe down over one of my shoulders to expose some of my chest.

When I opened the door, Mike's eyes feasted on me. He licked his lips and said, "I've been fantasizing about being with you since you left me Sunday morning. I think about fucking you all day and night." He kicked the door closed while kissing me and trying to remove my robe.

I liked his in-your-face style. Laughing, I pulled away from him and walked up the stairs to my bedroom. At the top I let my robe fall off. He followed me while leaving a trail of his clothing along the way. I hopped into bed and waited for Michael to hurry out of his clothes and take what I was offering.

I hadn't said a word to him. Yet, when he gently kissed me, testing my mood, I responded to his kiss aggressively. We began kissing wildly. When I started panting for breath, Michael flipped me onto my stomach and thrust himself inside me from behind. It hurt initially, but the deeper he went, the wetter I got.

We fucked frantically, changing positions rapidly. I was hungry for him and he was pounding me hard and fast. He was rough and I loved it. I could feel every inch of him as he plunged deep inside me. Before long we reached an intense climax together. I was surprised to hear him struggle to contain his cries of pleasure, because I let go and cried out in ecstasy.

I finally spoke once we were lying next to each other. "Wow, Michael, you give a good workout."

He locked his hands together behind his head and gave me a lustful smile. "That's what good pussy will do to a man. I can't get enough of you."

I smiled but didn't say anything. By "you" he meant "your pussy."

He didn't pretend to be interested in hanging around. He'd gotten what he wanted from me, and that was fine, because I got what I wanted, too.

We showered together and he was on his way after getting dressed.

I called Sean while I dressed for Michael's get-together. I had been thinking about him even more since last night with Michael. I could feel a shift. I'd enjoyed the sex, but I wanted more. I wanted closeness with a man. Like Sean. He didn't pick up, though, and I decided not to leave a message. I didn't have anything to say. I just wanted to hear his voice.

Ashley and I decided to meet at Jazzy's around ten o'clock.

When I came in the door, the first person I saw was Nicco's brother Mario. He rushed over and we hugged. "Jasmine, what a surprise. I'm so happy to see you, I've missed you."

His words were genuine. I hadn't really thought too much about Nicco's family and friends while I was out of his life.

"I've missed you, too, Mario. It's been a couple of years, but you still look the same, you're looking real good. How are Lyn and the kids?"

"They're all fine, everyone is doing well. Mama still talks about how much she misses you and that Nicco made a huge mistake. Hopefully he is trying to correct that mistake."

My smile dimmed. "He's trying, but I'm not interested anymore, Mario. I came tonight for Michael and to see some people I haven't seen in a very long time, including you."

He touched me lightly on my arm. "Whatever reason you came, I'm glad you did."

In retrospect, I had to wonder if I'd gone out with the wrong brother.

I looked around for an empty table and Mario offered, "What are you drinking? Rum and Coke?"

"Yes, you remembered."

He left to get me the drink.

At that moment, Nicco walked up behind me and slid his arms around my waist. Just as smoothly, I took a step forward and pulled free.

"I'm so happy you decided to come."

"Where is the guest of honor?" I asked, avoiding the faux intimacy.

"He had a late night or early morning with some chick he's been messing around with since he's been here. I guess she wore his ass out. He should be here any minute."

I didn't say a word. Mario came back with my drink. "Why didn't you tell me that Jasmine was coming, Nicco?"

"Because I wasn't sure if she would show up." Mario chuckled and winked at me.

Nicco had escorted us to a table when Michael walked in the door. Nicco waved him over. As he strolled to our table, I thought about how good he made me feel. I pictured him naked, and when he spoke, I thought about those lips wrapped around my nipples. Michael sure knew how to please me.

He flashed me a knowing smile. I'm sure he had thoughts of our last encounter on his mind, too. "Jasmine, it's good to see you again."

"How are you, Michael?"

"I'm doing well." He acknowledged Mario.

"How are you enjoying your visit to our great city?" Mario asked.

"I've had much more fun than I expected."

Nicco added, a touch annoyed, "Why didn't you bring your fun here so that we could all meet her?"

"She had to work," he replied smoothly. "I'll let y'all meet her next time I'm in town." He must have had that lie all prepared. I made a note to myself: *he could lie to me just as easily.*

I glanced at the door just as Ashley arrived. I excused myself and joined her.

"Hey, girl, I'm so glad you are here. I'm seeing all these people that I haven't seen in the past few years, and they all think that Nicco and I are getting back together."

Ashley was amused. "I'm sure you quickly put a stop to that."

"You know I did."

She leaned in a little closer. "Tiffany wanted to come, but I knew that would be a disaster waiting to happen."

"I'm glad you didn't bring her," I said sharply. "I'm not in the mood for her tonight."

"She's not that bad, Jasmine."

"She doesn't like me, Ashley, and me and her in the same place with liquor right now is not a good combination." I cocked my head toward the gathered group. "Plus, throw Nicco in the mix and things could get ugly."

"Yeah, you're right about that. She can't stop talking about him."

I glanced back at my ex. "Did you talk to her about him?"

"Yes," she said wearily. "I told her what type of man he is, but she's determined to get to know him."

"Did she get his phone number or give him hers?"

"No, but she's decided to make the connection."

I didn't say anything. I knew that if Nicco was interested, he would have gotten her number. "As long as you warned her, there is nothing more you can do. She's a grown woman."

"Yeah. Hey, did you get with Michael?"

I shifted nervously. I was uncomfortable talking about what I was doing here. "Yeah, he came by the house last night."

She laughed lightly. "Girl, you know you do some crazy shit."

"There's Michael over there by Nicco."

Ashley turned in their direction and said, "He reminds me of Morris Chestnut. He is cute."

I waved him over and made the introduction. "Michael, this is my friend and business partner, Ashley. Ashley, this is Nicco's college roommate, Michael."

"Ashley, it's nice to meet you. Come on over and join us. Can I get you ladies a drink?"

"Yes, any white wine will do. Thank you," Ashley said.

"I had a drink on the table, but I could use another one."

"Rum and Coke, right?"

"Yes, thank you."

Like a watchful hawk, Nicco walked over to us. "You remembered Jasmine's drink?"

"Yeah, I remembered. Excuse me."

"Ashley, I'm so happy you decided to join us."

She looked around and said, "This is a very nice club, Nicco."

"Thank you. I just wanted to create an atmosphere that my baby would feel comfortable in."

I rolled my eyes, nudged Ashley with my elbow, and mumbled, "See what I mean?"

Michael came back with our drinks and we sat down.

"So, Michael," I said, "what time are you leaving tomorrow?"

"I have an early-morning flight."

Ashley said, "Did you enjoy your stay?"

"Yes, it was very memorable. I look forward to visiting again sometime soon." He looked directly at me when he said that.

Nicco said, "He met some chick that he's hiding. I tried to get him to invite her tonight, but he said she had to work."

Michael clapped his friend on the shoulder. "Nicco, you'll get a chance to meet her, probably the next time I'm here."

"That's all right, Mike, keep your honey a secret."

"Man, you be trippin'." Michael turned to me and asked me to dance.

I have always thought that a man shows what he's all about on the dance floor, and I wanted to find out more about Michael.

We went out and danced through three songs. One of them was a slow R&B number that had us dancing cheek-to-cheek. Nicco watched intently from afar. I knew he would have something to say about it.

When we returned to the table, Nicco said, "You two look like you were enjoying yourselves."

I said, pleased to see him angry, "We were."

"Come here, Jazz, let me talk to you. Y'all excuse us."

Reluctantly, not wanting to make a scene, I followed him into his office. He had the nerve to have a picture of me on his credenza. Pictures of his daughter were everywhere. I picked one up and said, "She's beautiful, Nicco."

"Thank you." He quickly got to the point. "What's going on? Are you trying to make me jealous by dancing with Michael?"

I shrugged, not giving away anything. "He asked me to dance. I don't have any reason to make you jealous, and you don't have any reason to be jealous. I'm not your woman anymore. I'm free and single."

"Are you interested in Michael?"

I sat in one of the two leather chairs facing his desk and he sat in the other. "He's very handsome, Nicco, but no. Why would you ask me that?"

"Because you two were getting a little familiar on

the dance floor. I vividly remember you telling me that as a rule, you would never slow dance with a stranger."

I was keeping to that rule—Michael wasn't a stranger. "I told you before, Nicco, you don't know me anymore. There are things that I wouldn't do before that I do now."

"What's that supposed to mean?"

"It means just what I said—I do a lot of things differently now. Besides, I didn't consider Michael a stranger. I felt comfortable dancing with him."

Nicco was almost pouting. "I wanted to dance with you."

"But you didn't ask me to dance, Nicco, Michael did."

He had to pause to consider that. "I can't say I blame him for wanting to get close to you. That has got to be the sexiest dress I've ever seen, and you're wearing the shit out of it. You never dressed like that before. Did you wear that sexy dress for me?"

Rolling my eyes, I stood up to leave. "I better get back out there with Ashley."

"Don't run off, Jazz." He grabbed me by the waist and tried to kiss me. I turned my head before his lips met mine. I didn't want to lead him on.

"Jazz, wait."

I stopped and turned to face him. He took my hands and said, "I can't stand the thought of another man being with you. I must be the stupidest man on earth, Jazz. Everybody tried to tell me, but I didn't listen. I thought that you would be with me no matter what. I actually thought that I could marry Pat and keep you on the side. I never dreamed that you'd be able to walk away from me."

I pulled my hands away and laid it on the line for him. "You know, Nicco, in the beginning, I didn't think that I would survive through the hurt and pain, but life has actually gone on without you. I learned a lot about myself while I went through our breakup. When you think about being with me, you're thinking about the Jasmine you used to know, not the Jasmine you've created."

He was perplexed. "What are you saying, Jazz? You keep saying how I don't know you anymore. What's so different about you now?"

"I'm not looking to fall in love anymore," I said, nailing every word. "I'm not trying to be in a relationship with anyone."

"So you're saying you're just out here fucking now?"

I made a face at his insult. "If that's how you want to put it. I have a few 'friends.' I'm not trying to get my heart broken again in a so-called one-on-one relationship."

He stepped back and looked me up and down. "So this dress, the dress you had on last Friday, this is how you dress now?"

I fired right back, "What's wrong with my dress? You liked it a minute ago."

"I liked it when I thought you wore it for me, but I see now it's for general observation."

I started toward the door. "I'm going home now, Nicco. Enjoy the rest of your evening."

"Jazz, don't leave like this."

"I'm not going to be with you, okay!"

His voice dropped to a murmur. "All right, Jazz, I'll leave you alone. If you change your mind, you know where to find me."

I walked out. I thought about saying something to him about Tiffany, but I didn't want him to think I cared, so I let it go.

When I returned to the table, I told Ashley that I was leaving, then gave Michael a hug and said, "Have a safe trip home."

I didn't see Nicco standing in the doorway of his office, watching me. Michael whispered in my ear, "I want to see you before I go. Can you spend the night with me?"

I thought about what had just happened in Nicco's office. If I slept with Michael tonight, Nicco would think it was in reaction to him.

"I think, maybe next time."

10

Jasmine

Once my plane landed at LaGuardia and I was settled in the limo that Sean had sent, I called him. He insisted that I stop by the studio to pick him up, saying that we would get lunch or something and spend the rest of the day together.

The receptionist escorted me to Sean's office to wait for him. A huge flat-screen TV hung on the wall among the gold and platinum records that Sean had produced. The TV was tuned to MTV and Ray Cash was singing a sexy ballad.

Tired after my flight, I decided to relax on the black leather sofa. Soon enough, I ended up falling asleep. After an hour, Jimmy came in and woke me. "Jasmine! Hey, it's good to see you again."

I sat up and said, "Hi, Jimmy!"

"I'm sorry, but Sean wanted me to let you know that he'll be tied up here for a while and that you should go on to the condo. He'll meet you there later." He handed me a stack of twenty-dollar bills. "Sean's driver Samson will take you to the condo. Menus are in the drawer in the kitchen if you want to order something to eat, because there is no food in the fridge."

I was disappointed. Sean had asked me to come by the studio, but he couldn't pull himself away long enough to at least say hi.

Samson drove to Sean's condo on West Forty-second Street. We arrived at Sean's condo in no time. The doorman helped me out of the car and showed me how to use the elevator key.

This would be my first time seeing his new place. I knew it had to be spectacular because Sean always had the best of everything. He had sent the alarm code and elevator key to me by FedEx a few days earlier to use when I arrived.

I rode the private elevator to Sean's penthouse. I was at a loss for words when the elevator doors opened. I walked straight through the foyer to the balcony to see a spectacular view of the Hudson River. The rooms on the first floor of the duplex flowed into one another, with the bedrooms on the second level. I kept my bag on my shoulder as I walked around. I knew Sean couldn't boil water, but he had a beautiful gourmet kitchen. Again, only the best for Sean: Sub-Zero appliances, including a wine cooler, granite countertops with coordinating glass backsplash, hardwood floors, exposed brick walls.

Upstairs, I found the master suite and dropped my carry-on bag in there. Samson had dropped off my other bags earlier, which I saw in the open closet. I *guess I have my own closet while I'm here*, I thought. Nice.

After putting some of my things away, I searched

for something to eat, but, just as Jimmy had said, there was nothing in the house. I sat at the island in the kitchen and was reaching for the phone to call Ashley when it rang. I let the call go to his answering machine. The machine, I quickly discovered, was on some kind of surround-sound speaker. Some woman named Brenda said, "Sean, baby, I miss you. When are you coming home? I was hoping to see you before you left. I know you're in the studio, so I didn't want to call you on your cell. Call me when you get in."

I was stung. I'd always known he had other women, but being confronted with the honeyed voice of one was something else.

As I reached for the phone, it rang again. Another woman, using a very sexy voice, said, "Hi, Sean, this is Ebonie. I was so happy to talk to you yesterday. I just wanted to make sure that we're still on for this evening. I'll be sure to bring my overnight bag. If I don't hear from you, I'll be there at nine."

"Ain't that a bitch!" I muttered. "He's got more women than I have men. We definitely need to discuss this."

Annoyed, I found his answering machine and turned the volume down. Then I called Ashley and brought her up to date. Call waiting continued to beep while we talked.

After talking to Ashley, I found the menus. The phone rang again and I recognized Sean's number on the caller ID.

"Hey!"

"I'm sorry I couldn't get away. Are you settled in?"

"Yeah, I'm cool. Your new place is beautiful, Sean."

"I was hoping you liked it."

"I love it." Everything except the surround sound. "I need something like this for myself. I'm hungry, baby, where's the food?"

"Why don't you order something? Menus are in the drawer."

"I found those already. Will you be home soon?"

"About eight o'clock," he said with a sigh.

I could tell that some band was working his nerves.

"Do you want to go out for dinner?"

"Yeah, that's cool." Sweetly I added, "Hey, you better call Ebonie and cancel your plans so that she doesn't show up with her overnight bag."

He chuckled. "I'm sorry about that. I'll take care of it. Why don't you make reservations somewhere for nine o'clock."

"Okay."

"I'm really happy that you're here, Jasmine."

I was smiling when I said, "Me too."

"You can turn the volume off on the answering machine if you want."

I chuckled and said, "Yeah, okay."

I actually was starving. I grabbed my purse and keys and headed for the lobby, where there was a variety of amenities. I walked past a dry cleaner, an upscale restaurant, and, at the end of the long hallway, a convenience store, where I bought a prepackaged salad, a couple of bottles of water, and a bag of chips.

Back to the condo, I ate, then I showered and prepared for Sean. I planned to give him a homecoming he wouldn't soon forget. Better than any ol' Brenda or Ebonie could do. Going out to dinner could wait.

When Sean called to tell me that he was on his way, I pulled a rug into the foyer and lit candles and lay across the rug in lingerie. I heard the elevator rise to the top floor. When the doors opened and Sean saw me, he dropped his bag and stared. I sat up, feeling self-conscious, and said, "You don't like what you see?"

He stuttered, "I—I love what I see."

I didn't know how to interpret that. I didn't want my feelings hurt, so I didn't give his comment too much power. "Come here, Sean."

He approached and stood over me with lust in his eyes. "You did this for me, baby?"

"Whatever it takes to make you happy . . ."

He was surprised by my words. He reached for me and helped me up. "Give me a kiss," he said.

As we kissed, exploring with our tongues, I started unbuttoning his shirt. I slid my hands under his wife beater and ran my fingers across his nipples.

"That's it," he said as he pulled me close. "I want to make love to you."

I unbuckled his belt and helped him out of his clothes. I took his hand and led him to the couch. "Have a seat and let me have you," I purred.

He sat back, spread his arms, and said, "I'm all yours. Do what you want to me."

He watched attentively as I slowly removed my lingerie. He was fully erect when I dropped to my knees and took him in my mouth.

He let me have him for as long as he could take it before saying, "Let me taste you."

I looked into his eyes and said, "It's your night, Sean. Let me take care of you."

I sat on his lap, but he didn't enter me. I rubbed my hands across his chest, feeling the smooth skin. I looked into his eyes and kissed him lightly on his lips.

He wrapped his hand around the back of my neck and kissed me passionately. I lost my control and he took over.

"I know you want to do this, baby, but seeing you laying on the rug waiting for me got me really excited."

He kissed me again, this time gently.

"I'm excited about you being here with me, Jasmine," he said as he looked lovingly into my eyes.

At that moment, I believed that Sean was in love with me. I saw it in his eyes. Just as I moved to give him oral pleasure, I felt his fingers slide inside me. "Aaaahhh," I said, exhaling as he pushed deeper.

"You like that?"

"I love it, Sean. You know how to make me feel good."

"I feel good having you in my arms, Jasmine. I

want to make love to you all night. I don't want to let you go."

"I don't want to leave your arms, baby."

He lifted me by the waist and with one thrust pushed his dick inside me.

I gasped, and he began to move methodically beneath me. I began pushing hard, faster, trying to get all of Sean inside me. "Harder, baby," I panted.

"Can you take all of me?"

"Yes," I said, out of breath. "I want all of you."

He let me up and directed me onto my knees so that he could enter me from behind. He pushed himself deep inside me again. He started slow stroking and slapping my ass. I pushed back against him, forcing him to go deeper. He began stroking me fast and hard until I reached my climax, and he reached his a few strokes later.

We crashed on the couch, exhausted. After a few minutes he said, "You want to order in?"

"Yeah, I guess we should get dinner. What do you have a taste for?"

"You."

I smiled tenderly. "I mean to eat."

"You."

My smile spread wider. "How about some Chinese?"

"Get whatever you want, baby, I'm going to shower."

I ordered Thai food from a restaurant not far from

the condo. I walked into the bathroom nude. Sean had the multiple showerheads on as he lathered himself. When he saw me, he dropped the bar of soap. I opened the shower door and dropped to my knees to retrieve it. In that position, I wrapped my hands around Sean's dick and took him in my mouth. As I sucked the head of his dick, I felt him grow hard. Sean pulled me up and leaned me over the bench and took me from behind.

Sean's phone rang continually. He cleaned himself again and hurried out of the shower while I found a bottle of Axe shower gel and washed myself.

Sean was sitting on the sofa in the enormous bathroom, talking on his cell phone, when I walked past him naked.

I smiled to myself when I heard him lose his train of thought because he was gawking at me.

I threw on one of his T-shirts and was headed downstairs to wait for the delivery guy when the bell rang. I grabbed money off the dresser and hurried downstairs. When I unlocked the elevator and the door opened, though, a chick was staring at me with an overnight bag on her shoulder. The smile she was wearing quickly vanished. "Who in the fuck are you?"

I left her standing at the front door and headed to the stairs, shouting, "Sean, someone is here for you."

"Who is it, baby?"

"I don't know, but I don't think she's too happy about seeing me."

He was silent for a minute. When I went into the bedroom, he said, "Did the doorman call first?"

"No," I snapped.

Recognition flashed on his face. "Oh shit, I forgot to cancel with Ebonie. Where is she?"

"At the door."

"I'm so sorry about this." He slipped on a pair of shorts and headed downstairs. I followed, wanting to see where I stood with him.

When he saw her standing in front of the elevator, he said, "Ebonie, I meant to call and tell you that our plans changed."

The rug and candles were still in the middle of the floor. My lingerie and Sean's clothes were strewn across the rug.

"You changed our plans to be with her?" She eyed me nastily as I stood at the top of the stairs.

"Yeah. I'm sorry you came all the way over here."

With an attitude she challenged him. "You're not gonna ask her to leave?"

He answered her right back, "You know how it is, Ebonie."

"Yeah, all right, Sean." She looked at me like she wanted to kick my ass. In response, I walked down the stairs and put my arm around his waist. She hissed, "Y'all have fun." She stormed back to the elevator and left.

I turned to Sean and said, "How many women do you have?"

He started walking back upstairs. "Come on, Jasmine, not you, too."

I followed. "If I'm pleasing you, I should be able to ask you."

"All right." We walked into the bedroom and sat on the bed together. "I have a few friends here and there," he said, "but to be honest, none of them come before you, baby, and that's the truth. I'm not serious about any of them."

The doorbell rang again—it was our food delivery.

He dashed to the door.

I sat on the bed, thinking about what he'd just told me. I didn't know how much of it to believe.

We sat down to eat at the center island in the kitchen. His home phone and cell phones rang constantly. He took some of the calls, but let most of them go to the answering machine or voice mail. I was discouraged by most of the activity, but I didn't let it show.

"I'll be in the studio again all day tomorrow. Did Jimmy give you that package?"

"Yes. Thank you. I'll get out tomorrow and see what kind of trouble I can get into." That didn't sound right, so I added, "Maybe I'll call some of my friends here in New York and see who I can get together with for lunch."

"You're talking about girlfriends, right?"

"Of course I am. I wouldn't come here to see you and hook up with another man."

"I was just checking."

I wasn't sure why he thought he could be all possessive after the show I'd seen tonight. I let that pass, too.

"Do you think I can get another greeting like the one I had tonight?" he asked eagerly.

"Most definitely. I'm looking forward to it."

After dinner, Sean headed to his office to return phone calls and I went into the media room to watch movies.

Sean's media room was better than a movie theater. I loved the thickness of the wall-to-wall carpet as my bare feet sank into the cushiony padding. There was plenty of seating, but I chose to sit in the last of three rows of brown leather seats. Eight oversized recliners made up the first two rows, four chairs each, and the last row was a sofa with two recliners on each end. It had been a long day and I knew I would fall asleep soon. I found the remote and played with the buttons until I was able to operate the multiscreen console.

After taking care of his business, Sean joined me where I had fallen asleep. I woke up when I felt him sit next to me. I said neutrally, "Did you get all of your business taken care of?"

"Yeah, some of it, but I have to be out of here early tomorrow. Jimmy and Jamal will be in the studio all night. They let me leave so that I could spend some time with you, but I've got to put in some time tomorrow." His voice became anxious. "You understand, don't you?"

"Of course I do. I know you're busy. I'll do some shopping tomorrow, don't worry about me."

"Why don't you come by the studio?"

I'd done all the waiting I wanted to do today. "We'll see. I don't want to be in the way."

"You won't be in the way. I want to introduce you to some people anyway. Oh, before I forget again, my mother wants to meet you."

I almost screamed. "Your mother?" I said.

He looked wounded by my reaction. "Yeah, I told her that you were here, and Aunt Frances already told her about you."

I quickly tried to gauge what this meant. "You told her that I was staying here with you?"

"Yeah."

I was really uneasy. I didn't want his mother to think . . . I didn't know what I wanted her to think. "What did you tell her about me?"

"That you're special." He leaned over and kissed me. "I thought we could take her to dinner tomorrow. I want you two to get to know each other."

I was still flustered. "Doesn't she live in Detroit?"

"Yeah, she's here visiting my aunt." He saw that I was uncomfortable, but was wrong about the reason why. "If you didn't bring a dress, take my card and buy something tomorrow."

The fact was, I didn't like how he'd sprung that on me. "Sean, you can't just spring this on me."

"You don't want to meet my mama?"

"Yeah, I do, but I wasn't ready."

"Come here, baby."

I sat on his lap and he put his arms around me. "Don't worry, Jasmine, she'll love you."

I tossed and turned all night. I didn't know how to read him. Why would he want me to meet his mother? If he was getting serious about me, why hadn't he told me? Would his mother be able to tell that I was in love with him? What kind of person would she think I was, coming to New York to stay with a man?

When I woke up the next morning, Sean was gone. He'd left a credit card and a note on the dresser. The note also said for me to be ready to go at eight o'clock. A car would be waiting for me downstairs.

I checked my voice mail. There were two messages from Nicco, which I deleted. Ashley had called to check on me. I needed to check in with her anyway. I could not believe there were two messages from Tyrone. He had to be kidding.

After I showered, I called Kendall, a college friend I planned to meet for lunch the following day to discuss franchising her spa. She owned a spa/salon and I had begged her to squeeze me in for the works. Although I'd had a spa day before I came to New York, I wanted my polish changed and I needed a massage due to my lack of sleep the night before.

It was ten thirty when I arrived at Secrets. I still had to find a dress for the evening.

After getting a massage and my polish changed,

I decided to get my hair styled. It was three o'clock when I finally left. I promised Kendall that I would call her in the morning to schedule lunch.

I found a dress, shoes, and handbag at Versace on Fifth Avenue. I had to rush to the condo to get dressed. It was six thirty before I realized that I hadn't heard from Sean. I called his cell.

"Hey, baby. Where you been all day?"

"Shopping."

"Will you be ready by eight o'clock?"

"Yes. How's your day been?"

"It's been good so far. I'm looking forward to spending the rest of it with you, though. I'll be in the car waiting, just come down."

"Okay, I'll see you then."

I talked to Ashley while I dressed. She said that everything was going well at the dealership. I could tell that she had more to say, but she was hesitant.

"What's up, Ashley?" I said.

"It's Tiffany. I don't know what to do with her, Jasmine. I think she's sleeping with Victor."

"What! Victor is at least forty. What the fuck!"

"I know. I think she believes he has money, and that's what she's looking for. She came in smiling yesterday morning, showing off a pair of diamond earrings. I know she can't afford diamond earrings, and my father called me asking where she got them."

"Do you think Victor gave them to her?"

Her voice became testy. "I don't know, Jasmine.

I'm tired of this shit already. She spends so much time hanging around Victor, and I know that they've gone out a couple of times."

I couldn't believe what I was hearing. "Victor is married. Have you talked to him about this?"

"No. What can I say? He's a grown-ass man, and who am I to tell him who he can socialize with?"

"You're his boss, Ashley, and Tiffany is your sister," I said sternly. "If what he's doing is disrupting the business, then it needs to be addressed."

"Then Tiffany will be mad at me."

"And you give a shit?" My voice became as hard as stone. "I'll take care of it when I get back."

"No. Don't say anything. I'll talk to her."

"What about Victor?"

"I'll talk to him, too."

I wanted to bring up a larger issue as well, as long as we were on the subject. "How's her work? I mean, is all the aggravation worth it?"

"Yes, her work is really good, she's smart. Plus, my dad would be so upset if we let her go."

I heard the pleading in her voice, and I backed off. I could handle whatever when I returned to Chicago. "I'll talk to you later, Ashley. I need to finish dressing."

"This Tiffany shit is getting on my nerves," I said to an empty room, after we'd hung up.

I drank the last of the Moscato from my wineglass while I eyed myself critically in the mirror. I wanted to be sure that Sean's mother liked what she saw before I made my way downstairs. There was a limo waiting at the door, just like Sean had said.

I saw my reflection as I walked to the door. I winced, hoping I wasn't overdressed. The doorman held the door for me. I saw Sean waiting outside the car, talking to Samson. He was wearing a suit and tie and I instantly felt better about my outfit. He looked me over as I approached and said gently, "You're beautiful."

"Thank you, Sean, you look really good yourself."

Like the gentleman he was, Sean helped me inside the car. He spent most of the ride to the restaurant on his phone. We had reservations at Uncle Jack's Steakhouse in midtown. After a brief wait at the bar, Sean's mom walked in and joined us.

I had on a soft blue linen dress. Simple but elegant. My makeup was light and I wore pearl jewelry. I stood to greet Sean's mom. She looked me over as I stood next to her son, holding his hand. She wore an off-white suit, very elegant, very expensive. Sean released my hand to give his mother a hug. "Mom, this is Jasmine Taylor. Jasmine, this is my mother."

I extended my hand, which she shook. "Mrs. Williams, it's a pleasure to meet you."

"It's a pleasure to finally meet you, too, Jasmine. Sean and Frances have said so many nice things about you."

I glowed at the thought that Sean had talked about me. "The pleasure is mine, Mrs. Williams."

Sean said, "Come on, ladies, let's get our table."

The staff was familiar with Sean. We were taken to a semiprivate area on the upper level. Once we were seated, a waiter came by with a wine list and handed it to Sean. He ordered a Pinot noir for the table.

"So, Jasmine, you're from Chicago?" Sean's mother asked.

"Yes, born and raised."

"Are your parents in Chicago?"

"Both of my parents have passed."

"Oh, honey, I'm sorry to hear that. Do you have other relatives in Chicago?"

"No, not in Chicago. I have an older brother who lives in Santa Monica. Most of my relatives are scattered out West."

The waiter came with our wine. After Sean okayed the selection, we were all served. Sean also placed orders for our entrees.

"So this is great," he said when he was finished. "I have my two favorite women in the same place."

As dinner wore on, his mother told stories of Sean's childhood, and I enjoyed learning new things about him. I revealed things about my past to them, too. Sean didn't know that my mother had died giving birth to me and that I'd been raised by my father. I hardly ever told people about that.

After dinner, we took his mom back to his aunt Catherine's house in Brooklyn. We stopped in and visited with his family for a little while, and I met a few of his cousins, before we headed back to his condo.

Once we were in the car, Sean said, "That wasn't so bad, was it?"

"No, it was great, I had a good time," I said in a relaxed tone. "I wanted to touch you so bad while we were at dinner, I couldn't wait to get in this car. Come here, Sean."

He crawled over to me and put his head under my dress, and right there in the car he started kissing my thighs. My legs parted and he discovered that I wasn't wearing any panties. He dropped his pants to his knees, pulled my body to the edge of the seat, and slid himself inside me. I gazed at the stars, the streetlights, and the lights from the tall buildings through the moon roof while Sean and I made love.

When we arrived at his building, the doorman opened the door just as Sean zipped his pants. He had a smirk on his face as we got out of the car.

After showering, Sean put on some music. I grabbed a bottle of wine and glasses, and we headed for the patio. He sat on the chaise and I sat in his lap.

"Jasmine, I could get used to this."

"Get used to what?"

"To being with you all the time. I think about being with you too much."

He liked to get caught up in the moment. "Sean, you have too many other women to be thinking about me."

"None of them mean anything," he said, giving me a squeeze. "Just you. You know what I can't stop thinking about?"

"What?"

"How much my mama liked you."

"You really think so?" I was starting to feel uncomfortable. It sounded like we were going to talk about some stuff that I didn't want to discuss.

I tried to get up, but he pulled me closer. "Don't run, Jasmine. Talk to me."

I didn't want him to know that I was in love with him. Not yet, at least. "I liked your mother, too, Sean. It meant a lot to me."

"Oh? Why is that?"

I decided to be honest. "Okay, Sean, I think I'm in love with you."

I could feel him stiffen beneath me. "It took meeting my mama to tell me that?"

"I'm scared to fall in love again, Sean," I confessed. "I mean, come on, let's face it, your phone rings off the hook with women calling, and I know you're not ready to settle down with me. I know how much you hate it when women cling to you. I just don't want to get too attached."

He smiled.

"What are you smiling about?"

"You said you were in love with me."

"Okay, now you know," I said, worried as hell. "Can we just forget it and move on?"

"I'm in love with you, too."

I touched a finger to his lips. "Sean, don't say it because I did."

"I'm not just saying it, Jasmine. It's true, though I didn't realize it. I do know I couldn't concentrate until I had you here with me."

"Sean, let's try to keep things the way they are. We live in different parts of the country, and a long-distance relationship will be too difficult. I love you, and I believe you love me, but think about it. My coming to New York didn't stop you from inviting your friend over for a booty call. So, until we're ready to commit, let's not change anything."

A hard look came over his face. "I don't know if I can do that, Jasmine. I don't want another man touching you."

"Let's not do this, Sean. Let's just enjoy the rest of the evening."

We spent the remainder of the evening listening to music and talking. I had to admit, I felt more comfortable with Sean than with any other man I knew.

The next afternoon, while Sean was in the studio, I met Kendall for lunch to discuss franchising her salon and spa in Chicago. I also did more shopping while I was out.

Sean and I had a good time while I visited with him. I made it to the studio and met some of his artists. We ate out, I cooked a little, but most of all we spent time alone, just the two of us.

I was up early to finish packing, get a bubble bath, and make love to Sean once more before I left. When I came out of the bathroom after my bath, Sean was sitting on the side of the bed, on the phone. I walked over to him and let my robe drop to the floor. He quickly told whomever he was talking to that he would call back.

In another hour, Sean saw me off at the airport. During my flight I realized that this trip had caused me even more confusion. Did Sean truly love me? I didn't know if things would be awkward between us now, or if we could continue on the path we were on.

11

Jasmine

Ashley was in her office with Tiffany when I arrived at the dealership.

I waved at them and walked the short distance to my office. I logged on to my computer, returned some phone calls, and started digging through the pile of papers on my desk. A short time later, Ashley appeared in my doorway. "Welcome back, Jasmine," she said as she came over and gave me a hug.

"It's good to be back. How is everything?"

"Good." She handed me a sales report and sat down. "We will definitely exceed our sales goals for this month. People really love the new models, especially our hybrid SUV."

"That's great. I have a feeling that this will be a record year for us."

"That would be good." A new gleam entered her eyes and she switched the subject. "Did you talk to Kendall?"

I handed her a brochure with a detailed list of services. "Check this out."

She glanced over the brochure and said, "Wow, they do everything. It's a little pricey, isn't it?"

I handed her another brochure, from a spa in one of the downtown Chicago hotels. "I think Kendall's prices are competitive. She uses the best products, and her customers are willing to pay a little extra for the best."

Ashley compared the price lists. "So did you like the service?"

"Yes, it's heavenly, and her staff is top-notch. Ari has already checked out the financials and he says that it's a good investment for us. I think we should go for it."

"It sounds good so far."

I started to become excited. "Kendall's goal is for Secrets to be a national chain. She's making huge profits at all of her locations. All of her investors are getting big returns. I think it would be a gold mine for us, Ashley." I waved my arm toward the show-room. "We're running this business like a well-oiled machine, and I'm confident that we can run a spa even better. I mean, think about it, these luxury cars are easy to sell because it's a good product. People feel better about spending their money when they get what they pay for." Ashley was nodding, knowing just what I meant. "When it comes to pampering, people will pay extra to get the best. This business will thrive because it's a comfort service." I gave her a broad wink. "Plan to be pampered when we go to New York in two weeks."

She arched her back in pleasure. "You're right, Jasmine. I love to be pampered, and when I find a good masseuse, I don't really care what the cost is. Yeah, all right, let's get ready for New York. When are we meeting with Ari?"

"One day next week. He said that he'll have all of the legal documents ready for us to move forward."

"Cool. This sounds like a great opportunity."

"It is," I concluded. I felt a little funny, because here I was using my saleswoman skills on my partner. Then again, she knew me pretty well, and she didn't seem to mind. "So what else is going on? Did you talk to Tiffany?"

"I told her that we need to talk to her," she said, turning away.

"We?"

"Yeah, I think it should come from both of us."

I figured she just didn't want to confront her sister. "Okay. What time?"

"Main conference room at two."

"So, tell me, why did you change your mind?"

"Nicco came in looking for you a couple of days ago and then again yesterday. He talked to Tiffany both times, but yesterday she left shortly behind him and was gone for almost two hours."

I didn't like the sound of that. "Do you think something happened?"

"Yes. I don't know exactly what, but she's been inquiring about your relationship with him."

"I already told her that Nicco and I are no longer."

"I guess since he keeps coming in here to see you, she thinks there is something going on."

I let out an audible puff of breath. "I hate to see her get mixed up with him. He'll just use her."

"Yeah, I know. I wonder why Tiffany can't see that she's only a second thought. He isn't coming here to see her, he's looking for you."

"That's a problem in itself," I said irritably. "I don't know why he refuses to believe that I'm not interested in him."

She came closer and leaned across the desk. "You know, Jasmine, I'm really proud of you."

"Why?"

"I guess I was thinking the same as Nicco and I'm sure many others. I thought you would give in to him if he came back and said he wanted to be with you."

I'd been doing some thinking about that, and I had to level with her. "If he had done so a year ago, I probably would have, but now it's too late. I like my life the way it is, and if I was to get serious with anyone, it would be Sean. Guess what? He told me that he's in love with me."

She looked amazed. "Do you think he's bullshitting?"

"I don't know. I did confess I loved him first."

"You did?" As I nodded, she seemed even more impressed. Then she frowned. "I didn't think he was that into you, to do something like that."

"Neither did I."

"I guess both of you are masters at hiding your feelings. What will you do now?"

"I won't do anything. Sean's a player, Ashley. His phone rang off the hook while I was there. Off the hook. One woman even showed up at his condo because he forgot to cancel his date with her before I got there."

She started smiling, imaging how that must have been.

"Does Sean know about any of your friends?"

"He made a comment, but I told him it was nothing. I just don't want to start answering to anyone. He likes to control his surroundings."

That mean look of his came back to me and made me shift in my seat. I quickly changed the subject. "So, how are things with your new friend Joe?"

"Things are good," she said brightly. "We have another date tonight, so I won't be able to go to Sisqo's."

"I'm not going either. It seems like every time I go there, Nicco shows up."

After talking to Ashley, I called Sean to let him know I was home safely.

"Jasmine. I'm missing you already."

"I'm missing you, too. How much longer will you be in New York?"

"We should be done next week. Hey, I want to see you again. I was thinking about stopping in Chicago on my way home. You got time for me?"

"I've always got time for you," I said warmly. "Can you stay with me this time?"

"I would have stayed with you before if you'd offered."

"I never get a chance to invite you to stay with me," I said, "because you always call me after you're in town and checked into a hotel, so don't go there."

"I know, I'm sorry. Yes, I would love to stay with you."

"How long can you stay?"

"A couple of days. I should be there Friday and leaving Sunday."

When two o'clock rolled around, I saw Tiffany and Ashley engaged in conversation as I approached the conference room. They stopped talking when I crossed the threshold.

"Good afternoon, ladies," I said with a smile in my voice. I had decided to try a new approach with Tiffany.

Ashley answered, but Tiffany didn't.

"How are you today, Tiffany?" I said.

She looked me over before saying, "I'm doing just fine. I haven't seen you in a while."

"I was in New York."

"Nice. Does this job require traveling, because I really want to go somewhere."

I allowed her a tolerant smile. "After six months, you're entitled to a week of vacation. Maybe you should plan to get away then."

Beaten down, she said, "Yeah, I'm sure I can get one of my friends to take me somewhere."

"Speaking of friends, Tiffany," I said, warming to

my task, "there's been a lot of talk amongst the guys in the service department about how much time you spend back there. Your presence is disrupting the work flow, and I must ask you to stay out of the service area unless you have official business."

She looked offended. "I knew you felt threatened with me being here, but dang, Jasmine. These guys work in the service department, and I'm just having fun with them anyway."

"Victor is married."

"Yeah, he is, but I'm not, so I'm not concerned about hurting anyone. Being married is his problem. Is this about me going out with Nicco?"

I'd been half expecting that. "I didn't know that you went out with him and like I told you before, Tiffany, I'm trying to get rid of him. I have no interest in what Nicco does or whom he does it with, but I can tell you this." I pointed a finger at her. "He'll use you. Why would you want to be with a guy that you met while he was chasing me?"

"He's not chasing you, Jasmine. You're so full of yourself! He told me that the two of you dated and that he was coming around because he wanted to be sure that you were okay after he dumped you."

I didn't reply at first, to underline how ridiculous that idea was. "All right, Tiffany. Date Nicco. I don't care what you do with your free time." My voice instantly got tougher. "But what you do here at Taylor and Daniels is my business, and I'm telling you now, stay out of the service department and end your flirting with Victor. He's a married man, and so is Richard."

"Richard!"

"Yes, Richard. I heard that you were smiling in his face, too. This has been a family business for a long time, and we've managed to keep it drama-free until now." I pinned her down in my intense gaze. "Please, Tiffany, if you want to mess around with Nicco or whomever, that's your personal business, but don't disrupt the other people who work here with your business. Do you understand?"

She didn't like giving in, but she did. "Yes, very much. Is that it?"

"Yes, Tiffany, that's it."

She abruptly stood, brushed past Ashley, and marched off to her office.

I turned to Ashley and sighed. "That went well."

"Yeah, a little progress."

"At least she's not dressing like a hootchie anymore."

When I pulled into my driveway later that evening, Nicco was sitting on my porch, waiting for me.

I didn't know what to think. *I'll give him a minute to explain himself,* I thought, *before I ask him to leave.*

I stopped at the stairs and stared at him. "What are you doing here, Nicco?"

"I just wanted to see you and make sure you made it back safely from your trip."

"I'm fine."

"Can I come in?"

He looked so pathetic, I nodded. I'd kick him out soon enough. "Come on."

Nicco took a seat in the living room.

"Can I get you anything?"

"Do you have any juice?"

"Sure."

I went into the kitchen and poured some apple juice for him.

"So, Nicco, what's up?"

"Nothing. I thought maybe we could hang out, you know, go for a ride or something. Are you going to Sisqo's tonight?"

"No, I'm not in the mood."

"Come on and go for a ride with me, then. Let's talk. We really haven't had a chance to talk since I saw you a couple of weeks ago. I'm not trying to pressure you into getting back with me, but I do miss talking to you as a friend. Can we be friends, Jazz?"

"Nicco," I said cautiously, "I don't want to lead you on. I remember how possessive you are. Don't think that just because we're trying to be friends, you can show up at my house when you want to or question me about anything I do."

"I can be your friend without trying to control you. Come on, let's take a ride, get some dinner and catch up. I really don't know what's going on with you, and you don't know what's going on with me. I miss that."

"Okay. Give me a minute."

I went into my bedroom and slipped on a pair of jeans.

"Hey, Jazz," he shouted up the stairs. "I was thinking about having steppers sets at the club on Friday nights and was hoping you were interested in being my partner again."

"No, I don't think so," I shouted.

"Why not, Jazz? We dance so well together."

"I know, Nicco, I just don't want to make that kind of commitment."

We had a nice dinner and decent conversation, and Nicco didn't pressure me about getting back together.

When we returned to my house, he opened the door to help me out of his SUV, then he walked me to the door.

"I had a great time, Jazz. I hope we can do this again."

"I had a good time too, Nicco." I avoided offering to spend any more time with him.

He kissed me on the cheek and said, "Good night."

I watched him walk to his car. When I closed the door, I worried that this evening would give Nicco the wrong impression. I hoped he wouldn't make more out of it than what it was.

I called Kendall and told her that Ashley and I would be in New York to discuss the deal. She was just as excited about the idea as we were.

• • •

On Friday, Sean arrived at my house around noon. I had prepared for him all week. My house was spotless. I'd even gone grocery shopping so that I could cook for him.

Before speaking, Sean looked into my eyes and pressed his warm lips against mine. I opened my mouth to receive his probing tongue. His kiss was sensual and full of passion.

"Sean, I'm so happy that you're here."

"It's getting hard for me to stay away from you, Jasmine."

I kissed him for that and said, "I know."

After he put his things away, we went to the movies, then we spent the rest of the afternoon doing a little shopping and relaxing along the lakefront.

Sean asked if we could go to Sisqo's. He'd heard me talk about Sisqo's so much over the years, he wanted to check it out for himself.

I was happy to take him there and introduce him to some of my friends. We got dressed around nine thirty. I wore a low-cut, hip-hugging dress that I knew would keep Sean's attention.

When I appeared in the living room, he said, "You look so sexy in that dress. Why don't we stay in? Now that I think about it, I don't want to share you."

I tugged his shoulder as I walked past him. "Come on, Sean. You wanted to see what Sisqo's was about, and we're going. Believe me, I don't want to share you,

either, but I can for a little while." I lowered my voice
to a sexy timbre. "We won't stay long, okay?"

I hadn't heard from Nicco, and I'd thought that we
had an understanding, until we pulled into the parking lot at Sisqo's and I saw his truck. I had hoped that
he would leave me alone.

When Sean and I walked in the door, I spotted
Nicco immediately. He was at the far end of the bar,
facing the door and talking to some guy. I turned my
face away, hoping he hadn't seen me, but I knew he
had. Sean and I sat at the bar. I could feel Nicco staring
at me, but I refused to look his way. Instead, I gave all
my attention to Sean. He looked so good, as usual. I
saw other women in the bar eyeing him like a prime
rib, but I wasn't concerned. Sean would never do anything to disrespect me. His eyes never strayed once.

Sean's and Nicco's dress styles were like night and
day. Nicco almost always wore a suit. Very rarely did he
buy off the rack. Sean, on the other hand, loved urban
wear. He wore lots of expensive designer clothes,
shoes, jewelry. They were both very well groomed, just
two different styles.

Sean ordered a second round of drinks and then
said, "I'll be back. Where is the bathroom?"

I pointed him in the right direction. After he left,
I sat nervously hoping that Nicco wouldn't start any-
thing. I was relieved when I saw Ashley and her friend
Joe come through the door. Sean came back just as

they were approaching the bar. Ashley saw him first and said, "Sean, is that you?"

"Ashley, how are you?" he said as they hugged. Ashley introduced Sean to Joe, and Joe and I said hi. The bartender set drinks in front of Sean and me and said, "Jazz, these drinks are from Nicco."

Sean looked around sharply and said, "Nicco!"

I hadn't told him that Nicco was still coming around, and I grabbed his arm to prevent any confrontation. "Come on, Sean, let's just go," I said.

He patted my hand and said, "Naw, baby. I think it's about time I met Nicco. Where's he at?"

At that moment, Nicco started walking to our end of the bar. I wanted to run, but it was too late. Nicco stopped in front of me and said, "How you doing, Jazz?" His eyes were freely roaming all over my body. "You're wearing the shit out of that dress, damn!"

I said flatly, "Nicco, please don't do this."

"Did you and your friend get the drinks I sent?"

"Yes, thank you." I turned to Sean and said, "Sean, this is Nicco. Nicco, this is Sean."

Ashley was staring, her mouth open.

As Nicco started to lean on my chair, Sean stood up to block him. Sean was slightly taller than Nicco and a little bigger, but Nicco was unpredictable. I grabbed Sean's hand and said, "Are you ready to go?"

Nicco edged back. "Don't leave on my account." He smiled and said, "I guess you won't need me to take you home tonight. Call me when you need me, Jazz." He turned to walk away.

I felt Sean's body tense up. I knew he wouldn't let Nicco have the last word. "She won't need you for anything, and I would appreciate it if you'd leave her alone."

Nicco turned back and said, "Who are you?"

"I'm her man."

A puzzled look came over Nicco's face. "Jazz, you didn't mention that you had a man while we were at dinner the other night. I thought you said you were playing the field."

"Oooh!" Ashley said.

I closed my eyes for a second, took a deep breath, and slid off the bar stool. I grabbed Sean's hand and in a pleading voice said, "Let's go, Sean."

He pulled away. "No, we came here to have a drink and I'll be damned if some old boyfriend is gonna run me out of here." Then he addressed Nicco. "Look, man, Jasmine don't want you no more. I don't understand why she has to keep telling you, but I promise you, she's not getting back with you."

"Who are you, Jazz's spokesperson?"

Sean moved closer to Nicco, right into his personal space. "Yeah, that's exactly who I am, and I'm telling you to step off, man."

"Or what? What you gonna do from the West Coast?"

Sean was surprised that Nicco knew that. "What do you know about me?"

"More than you think." Nicco was pleased as hell

with the trouble he'd created. "Look, I just wanted to buy y'all a drink. I'm out of here." He turned to me and said, "Jazz, I will see you around."

In a defeated voice I said, "No, Nicco, you won't."

"All right, baby, I'll holla."

Sean was steaming mad and didn't say anything to me for at least ten minutes after Nicco had left. He ordered four shots in a row and paid for the drinks that Nicco had sent to us. I sat silently and sipped my drink. When he finally spoke, I was heartbroken.

He looked me in the eye and said, "You fucking him again, Jasmine?"

My eyes watered, but I was able to keep my composure. "No, Sean. I told you I wasn't interested in being with Nicco again and I meant it."

"Then why did you go to dinner with him?"

"I don't know. He asked me to go, I wasn't doing anything, and he wasn't pressuring me about us getting back together. I thought it was harmless. Nothing happened." I found myself pleading again. "I swear Sean, nothing happened."

I could tell he didn't believe me. He stood up and paid the bar tab, then he grabbed my hand and said, "Let's go."

I said bye to Ashley and Joe. When we walked outside, I saw Nicco's truck idling in the corner of the lot. I knew that he was watching us. When we got close to Sean's car, he stopped and said, "Why was he saying he'd see you around?"

"Because he won't leave me alone," I protested.

I moved close and tried to kiss him, but he opened the car door for me and waited while I slid inside. Once we were on the road, Sean stared straight ahead. He didn't even turn on the music. The silence was deafening.

"Sean."

"What?" His tone was harsh.

"I didn't know that he would be there. Why are you letting him mess up our evening?"

"Because I don't trust you, Jasmine. He sure as hell wanted me to know that you spent time with him. How does he know who I am?"

"I don't know," I said, feeling a headache coming on. "He's mentioned knowing about you before."

When we got back to my house, Sean had some phone calls to return, so I took a shower and put on something sexy that I knew he would like. When he finished his calls, he came into the bedroom and stripped down to his underwear, got into bed, and turned on the TV. I pretended to look for something on the armoire next to the TV. I wanted him to get an eyeful, but he picked up a magazine and looked away. I didn't like the way Sean was ignoring me, so I walked over to his side of the bed to show him some love. When he saw me coming, he put his arms up and said, "Not now, Jasmine."

I had never been rejected like that, and he really hurt my feelings. Besides that, I was getting mad. I stormed into the bathroom, slamming the door behind me. I stared at myself in the mirror, wondering why I felt compelled to kiss Sean's ass when I hadn't done anything wrong. I changed into my nightgown. When I got into bed, I turned my back to Sean and eventually fell asleep.

Sometime during the night, he woke me up with kisses and we made love. Naw, I think he fucked me.

All the anger had faded by the next morning, though. Sean wrapped me in his arms and planted kisses on my face. He turned on the TV and began channel surfing. I had an uneasy feeling when my phone rang. I reached over Sean and picked it up.

"Hey, Jazz, what's up?"

"Stop calling me!" I said, then I hung up on him.

Sean got out of bed and headed to the bathroom, slamming the door. I went down the hall and showered in another bathroom. When I returned to the bedroom, Sean was waiting for me.

"Come here and sit down, Jasmine, I need to talk to you."

I didn't like his tone. It scared me. I sat next to him while unpinning my hair and shaking it loose.

"Listen, Jasmine. I love spending time with you. You're smart and beautiful, and just about everything about you is all that I could wish for." He paused. "The problem is, I don't trust you, and trust is really important to me. It took me a long time to find the courage to say I love you. I've never told any woman that, so that was big for me. Even after you knew how I felt about you, you went out to dinner with Nicco. You can't imagine how I felt last night. After you told me that you didn't want to be with him, I believed you. I'm all mentally fucked up now. I ain't even gonna lie. I thought about it all night and today, and I just can't do this with you."

I had tears in my eyes. "Can't do what, Sean?"

He looked away. "I can't be serious with you. I thought I wanted to, but even after I told you how I felt, going out of my way to spend time with you, doing shit you know I don't do, you turn around and go to dinner with your ex. We can still be friends, but I can't handle any more than that."

I was stunned. "You don't want to be with me anymore, Sean?"

"I wish I could, because I love you, but I don't trust you and I can't have a woman that I don't trust."

"What about all of the other women you're seeing? I'm not trippin' about that, Sean." I was openly crying. "What about last night? You already knew that you didn't want to see me anymore, didn't you?"

He didn't say anything.

"Sean. You knew, didn't you?"

"Yeah, I knew."

"Then why? Why did you have sex with me?"

"I'm sorry, Jasmine," he said tonelessly. "I shouldn't have. I should have left last night."

"So that's it? You tell me you love me, I tell you that

I love you, too, and just like that, it's over. You walk away from me because Nicco won't stop bothering me?"

He stood. "Once you knew how I felt, I thought you were smart enough to know that what's mine is mine and I don't like to share."

"But I didn't do anything, Sean. Won't you give me a chance to show you how much I love you?" I knew the answer, though.

He started packing his bag. "I can't."

I sat on the bed and silently cried. When he had all his things packed, he walked past me, but stopped at the door. He looked back and said, "It was fun, baby, be good."

12

Jasmine

I woke up the next morning in the same clothes that I had worn the day before. My eyes were swollen and red from crying. I couldn't believe that I was in this situation. Since Nicco, I had promised myself that I would never let a man make me feel miserable again. I hadn't seen this one coming. A few days ago, I'd been happily in love—and now look at me.

I took a shower, put on a robe, and lay in bed. There were messages on my answering machine and my phone was ringing. I didn't have the energy to speak with anyone, so I let the call go to the answering machine.

Nicco's voice came across strong and clear: "Jazz, it's me. I hope you got that man out of your house. Look, I'm sorry about what happened the other night. I hope I didn't cause any trouble for you and your man. I'll leave you alone, but if you ever need anything, call me and I'll be there."

I had started crying again when I heard my front door open. When I looked up, Ashley was standing in the doorway of my bedroom.

"Jasmine, what is wrong with you? I've been calling you since last night. What's going on?"

"I'm sorry, Ashley, I just haven't been feeling well."

When she'd had a good look at me, she said, "Damn, girl, you look terrible. What's wrong?"

"Nothing," I said, sniffling. "I'll be okay."

"You've been crying. What is it? Is it Sean?"

I started crying again and Ashley put her arms around me.

I told her that Sean had left me.

"He did?" She wouldn't let me feel sorry for myself any longer. She clapped her hands. "Come on and get out of the bed. Get up, get dressed, and let's get out of the house." She clapped her hands a few more times. "You have messages on your machine. Has Sean called?"

"No," I said sullenly. "He made it clear that he doesn't want me anymore. He's not one to mince his words. He says what he means, and he meant it." I couldn't help feeling stricken. "It was so cold and so final. What's wrong with me, Ashley? Why do I keep meeting these men that walk out on me?"

"There's nothing wrong with you, Jasmine. It's not you, it's them. Nicco and Sean are a lot alike. I hate to say it, but it's true. They're both possessive, and they want to have all of you, but don't want to give all of themselves."

I nodded in agreement. Sean had been too willing to believe I was guilty. That told me he really wasn't ready to make a commitment. "Why do I keep falling for the same type of man?"

"Power," she said simply. "They are both powerful men."

I shook my head, realizing how stupid I'd been. "I knew not to get involved with Sean like that, but I did anyway, and he just walked away from me like I didn't mean anything to him."

I sat up and made an effort to get going. "I can't go through this again, Ashley. Fuck both of them."

I jumped out of bed and headed for the bathroom. "I talked to Kendall and we have a meeting with her next Thursday at three o'clock. We'll go to the spa and get the royal treatment first, so that you'll know first-hand what we're investing in. Afterward, we'll meet with Kendall."

She saw what a strain it was for me to act all professional. "Jasmine, we don't have to talk about business right now. Take some time to get it together. Are you still coming to Richard's party tonight?"

In my misery I had forgotten all about it. *A party*, I thought, *that's just what I need*. "You know I'm not going to miss that."

I don't know if Jason just happened because I wanted it or if I was looking for something different when I went to Richard's house. I just knew that Sean had done me wrong.

Ashley and Joe were already there when I arrived. Joe was very personable and had found some guys to hang out with. Ashley and I were sitting on the deck, checking everything out, when Jason walked outside. He was dressed in jean shorts, a white T-shirt, and white Air Force Ones. He wore his hair in a short fade, diamond earring in his left ear, dark brown skin, almost six feet and weighing around 190 pounds. I was mesmerized. I knew he caught me staring at him. I'd seen him somewhere before, but I couldn't put my finger on it.

Richard came outside a few seconds later. "Jasmine, Ashley, I want you to meet my cousin Jason. Jason, these are my bosses."

I kept my face neutral. "It's nice to meet you, Jason."

"You too. I'll be at your dealership one day soon, probably Monday. I'm looking at the new LS460. Richard said you can give me a good deal."

I said, "We'll take care of you. I've seen you somewhere before. . . ."

"You may have seen me in the paper, on the news or something. I'm the press secretary to the mayor."

He was looking better and better. "I believe that's it. Come on, sit down and talk to us."

"Okay. Can I get you ladies another drink?"

Ashley wanted a glass of white wine, and I asked for a rum and Coke.

"I'll be right back, ladies."

Ashley and I were grinning from ear to ear. I said in a hushed tone, "Girl, he is fine as hell."

"Ain't he? I wonder if he's single."

"We'll soon find out, now won't we?"

She raised an eyebrow at me, guessing my game. "I'm sure you will."

I adjusted my clothes and checked my hair before Jason returned. "Whatever, girl. I could go there."

"I see the ho is back."

"Not completely, but damn, Ashley, did you see him? How can you pass up an opportunity like that, if he's available. I'm gonna see what's up."

"You go on and do what you do."

When Jason returned, he handed us our drinks and took a seat. "So, ladies, you two here alone?"

Ashley said, "No, my man is around here somewhere."

"I don't have a man," I said sadly.

"I find that hard to believe." He was showing a lot more interest than he had a moment ago.

"It's true, Jason. I'm here all alone," I said, continuing in my alluring tone.

Ashley said, "Excuse me. I need to find Joe."

After she left, Jason moved to the seat closer to me. "So, Ms. Jasmine, what's it gonna take to get to know you better?"

"Conversation."

"What do you say we go for a walk and talk?"

Since Richard's house was close to a forest preserve, we decided to take a walk along the bike path. Not far along, we sat on one of the decorative benches.

"So, how do you spend your free time since you're a single woman?"

"I don't really have a lot of free time. Ashley and I run the business, and it takes a lot of time. I date when I get a chance, but that's not very often."

"So what do you do for pleasure?"

I folded my hands together across my lap. "I haven't had a lot of that lately."

"I can help you out with that."

I remained calm and looked at him innocently. "Can you really?"

"Most definitely. There's no reason for a good-looking woman like yourself not to have a man around when she needs him for whatever reason. I'd like to be there to take care of your needs." He came closer, so we were almost touching. "Are you in need of anything right now?"

"Actually, I am."

"What can I do to help?"

My tone became more stern. "Are you married?"

"No. I'm free and single. Why don't we go back to the party, say our goodbyes, and get ourselves a private spot?"

He was coming on strong, but I didn't mind a bit. "Okay, Jason. I like your take-charge attitude."

When we got back to the cookout, some people were playing cards, and Richard insisted that Jason play with him. We stayed at the party for a few more hours, talking and getting to know each other, before Jason asked me again if I wanted to find a private spot.

I found Ashley and told her I was leaving to go for a ride with Jason.

She was a little drunk and said sloppily, "All right, Jasmine. Just go for a ride in the car, please. Don't go riding anything else."

I said bye to Richard and his wife and thanked them for inviting me. When we got outside, Jason told me to follow him. He was driving a Porsche Cayenne. He looked good in it. I'd sell him another car that would look even better.

I followed Jason for about ten minutes to a Hampton Inn.

In the room, he pulled out a bottle of champagne and two glasses that he had taken from Richard's house. As he handed me a glass filled with bubbly, I said, "Thank you, Jason."

"You're welcome."

I took a sip and set the glass on the table. He had such a commanding presence, I was turned on and couldn't wait to get close to him. The champagne went straight to my head on top of the rum and Coke I had been drinking. I hoped I wouldn't get sick later, but right now I was feeling just right.

Jason sat in the chair next to the bed. I took another sip of my drink and started dancing to the music while slowly removing my clothes. Jason enjoyed my strip-tease and kept trying to lure me closer, but I playfully stayed out of reach. He removed his shirt, revealing his muscular chest. His shorts and underwear also came off.

I couldn't wait to feel him inside me, but I wanted him to be hungry as a lion before I let him touch me.

I removed my bra and my breasts jumped out. I walked over to Jason and made him an offer. As soon as his warm tongue touched my nipple, it became hard as stone, and my pussy instantly started throbbing. I pulled away, turned my back to him, bent over, and slowly pulled my thong off. I heard the chair fall over as he got up. He was on me within seconds. I felt his hard dick against my lower spine. He started kissing my neck and down my back. Jason turned me around and started sucking and kissing my breasts again. I was hot and wet, but I managed to pull away. I dropped to my knees and took him in my mouth. Gasping, he grabbed on to the dresser to keep his balance. When I felt him getting too excited, I got up and walked over to the bed. I didn't want him to come in my mouth. I had a better place.

I climbed onto the bed, lay across it, and opened my legs. He came over and started right in kissing my inner thighs. When he saw my tattoo, he had a smirk on his face, and he started kissing and licking his way up to my pussy.

The soft and warm kisses were driving me crazy. Jason knew how badly I wanted to feel his tongue inside me just from my reaction to his touch. I arched my back when he finally parted my pussy lips with his tongue.

"Ahhhh!" I exhaled a cry of pleasure. He pushed his tongue inside me and slowly licked me wide open.

He rose above me and held his dick in his hand as he pushed deep inside me. His strokes were slow and methodical. He didn't say a word while he fucked me. He brought me close to another climax and then pulled out. I felt almost desperate, but he was merely teasing. He did this to me a couple of times before he started stroking me hard and fast. We came together, and although I'd promised myself I wouldn't, I couldn't hold in the scream that escaped.

He rolled off me and we lay next to each other, sweating and panting for the next few minutes. Finally, I jumped up, grabbed my clothes, and took a quick shower.

When I came back into the room, I found Jason sitting on the side of the bed. I walked over to him, gave him a last kiss, and walked out the door, leaving him staring after me.

By the time I got home, though, I was feeling worse than ever. I'd thought that spending time with Jason would help me move past Sean, but it had only made me miss him more. I had to get Sean out of my system. I was sure he wasn't thinking about me.

All day I had constantly checked my cell phone, hoping to hear from him, but I knew he wouldn't call. He'd moved on to someone else. Maybe that chick Brenda or even Ebonie. He had choices.

13

I couldn't remember ever being as mad as I was when I found out that Jasmine had gone out to dinner with Nicco. I should have left right then and there, but I couldn't. I needed to sort out my thoughts.

When she'd walked into the bedroom wearing that thong and bra, I'd had to act like I wasn't interested. I wanted her bad, but I'd had to do it my way. I had let her fall asleep mad. My anger wouldn't let me sleep, though, so I'd lain awake, watching her. I loved this woman, but I couldn't have this kind of drama in my life. I had to be strong and let her go. I knew I was getting too attached to her, and this incident gave me the excuse I needed to break away. I didn't want to be tied down, and she obviously didn't want to be, either.

After I broke up with Jasmine for good, I headed to the Sheraton, where I emptied the minibar and passed out for the night.

When I got home, I threw myself into my work. I had thought I would break up with her and that would be it. Yet I was thinking about her more now than I had before we'd broken up. I needed to get out of the house, so I headed to the studio downtown. I loved the bustling atmosphere, and being in the studio usually kept me focused on my work.

I was in the engineering booth when Ray walked into the studio with four women. He was holding a cup of something, and right then I knew our day would be unproductive. Ray was one of those people who shouldn't drink. I believe he was allergic to alcohol. He got stupid and then into trouble.

Jimmy groaned at the sight of Ray and his entourage. "Look at this shit, Sean. We won't get any work done."

Ray asked, "Are you talking about me, Jimmy?"

"All these women mean trouble. Oh, why waste my breath?"

He sat down and said, "Come on, Jimmy, that was two years ago. The charges were dropped."

"The charges weren't the problem, Ray. You interfered with the trust in my marriage. To this day, my wife doesn't trust me. I can't do shit without her thinking I'm at a strip club or some shit, thanks to you."

Ray didn't seem to mind, but he said, "I'm sorry about that, man. Let's try to move past this. We were once really tight. Seriously, though, Jimmy, I'm truly sorry for getting you in trouble like that."

"Yeah, all right, Ray."

Ray sat in a rolling chair, opened his arms, and said, "So, we're all good?"

"Yeah, Ray, we're good."

Ray was in a talkative mood, loosened up by the liquor. "So, Jimmy, tell me what's up with this chick Jasmine? I think Sean is gonna be settled down soon."

I said with a dangerous undertone, "Don't go there, Ray. Me and Jasmine are just friends." I was hoping that Jimmy wouldn't jump on the bandwagon, but that was wishful thinking.

"I know, right?" he said with this big grin. "Man, you don't know the half of it."

"What's up, Sean? She's fine as hell and she seems smart."

"She is," Jimmy said. "She owns a Lexus dealership. She has her own money and she doesn't chase him like these other women. She's perfect for him."

"So what's the problem, Sean?" Ray said, enjoying my discomfort.

I played it off. "There is no problem. Things work just fine between me and Jasmine the way they are."

"How old are you, Sean? Thirty-four like me, right?"

"What does my age have to do with anything?"

"You're thirty-four years old, no kids. Hello, I've never known you to have a real girlfriend since Toni Hall back in Detroit. It's always been a different woman every time I see you. What's up with that?"

"I like variety, and I haven't met a woman that I wanted to settle down with."

Jimmy said, "Yeah, not until Jasmine. I keep telling him that she won't be available forever."

Little did he know, I wasn't taking what was offered. I said, "Can we get to work?"

"All right, Sean. You know that Jimmy is right," Ray said.

"I know you two are a couple of matchmakers. You should call up my mother and have a hen party."

They busted out laughing.

I was right. Ray was worthless as a singer that day. After too many blown takes, I finally told him to get lost. That left me and Jimmy alone in the engineering booth.

"You've been acting all fucked up ever since you came back from Chicago," he observed. "I don't know what happened, but whatever you did, you made the wrong decision."

I didn't want to hear it. "Man, you don't even know what you're talking about."

"Whatever got you like this ain't good for nobody around here. You snappin' on people and shit. You keep it up and somebody is gonna kick your ass."

I turned my chair away from him. "Leave me alone, Jimmy."

In a kinder tone, he said, "What's up, Sean? What happened? Is it Jasmine?"

"Fuck her."

He let out a groan. "Yeah, I guess it's Jasmine. What happened? You were all in love a few days ago, and now all you can say is fuck her. Come on, Sean, what's up?"

I turned back to him and told him what had happened. He'd helped me through some stuff before and I trusted his advice.

"Sean, man, are you gonna be all right?"

I smiled and said, "Yeah, I'm good. I just don't understand how she can tell me she loves me and then turn around and go out with old boy."

"Did y'all have that kind of relationship?"

"Man, I told her while we were in New York that I couldn't deal with her seeing other men."

Jimmy had a puzzled look on his face. "So it was okay for you to see other women, but she couldn't see anybody else, right?"

"Man, I was ready to give up this lifestyle for her." I put my head down and said, "I fucking told her that I was in love with her, and she turned around and did this to me."

Jimmy pulled back, taken by surprise. "Hold up. Did you say you told her that you were in love with her?"

I whispered, "Yeah."

Jimmy tried to contain his laughter but could not. "So that's really why you're all fucked up, ain't it, Sean? You're in love with her, and you're pissed off that somebody else is interested in her. You thought she was going to stop doing what she was doing because you made a confession, even though you didn't stop seeing other women when she told you how she felt about you."

"No, that's not it."

"Yeah, that's it," he said in triumph. All these years he'd been telling me to settle down, and now I'd said I loved someone.

"You know what, I don't want to talk about this anymore. Let's go."

At home, I listened to some slow ballads, sat out on the deck and watched the sun set. I didn't know how to deal with what was happening to me. I really did need to talk to somebody about this. Jimmy tried, but I didn't think he could help me. I wanted to call my mother, but I've never had this kind of conversation with her. I poured myself a shot of whiskey and then the phone rang.

"Hello."

"Sean, why haven't I heard from you since you left New York?"

I was shocked that she knew I'd been thinking about her. "Mama? I was just thinking about you, and you called."

"Is everything all right?"

"Yes. No. Well, I sort of have a problem that I don't know how to handle."

She was delighted that I'd turned to her. "Talk to me and let me see if I can help."

"I think I'm in love."

"With Jasmine?"

"Yeah."

"Why is that a problem?"

I sighed. "I told her I didn't want to see her anymore."

With an edge in her voice she asked, "Are you running from your feelings?"

"No, I don't think so. I don't know, Ma. She has been seeing her ex and I don't like it."

"Is that why you told her you didn't want to see her anymore?"

"Well, yeah," I said defensively. "I don't think she should be seeing anyone else. She told me that she loved me, too. Why would she see him again?"

As usual, she cut to the heart of the matter. "Did you two agree that you wouldn't see anyone else?"

"No."

"Then what is the problem, Sean? Did you stop dating all of the women you see?"

"No," I said, then tried to explain. "But she said that she was in love with me and was able to deal with me seeing other people. She said she just didn't think about it. I even told her that I didn't want her to see anyone else. I thought we had an understanding."

"You obviously had some miscommunications. Just call her, Sean. Maybe you can work something out that works for both of you."

"Okay, Ma, I'll call her," I said, just to please her.

I knew that I wasn't ready to talk to Jasmine yet. I

had to let more time go by. Besides, she hadn't tried to call me, so I guessed that not being with me was okay with her.

Just the thought made me want to shout, *Why did I ever allow myself to get into this mess?*

14

Jasmine

Ashley and I were tying up loose ends before leaving for New York the next morning. She had talked to Tiffany after our explosive meeting and said that Tiffany was cool with everything we'd talked about.

Knowing I was heading into Sean's territory, I decided to spite him. I called Michael to see what was going on. "Hey, stranger," I said. "How are you?"

"I'm good, but I'm feeling much better now that I'm talking to you, Ms. Jasmine. What's up?"

"I'll be in your part of the country tomorrow, and I was hoping that you can spare a few minutes of your time to say hi."

I heard the excitement leap in his voice. "Yeah, of course. I've got plenty of time for you."

I smiled. "Maybe we can get together tomorrow evening."

"Let's get some dinner and take it from there."

Ashley was waiting when I arrived to pick her up and we headed to Midway Airport. She fell asleep shortly after takeoff. I plugged in my iPod and thought about my future and how I planned to live it. Opening a spa in Chicago would keep me busy.

My thoughts eventually drifted back to Sean and my behavior with men in general over the past few years—well, since Nicco. I had given too much of myself to him, and I'd never do that again. I needed a man that could love me for who I am. I'm a flirt, I know that, and I thought Sean accepted that about me. I was surprised that he'd been so upset because I still allowed Nicco to see me. But I think Sean was just looking for a way out. So I'd let him out. I had to realize that he wasn't the man for the job, and it was time that I stopped settling.

I just wished I could stop thinking about him.

When we arrived in New York, we went directly to Kendall's spa for our eleven-o'clock meeting. After making the introductions, Kendall, Ashley, and I started our meeting on the massage table. We did a full tour of the facility and indulged in most of the services as we talked about our future franchise in Chicago. I wanted to be smooth and soft for my dinner date with Michael.

We scheduled a second meeting with Kendall and a few of her key staff members for two o'clock the next afternoon. That would be the final pitch, and Ashley and I would give Kendall our decision at that time. I was already sold on the idea.

We flagged down a cab and headed to the W Hotel on Lexington.

"So, what did you think?" I said.

"I love it, girl. A Secrets Spa would do very well in Chicago. Did you have a location in mind?"

"Yes. There's a vacant lot not far from the dealership that I need to call Trina about. She'll give me the details, and if things work out, we can start building soon."

Ashley grabbed my arm and gave it a slight tug. "I'm excited, Jasmine. I'm really excited. I'll be our best customer."

I patted her hand. "You and me both. Hey, do you mind if I get away for a little while this evening?"

A caution light went on instantly in her eyes. "Michael?"

"Yes. He wants to take me to dinner."

"Yeah, I'm sure that's it," she said with a wink.

I saw him the moment I stepped into the lobby. He looked relaxed. His long torso was stretched out with his legs crossed as he read a magazine. He looked up and smiled as I approached.

"Jasmine," he said. A flood of heat ran through my entire body when he stood. He wore a pair of charcoal slacks and a white shirt, and his Burberry tie was loose at the neck.

We greeted each other, then Michael offered his arm and I took it as we headed for his car. When the doorman saw us step outside, he signaled for the valet to retrieve Michael's Mercedes sedan.

Once we were in the car, Michael looked at me and smiled before pulling into traffic. "How are you enjoying your visit so far, Jasmine?"

"It's been very nice. I had a full spa day, and now I'm spending time with you. I don't think it can get any better."

He gave the steering wheel a little tap. "It will get better. Let's see where the evening takes us."

Michael had made reservations at Le Bernardin. I wasn't easily impressed anymore, but I did like this restaurant.

"Nice decor," I said.

"Only the best for you." As we waited to be seated, Michael said, "I'm so happy that you're here, Jasmine. I enjoy your company and I can't stop thinking about you. If only we had met under different circumstances."

"I know."

After we were escorted to our table, Michael handed me a gift bag. "I saw this and thought of you."

Intrigued, I looked inside. I opened the jewelry box to reveal a beautiful silver bracelet. "It's beautiful, Michael. Thank you."

He brushed his hand along my face. "You're welcome, beautiful."

I blushed and looked away.

He must have truly enjoyed our time together in Chicago.

He took the bracelet and hooked it onto my wrist. I smiled and thanked him again.

Our eyes were locked on each other until the waiter arrived to take our order. Michael ordered lobster for me and red snapper for himself. Within minutes of placing our orders, Aldo, the restaurant's sommelier, was at Michael's side to recommend the perfect bottle of wine.

After completing our orders, Michael sat back and relaxed. I couldn't keep my eyes off him. If the situation were different, I wondered, would we have had a chance at a relationship? I liked Michael more than I should have. He was very masculine, and I loved his style and the way he carried himself. He was almost enough to erase Sean from my mind.

As we talked, we stayed away from the subject of Nicco, and I was happy about that. The food was superb, and we enjoyed a great conversation about everything else before heading out.

Inside the car, Michael asked, "Would you like to come by my place for a nightcap, or are you in a hurry to get back to your hotel?"

"A nightcap sounds good."

His loft was beautiful. If it had been mine, I wouldn't have changed a thing. I loved the dark wood floors, the floor-to-ceiling windows, the spacious and open floor plan. Michael let me roam around freely as he flipped on lights. He watched me in a lustful way, and I made sure to keep his attention riveted on me. I kicked my shoes off and swung my hips as I strolled from room to room, checking out the artwork on the walls, the sculptures, and the family portraits.

I wore a short, low-cut dress that exposed a lot of skin. I finally found my way to the couch and waited for Michael to join me. He stood at the bar and fixed drinks for us. I watched as he removed his tie and rolled up his shirtsleeves before walking over to the couch and handing me a glass.

With a push of a button, Usher began singing in surround sound.

"Dance with me, Jasmine."

I set my glass on the cocktail table and stood up. He pulled me close and ran his fingers through my hair while we kissed. Slow at first, but when we started a slow grind, our kiss became hungry.

I pulled away and sat down. Michael sat right next to me.

"Everything all right?"

"Yes." I picked up my drink and took a sip. "I don't want to rush, and being close to you like this gets me too excited."

He smiled at hearing that. With his forefinger, he pulled the top of my dress aside, and slipped his hand inside my bra. I leaned back, feeling blissful as he began kissing my breasts and teasing my nipple with his finger. He unbuttoned my dress and slipped it off my shoulders.

"Mmmmm, Michael. Why did I have to meet you like this?"

He sat up when he heard the questioning tone in my voice. He picked up his drink, took a sip, and asked, "What do you mean?"

"I like you. We could have been really good friends."

"I thought we were friends."

"We can't really have a full and free friendship because of Nicco. I'm just saying, Michael, it would be nice to spend more time with you."

"We can continue to see each other like this. You come here or I come to Chicago. Or we can meet somewhere else and spend time together."

I put my drink on the table and climbed into Michael's lap. I began a slow grind on him. After a few minutes, I got up, grabbed my drink, sashayed around in my bra and thong. Soon, he came up behind me and wrapped his arms around my waist.

He whispered in my ear, "I want you, Jasmine."

I turned to face him. "How much of me do you want?" I said in a sultry voice.

"All of you. I want to go deep inside you."

He took his shirt off and I ran my hands across his finely sculpted chest and muscular arms.

"Mmmmm," I said. "Look at you. I've been dreaming about what I know you can do for me."

"What can I do for you?"

"Fuck me."

He unhooked my bra and filled his hands with my breasts. I reached for his belt buckle and we continued to kiss while I opened his pants and helped him out of them.

We climbed onto the leather sectional and practically clawed each other as he tried to get inside me. Sex was rushed the first time because we were both so eager to come together again.

We opened another bottle of wine, and sex was better the second time.

After more wine, we went for round three. I was drunk and so was Michael when we finally fell asleep.

We woke up to someone banging on the door. The music was still playing, and it seemed louder than I remembered. Michael kissed me before slipping on his pants. I smiled and closed my eyes again. I needed to get up, but my head was pounding and I needed a little more sleep. Michael found the remote and turned the music off.

The banging started again.

"Okay, dammit, I'm coming!" he shouted.

When he opened the door, Nicco pushed his way inside. "I stood outside pushing that damn buzzer for ten minutes, man. Thank God someone came out of the building and let me in. You got your music all loud and shit early in the morning, man. What's up with you?"

When I heard Nicco's voice, I froze. What was he

doing in New York? He stepped farther into the condo, looked at the couch, and stopped in his tracks.

"Jazz, is that you?"

Michael rushed in front of Nicco before he reached me. "Let me explain, man."

Nicco turned to Michael and in an angry voice said, "There ain't shit to explain, man. This who you was fucking while you was visiting me, ain't it?"

"Nicco, man, listen."

He looked directly at me as I tried to cover my naked body. "Jasmine, you were right. I guess I don't know you anymore. I didn't know you'd become a whore."

"Nicco, man, come on. Don't talk to her like that."

I sat frozen. I tried to reach for my dress or Michael's shirt, but I couldn't reach either.

"Fuck you, Mike. You supposed to be my boy, and you're fucking my girl. I tell you how hard I've been trying to work things out with Jazz, and you've been fucking her since the day you two met." He paced to the window wall. "I knew something was going on with y'all. That's all right, y'all are meant for each other, because ain't neither one of y'all worth shit! Fuck both of y'all!"

I finally found the courage to move. I didn't care that I had to walk past both of them while butt naked. I grabbed my clothes and ran into the bathroom. I sat on the edge of the bathtub and started crying. I was surprised by my reaction. I knew there was always a chance of Nicco finding out about us and I thought I wanted that, but when it actually happened, I felt like a worthless tramp. I stood up and looked in the mirror and started crying harder. I didn't like the person I saw.

When I finally recovered, I dressed and went back into the living room. Michael was sitting on the couch with his head in his hands. Nicco was nowhere to be found, and I was thankful for that.

I said, "I'm going now, Michael. I'm sorry about what happened. I didn't want to come between you and Nicco. I know he won't talk to me again, but I hope the two of you can work it out."

Michael didn't say anything. I grabbed my purse and walked to the door. Before I opened the door, he rushed over. "Wait, Jasmine. I'll take you to your hotel."

"I can take a cab. I need a little time to myself."

"I hope you don't regret what happened with us. I know the outcome isn't what either of us wanted, but I'm attracted to you, Jasmine, and like we said before, I wish we had met under different circumstances."

I wasn't going to tell Michael that it was over.

He went on. "We're attracted to each other, what's wrong with that? I know that we broke some friendship rules, but what's done is done. I still want to be your friend."

"I don't know, Michael."

"Nicco and I will work things out, okay? Don't worry about it."

"Okay, Michael. I've got to go."

I returned to my hotel tired and very unhappy. I lay in bed, thinking about the things that I'd done since Nicco and I had broken up, and I wasn't very proud of myself. I'd had an opportunity to be with the man I loved, but I had messed that up.

I decided to make some changes in my life. I thought that maybe I should try to open the door to Sean again. But would he ever bother to walk through that door?

Soon I had to dress for our meeting with Kendall and her people. Ashley had called and said she would meet me in the lobby at one thirty. We headed over from there.

I did my best to concentrate, but I was out of sorts because of my earlier encounter with Nicco. I don't know why I felt guilty after all the things he'd done to me. Plus, he was the reason that Sean and I were not together anymore.

At last I focused my attention on the speaker. Kendall's group laid out their plans for a spa in Chicago. They had several desirable locations, one of which was an empty lot in Hyde Park. Ashley and I were very excited about this opportunity and were ready to get started. Once our attorneys negotiated an agreement, we could move forward.

After the meeting, Kendall took us to dinner at Uncle Jack's Steakhouse, in midtown. I had a flashback of the time I'd spent there with Sean and his mother, but I quickly put that out of my mind. I was happy to have something new and exciting to think about. A Secrets Spa in Chicago would be a huge success. The car dealership practically ran itself, and we could concentrate on getting the project off the ground.

After lunch, we did some shopping.

Everything was going ahead smoothly except for one thing: I still had a big hole in my heart.

We had a light dinner. I didn't have an appetite, but I didn't want to leave Ashley to do everything alone.

"Are you okay, Jasmine? You've been so quiet this afternoon."

"I'm just a little tired. I need a nap."

She smiled sheepishly. "You must have had a good time with Michael last night."

I mustered a weak smile. "Yes, it was fine."

I hadn't told her what had happened between me, Michael, and Nicco. I was too embarrassed.

Ashley said that she was tired, too, and when we returned to our hotel, she went to her room. I decided to take a walk, hoping to clear my head of Sean. He was heavy on my mind.

Our hotel wasn't far from Sean's studio. I had booked our rooms there purposely before the breakup. I also remembered a Cold Stone Creamery a few doors down. I suddenly had a taste for ice cream.

I was excited when I walked past the studio entrance. Being this close made me want to see Sean. I slowed as I walked by, but quickly lost my courage. I walked into the ice cream shop and ordered a Chocolate Devotion. I thought the chocolate would make me feel better.

As I walked to the exit, Sean came through the door with a woman. I almost choked as I scooped a spoonful of the delicious ice cream into my mouth. We looked at each other, but I turned away and walked past him. Out of the corner of my eye, I saw him stop.

"Jasmine," he called.

I stopped and turned around. "Yes, Sean?"

He looked at me. "Why did you ignore me?"

I shrugged my shoulders. "I don't know."

"Come here."

Shit! I thought. I felt grungy, and he looked as good as usual. He took my breath away with his style and class.

The woman he was with kept walking.

"What's up, Jasmine? What brings you to New York?"

"I'm here on business."

"Oh, yeah? You staying nearby?"

"Yes. The W around the corner. I hadn't realized that I was so close to your studio until I walked past."

"Yeah, I'm right here, Jasmine." He looked serious as he added, "Jasmine, I've missed you."

I looked past him at the woman waiting at the ice cream counter, and I smiled politely. "It was really good seeing you, Sean." Seeing him with a woman had changed my mood. I just wanted to get away.

He looked flustered. I guess my response wasn't what he'd expected. "Okay, Jasmine. Can I call you?"

"I don't think that's a good idea, Sean. I can't go back."

"You can't or you won't? Which is it?"

"I guess both. I've got to go." I was suddenly in a terrible hurry to get out of there. "Your date is waiting."

I rushed back to the hotel. Seeing Sean had me messed up all over again. Those old feelings resurfaced with a vengeance. I still loved him.

I replayed the entire encounter in my head from beginning to end. He'd been wearing the Rolex I bought him. I remembered the night I gave it to him. He had given me so many nice and expensive gifts, and I wanted to give him something to always remember me by. I had the Rolex inscribed, *Friends Forever*, JASMINE.

He loved it, I saw it in his eyes. He wore it often and it warmed my heart to see it on his arm.

I snapped back to the present and realized that I had to get out of New York before I did something stupid like try to see him again.

15

The week was going by pretty fast and we'd accomplished a lot in the studio. It was after two in the morning that night before we made it back to the condo. Jimmy and I both crashed on the couch. Just as I lay back, my cell phone rang.

"Hey, Sean, baby," she slurred.

I sat up. "Jasmine?"

"Yeah, it's me. I was just thinking about you, and I wanted to let you know."

I was alarmed by her numbed-out voice. "Where are you?"

"Sisqo's."

I glanced at my watch. "Don't you think you need to be getting home?"

"It's just one o'clock. The bar doesn't close until two."

I could tell that she was drunk already. "Why do you need to stay until closing?"

"I don't have to," she said in a little-girl voice.

"You must not be having a good time if you're calling me."

"You're not happy to hear from me?"

I ignored that question. "How much have you been drinking?"

That sobered her up. "I think a little more than I should have. I should probably go home."

"Is Ashley there with you?" I said. I was becoming concerned about her driving while drunk.

"She's somewhere around here, talking to her friend."

"Why don't you ask her to give you a ride?"

"I'll be okay." After a short pause she said, "Shit! I can't believe he's here. Why can't he get the message?"

"Who, Jasmine? What are you talking about?"

"Nicco. He's been hounding me all night. I told him that I don't want to be with him. I thought he got the message, but here he is again."

I was instantly angry. "Tell dude to step off."

"I did, but he won't leave me alone. Sean, I want to be with you. I want to see you."

Her words were like a shot to my gut. "I want to see you, too, but I can't come all the way to Chicago tonight. Why don't you go home now?"

She sounded defeated. "Okay, Sean, I'll see if Ashley can take me. I can't drive right now."

I was getting more and more worried. "How did you end up like this?"

"I'm stressed from dealing with Nicco. He's been sweating me, baby, you just don't know."

I wanted to strangle that motherfucker and leave him on the side of the road. "Go on," I said, like helping a little kid, "and ask Ashley if she can take you home."

"Okay. I don't see her. Hold on, Sean."

I heard her asking people if they'd seen Ashley.

She got back on the phone and said, "Sean, I forgot. She already left."

I heard a male voice: "Jasmine, I thought you might be gone. I'm glad that I was able to catch you."

I was sitting on the edge of my seat at this point. "Is that him, Jasmine?"

"Yes. I'm walking away. I'll get a cab, okay?"

"Call me when you get home. I'll be waiting to hear from you."

"I don't feel too good."

"You drank too much," I told her patiently. "Have the bartender call you a cab."

"Okay, I will. Listen, Sean, you know I still love you, baby. There, I said it. I'll talk to you later. Bye."

I stared at the phone after Jasmine hung up. "Now I know she's drunk."

Jimmy said, "What's up?"

"She just told me that she's still in love with me."

Jimmy was amused at my expense. "You know liquor is a truth serum."

I was wide awake now and on edge. I paced around the room, trying to figure out what to do.

"I'm thinking about going to Chicago to get her," I said. "She's drunk and can't drive, and her ex is there.

You know he'll insist on taking her home, and then what?"

Jimmy could tell I was serious. "Sean, she'll be sober and have this incident behind her before you can get there. Man, be realistic."

I didn't want to be realistic. I wanted to go to Chicago.

16

Jasmine

Friday after work, Ashley and I had met at Sisqo's. The usual crowd was there and the rum and Cokes were flowing. On average I have two, maybe three drinks, but tonight, at last count, I was at seven. I was drunk.

I think, maybe because it was a full moon, I felt that the night would bring some changes in my life. I didn't recall seeing Ashley leave, but I was sure she hadn't left without telling me and making sure that I was okay. The numerous drinks I'd had gave me that loving feeling, so I called Sean and told him that I was still in love with him. He sounded stressed on the other end.

I thought Nicco got the message when I walked away from him the first time, but he kept coming. I knew I didn't have the strength to fight him, and I hoped he would leave me alone.

He stopped in front of me and began talking. "I want to ask you a question, Jazz. Why? Why would you sleep with Michael? I don't understand."

"I never thought that you would find out about us. We are attracted to each other, but we knew you would never approve of us, so we kept it from you. Don't take it out on him, Nicco, it was me."

"But you knew we were best friends."

"I'm sorry, Nicco. That's what I told Michael." I put my head down.

When he realized that I wasn't listening, he said, "Jazz, I think you've had too much to drink."

"I called a cab and I'm on my way home."

"Why don't you let me take you? I don't want you in a strange cab, drunk like this. Who knows where you might end up?"

I sat up abruptly and said, "No, thank you."

He sat on the bar stool next to mine and said, "Come on, Jazz, it's just a ride. I'm just trying to help."

"What are you doing here, Nicco?" I slurred.

"I wanted to see you. Come on, let me get you home. You shouldn't be out here like this by yourself."

Finally, I gave in. "Okay, Nicco, thank you."

He helped me to his car. Once inside, he reclined the seat so that I could lie back. I felt his body heat as he reached over me to buckle the seat belt. That was the last thing I remembered before waking up as Nicco carried me to my front door.

"Where are we?" I managed to say.

"You're at home."

"Thank you, Nicco. I can walk the rest of the way."

He put me down, but I still needed to lean on him as I pulled my keys out of my purse to open the door. I staggered to the sofa and crashed. I felt Nicco trying to remove my shoes. I sat up and said, "I can do it, Nicco."

We were quiet for a few seconds. I said, "Thank you for bringing me home. I don't think I could have done it by myself."

I closed my eyes, trying to stop the room from spinning. I felt Nicco move closer to me, but I didn't have the energy to protest.

I kept my eyes closed as I asked, "What's up with you and Tiffany? You know she's Ashley's little sister, right?"

"Naw, I didn't know that, but nothing is up. She wants to go out, but I'm not interested. You know I'm not interested in anyone but you."

He tried to kiss me, which made me jump up and run into the bathroom to throw up. I turned on the cold water to wash my face and brush my teeth. I took off my dress and slipped on my nightgown and a robe.

While I was in the bathroom, I heard my phone ringing.

Nicco answered it.

When I returned from the bathroom, he walked up to me, put his hand under my chin, and asked if I was all right.

I turned my face away and said, "Yes, I'm better now, Nicco, thank you."

He ran his finger around the collar of my night-gown before sliding his hand inside to fondle my breast. I was wet instantly.

"What are you wearing under here?" he said as he exposed my breasts.

I recovered quickly and pulled away. I closed my robe tightly. After he saw that I wasn't receptive to his advances, his demeanor changed. "Why did you fuck my boy, Jazz?"

I headed for the couch, trying to escape him. He followed.

Before I could sit down he grabbed my arm. "Answer me." I could smell the liquor on his breath.

I pulled away and said, "What are you doing, Nicco?" I was uncomfortable with his aggression and sat down.

"I just want you to answer my question. You knew he was my boy, you knew how tight we were, and you were doing what? Being a whore, or did you just want to hurt me?"

"I guess I was doing a little bit of both."

"Why?"

"You know why, Nicco," I said defiantly. "You hurt me. Every time I was with Michael, even though you didn't know about us, it felt good knowing that if you did find out, it would hurt you."

He whirled toward me and shouted, "Every time! How many times were you with him?"

"Uh, just once."

"Nah, it was more than once. Tell me the truth."

"I don't know, a couple of times."

"When?"

"It's not important."

His stare was cold. "You still fucking him?"

I quickly said, "No. No, not since you found out."

"Have you seen him? You know he was in town last week."

"Uh, no. I haven't seen him."

He sat back, closed his eyes, and rested his head.

After a few minutes of silence he asked, "Can we work on us?"

"Nicco, I can't," I said flatly. Talking to him was sobering me up fast.

He opened his eyes and said, "You can't or you won't?"

"Both."

"Jasmine." He was quiet for a few minutes. Then he faced me and grabbed my hands. "Jasmine. I did love you. I know it didn't seem that way sometimes because of the way I treated you, but I did care about you and I still do love you."

I pulled my hands away. "No, Nicco. I'm cured of you. I know it's hard for you to believe, but I promise you, I'm done this time. I'm so ashamed of myself for letting you disrespect me the way you did. I knew better—I knew that I should never have let you treat me the way you did, but I fell so hard for you, and you took advantage of my love. I did things for you that I had promised myself I would never do for a man."

"Like what?"

"Like sleep with you on our first date. Two hours

into our date, you were fucking me. Two hours. That's my fault for being so easy, and I had to suffer the consequences of the decision I made that night."

A lot of what I'd kept inside for so long was spilling out. "I wanted so badly to impress you sexually. I was young, I had only been with two other men. But when I met you, you were mature, so masculine and good-looking, and I was intrigued by your lifestyle and wanted to be a part of it." I made a snorting sound. "After you fucked me, like a fool, I believed you wanted a relationship with me. I was seeking you aggressively for a relationship and you were seeking me aggressively for sex. Sex was the most important thing you saw in me. I guess Pat was the good girl, the wife material, and I was just some good pussy."

He tried to explain, like the dog he was. "I didn't want to marry her, but she was carrying my child. I didn't want to get married behind your back. I wanted to be honest and explain to you that I had to marry her."

That song wasn't playing. "Finally," I told him, "someone came along that you loved more than you loved having sex with me. I knew about your other women, Nicco. I turned a blind eye to your infidelities, pretending to believe the bullshit you were telling me. I was a fool, I knew it and so did everyone else." I chuckled. "Believe me, everyone begged me to leave you alone, my friends and yours, but I was under your spell. I was dumb and faithful while you were out getting other women pregnant."

He listened without interruption while I talked. He didn't look at me when he said, "I guess the saying is true that you don't know what you have until it's gone."

"It looks that way, doesn't it?"

He slowly shook his head. "Jazz, I miss you. I knew that I should have left you alone back then. But no matter what I did wrong, you would let me come back. I'd tell you my lie, we would make up with sex, and we were all good. I couldn't walk away from the sex." He was now drunken gloomy, but at least he was being honest.

"I did things that I knew would make you leave me alone, but what did you do, Jasmine, when I came back from Jamaica with Lisa?"

A tear rolled down my face. "I slept with you that night."

"That's how it always was."

I sucked up the snot, wiped my eyes with the back of my hand, and said, "Well, I'm a different woman now, Nicco. I finally found my self-respect and I have no desire to go back into a relationship with you."

"I've changed, too, Jazz. I want what you were offering me. I want to give you the happiness you always deserved from me."

I giggled. "I can't believe I revealed myself like that. I never confessed my stupidity out loud before."

I closed my eyes and rested my head on the back of the sofa.

He ran his hand alongside my face, and I opened my eyes in alarm.

"You weren't stupid, baby, you were in love."

He wrapped his hand around my neck and pulled me close and tried to kiss me, but I pulled away.

"No, Nicco. This is truly it for us."

When he saw how serious I was, he said, "Okay, Jasmine. I hear you. I want you to know that if you need me for anything, I'll always be here for you."

"Thank you, Nicco. I really appreciate that."

"Do you mind if I rest here for a few hours? I'm sleepy, baby, and I'd like to sleep off a little of this liquor before getting on the road again."

I closed my eyes and said, "That's fine, and thank you again for bringing me home."

We passed out on separate ends of the sofa.

17

Sean

had grown tired of waiting for Jasmine to call, so I called her house and Nicco answered the phone. I couldn't believe my ears. He had hung up on me like I was intruding. I knew he wouldn't tell Jasmine that I had called.

I was beyond pissed off, because I'd told her to get a cab. Out of all the people in the world, I didn't want that dude around her.

Questions were swirling around in my head. She'd told me that she was still in love with me, yet she had allowed him to prey on her when she was drunk and vulnerable. Shit! Why had she let him take her home, and why had he answered her phone? How could he tell her that I called when I hadn't even told him who I was?

Jimmy had fallen asleep. I shook him until he was awake and told him I had to go to Chicago. "I've got to see what's up with Jasmine. I just called to make sure she made it home, and Nicco answered her phone."

"Do you think they hooked up?"

"I know that he's trying to get something going with her again."

Jimmy was trying to piece everything together. "What you gonna do when you get there?"

"Man, I don't know. I guess I need to see what's up first." I started pacing in front of the couch. "She said she told him that she didn't want to be with him, but he won't leave her alone." I took a few more steps, then came to a dead halt. "Do you think you can handle the studio tomorrow?"

"Yeah, you know I got this. Everything should be cool until you get back."

I called my pilot to see if he was still in town. He sleepily told me to be at Teterboro at four thirty.

During my flight, I thought about Jasmine telling me that she loved me. I had never acted like this over a woman before. I didn't know how I would deal with my feelings for her, but I knew that I was acting crazy because of her.

When I arrived in Chicago, I rented a car and drove directly to Jasmine's house. When I saw Nicco's truck in her driveway, I almost turned right around, but I had to see things for myself so that I could end this thing between us for good.

It was seven thirty in the morning. After standing outside for a few minutes, ringing the doorbell, Jasmine finally opened the door.

She looked surprised and nervous at the same time. "Sean, what are you doing here?"

"Are you going to let me in?"

She stepped aside.

Nicco was stretched out on the sofa, but he began to stir when he heard voices. At least he was fully dressed.

I turned to Jasmine and said, "What's going on here?"

She was flustered. "Nicco gave me a ride home from Sisqo's last night."

I looked her over. "Why is he still here?"

She pulled her robe together at the collar. "He was tipsy and wanted to get a little sleep before hitting the road."

Under my breath I asked, "What else did he get, Jasmine?"

Nicco sat up, looked at me with a smirk on his face, and said, "What's up, man?"

I looked at him and nodded stiffly.

Jasmine finally said, "Nicco, thank you for the ride, I truly appreciate it."

Nicco stood, tucked his shirt inside his pants, and said, "No problem, baby, I'm just glad that I was there for you when you needed me."

He slipped his feet into his loafers, grabbed his car keys off the cocktail table, and walked to the door. As Jasmine walked behind him, I could see through her robe—she wore nothing underneath.

Nicco kissed her on the cheek. "Call me if you need me, okay, baby?"

"Thanks again for the ride, Nicco," she said. After she closed the door, she stood with her back to me for a few seconds before turning around.

I was pissed off and she knew it. I wondered why her hair was all over her head, and why her makeup and lipstick were smeared.

"So, what was this all about?" I asked, fanning my hand in front of me.

She didn't look at me when she said, "I needed a ride. I just wanted to get home."

"I can't believe that I'm here chasing you," I said, disgusted at my own behavior. "I never thought I would find you looking like a fucking slut with Nicco in your house. What happened here?"

She pretended not to know what I was asking. "Nothing happened," she said with a slight attitude.

She sat on the sofa and I sat next to her. We were right back to our last fight, but I was scripting a different ending. I didn't know if I believed her, but I wanted to see if there was a chance of us working things out. "Come here, baby."

She moved close and laid her head on my shoulder. "Did I call you in New York last night?" she asked.

"Yeah, that's why I'm here now. You got me doing crazy shit, Jasmine. I couldn't relax after your ex answered your phone."

She lifted her head in alarm. "Who answered my phone?"

"Nicco! That's how I knew he was here. Why did he have to come inside the house?"

"He was being helpful, Sean."

Now *she's defending this motherfucker.* "Did he help

himself into your panties? Oh, I forgot, you're not wearing any."

She took a deep breath. "He just made sure I got in the house safely. We talked, on this couch, and that's it."

"Talked about what?" I said sternly. I saw a tear roll down her face, but I wasn't moved.

"We talked about our past."

"What the fuck did you call me for, Jasmine?"

"Because I love you," she said quietly.

"Yeah, but you brought Nicco back to your house for the night. You fucked him, didn't you? Just tell me the truth."

She shook her head firmly. "I told you, we talked. We talked about our past, and I let him know that I was finally done."

"Did you offer him some pussy?"

She looked disgusted. "What are you talking about, Sean? I told you I didn't sleep with him."

"Is this what you had on while you talked to your ex?"

I looked at my nightgown. "Yes. I have a robe on. Sean, I threw up and I had to get out of my clothes."

"You couldn't find anything else to put on? And why did you have to take your panties off, too?"

"I wasn't wearing any."

That pissed me off even more. "I know how you get when you drink."

"What's that supposed to mean?"

"It means that you're loose and easy when you have alcohol in your system, and I believe that you fucked Nicco."

Now she was pissed. "I don't give a shit what you think, Sean. Yes, I was drunk, but I knew what I was doing. I called you to tell you that I was still in love with you, and I guess the liquor gave me the courage to do that. I drank too much and Nicco brought me home. I'm sorry that you saw him here, and I can't change that, but nothing happened. Why do you give Nicco so much power over you?"

I was quiet for a few seconds. "I guess you don't remember the conversations we had when we first met, but I remember them all, word for word, Jasmine."

"I remember our conversations, too."

"Do you remember telling me that all Nicco had to do was ask and you were his?"

She shook her head. "That was almost three years ago. Yes, Nicco did have a strong influence over me, but that has passed." She looked at me. "I called you because I wanted us to start over."

I couldn't believe she was sticking to this story. I said tiredly, "It just doesn't seem like we can make it work, Jasmine. You are too much work."

"If I'm so much trouble, why are you here?"

"I don't know. I thought you were ready to act right."

"Act right?" she screamed.

I'd had enough of this bullshit. "Yes, act right. You

know what I want, Jasmine, and you're not willing to give in."

She waved a finger in my face. "You want a submissive woman, Sean. You want someone you can control."

"You don't need to exaggerate."

"I'm not exaggerating and I'm not that girl, Sean. I guess I thought because I loved you so much that we could overlook some of our differences and make things work, but you're right, I'll never act right. And you can't compromise. If you make up your mind about something, then that's it, and if it's not your way, it won't happen."

"We finally agree on something."

She stood up and said, "You know what? You don't have to worry about me calling again. I'm through this time."

I stood up, too. "Good. So am I. Nicco probably didn't get too far away. Maybe you can call him back."

"Get out! Get the hell out of my house, Sean! I never want to see you again!" she screamed.

18

Jasmine

Over the next months I spent most of my time working on getting the spa up and running. Sean kept calling, leaving messages saying that he was sorry, but I didn't need some possessive, controlling man ordering me around.

I guess he felt guilty about calling me a slut and accusing me of sleeping with Nicco when I hadn't. I never returned his calls. But I hadn't been with a man in over three months.

We worked with a party planner for our grand opening. Our staff was sent to New York for training, and Ashley and I put the final touches on the spa. I was happy to have a project that kept my mind off Sean.

Ashley kept offering to fix me up with men she knew, but I wasn't interested. She couldn't understand why I didn't want to be with anyone. I finally learned to keep my mouth shut and stop telling all my business, even to Ashley. I didn't want anyone trying to convince me that I needed a man to make me complete.

Friday evening before the official opening, we had a formal cocktail party at the spa. One of the managers from the car dealership was my date. The turnout was fabulous. Kendall and her executive staff flew in from New York. Guests were able to schedule appointments as they toured the complex.

I was very happy with what Ashley and I had accomplished with the dealership and the spa, and I was finally content. For the first time in a long time, I felt like I could go on without Sean in my life. I felt empowered and I was happy with the face I saw in the mirror.

Once the spa was up and running, I split my time between both businesses and so did Ashley. It was great. When Tiffany became too much, I'd go to the spa. I was very happy to have a place where I could get away from that drama. Tiffany had asked Ashley if there was a position open for her at the spa. When Ashley told me about their conversation, I didn't hesitate to tell her that I didn't think it was a good idea to have Tiffany involved in the spa business. Ashley agreed, and that was it.

The atmosphere in both establishments soothed me in different ways. Both places were customer oriented and required personal contact, and I loved meeting new people and promoting our businesses. After things settled down, I was ready for a change of scenery.

Ashley wasn't seeing anything new, though. "I don't understand you, Jasmine," she told me one day. "You were hot, juggling three, four men at a time, and now you don't date at all."

"I know. To be honest, since Sean, I haven't wanted to be bothered with anyone. I just need to keep to myself, and eventually the right man will come along."

"Do you really believe that? Don't you already know who the right man is, and maybe you should give him a call?"

I was instantly defensive. "Why would I do that? He doesn't care about me in the right way. He wants to own me."

"But he still calls you, Jasmine. If he didn't care about you, he wouldn't call."

"I can't go back to being at his beck and call. It's best that I don't talk to him." I added sourly, "He doesn't call that often anyway. He hasn't called in over a month."

"He called yesterday while you were at the spa. I didn't say anything because you never call back anyway, so what's the point in giving you the message?"

My heart gave a little leap, but I pressed that emotion right back down.

"He loves you, Jasmine. I bet he's missing you as much as you miss him. If it was so easy for him to let you go, like you make it sound, he wouldn't keep calling."

"Girl, please. If Sean wanted to be with me, I would

have seen him by now. He's not ready to give up his playboy lifestyle. If he wants a girl, all he has to do is snap his fingers."

I was in the kitchen, boiling water in the microwave for my tea, when Tiffany walked in. "Good afternoon, Jasmine. I haven't seen you in a while."

"Hi, Tiffany. I've been spending a lot of time at the spa, but it's good to see you."

"You too." She looked in the refrigerator and pulled out a lunch bag.

She turned to me. "Do you know if Nicco made it back from Florida yet?"

I allowed a slight smile to cross my face as I realized that she wanted me to know she was into him. "I don't talk to Nicco like that, Tiffany. I don't know what's going on with him. I see you're still seeing him, though."

She smiled. "Yeah, we see each other sometimes. Nicco's sweet."

I had an answer for that. I grabbed my cup and headed back to my office.

The day dragged on, and when closing time finally rolled around I was ready to leave—but not ready to go home to an empty house. I didn't want to go out to a club, but I was lonely. I had always had a man somewhere, and I had to admit, being by myself wasn't working for me. I thought maybe I'd let Ashley introduce me to one of her friends.

The next time I saw her, I told her that I was ready to meet someone.

Ashley was delighted—a chance to play matchmaker. "It's about time, Jasmine. I have just the person for you. His name is Paul. I already told him about you, and he's been waiting to meet you. He's a doctor—an orthopedic surgeon. I met him about two months ago, when I had to take my dad in for surgery after he hurt his wrist."

"Why didn't you get with him?"

"Because things are going great with Joe and I'm not interested in meeting anyone else. Anyway, let me tell you about Paul. He's medium brown, kind of tall. He definitely works out and he has a beautiful smile. Seriously, Jasmine, if it wasn't for Joe, I would definitely go there."

The outside sounded good. "Why is he single?"

"He said he doesn't have time to date. He's a young doctor, on call at the emergency room at Northwestern. He's looking to meet someone who is patient and not too demanding." She started clicking keys, pulling up his contact information. "When do you want to meet him? I can call him now and set something up for this evening if he's available. Oooh, how about a double date with me and Joe? That way it won't be uncomfortable."

Her enthusiasm was starting to make me regret this idea, but I told her to call him.

"You won't be disappointed, Jasmine, I promise."

• • •

I prepared all day for my date with Paul. I went by the spa and got the royal treatment. Paul wasn't able to get away Saturday, when Ashley had called, but he'd called me later that night and asked if I was available Sunday evening. We had also decided not to double date.

I happened to walk by the window as Paul parked in front of my house. He drove a black Mercedes, shining like new money. I gave him a point for having it freshly detailed.

I watched as he got out of the car. He did look good. "Mmmm, I like," I said out loud.

When the bell rang, I took my time getting to the door. I didn't want him to think I was desperate.

I was impressed when I opened the door. Paul wasn't a pretty boy, he was just nicely put together. He looked like he took care of himself.

"Jasmine, it's so nice to finally meet you. These are for you." He handed me a bouquet of flowers.

"Please come in while I put these in water. Can I offer you anything?"

"No, we should be going. Our reservation is for nine o'clock."

He sounded like time was precious to him. "Okay, I'll be ready in a minute."

I opened the wrapping to find beautiful germinis, tulips, and lilies. I found a few little button poms inserted throughout. After getting the flowers in a vase, I grabbed my purse.

He helped me into the car, got in himself, and we were on our way.

"Ashley talks about you every time I see her, you know. I was beginning to believe that she was making you up."

I laughed lightly. "I have been very busy lately with the spa. I'm sure Ashley has told you about our businesses."

"Yes, she has. I am so impressed with the two of you."

"Thank you. I'm really enjoying what I'm doing. Tell me a little bit about you. Was being a doctor your career goal or was it a family obligation?"

"A little of both. My dad is a neurosurgeon. My mom is an RN. I guess you could say that medicine is in my family."

I admired Paul's handsome features while he talked. "Do you live near the hospital?"

"I live in the John Hancock Building right now, but I'm closing in about a week on a condo in the South Loop and should be moved in about two weeks."

"You'll have to travel a little farther to get to work," I said.

"Yeah, but that's okay. I really like what they're doing with the South Loop area, and I need a change of scenery."

So, he wasn't married to his job. "Tell me about your family. Do you have any siblings?"

"Three sisters. One is a cop in New York, one is an RN in Florida, and the youngest is a housewife here in Chicago."

I'm sure he understood women better than the average man. "Where do you fit in this mix of females?"

"I'm the second child. What about you? Any brothers or sisters?"

"I have one brother. He lives in Santa Monica. He's an investment banker."

"It's just the two of you?"

"Yes. Both my parents passed."

"I'm sorry to hear that."

We pulled up to Fogo de Chao, where the valet took the car, and we made our way into the restaurant. After a very short wait, we were seated. The conversation was great and we realized that we had a lot in common. I thought Paul was cool. I liked him instantly. After dinner, we left for the Peacock Club, where we danced until last call.

When we left the club, Paul asked me if I wanted to get something else to eat.

"You're hungry again?"

"Yeah, I want some White Castle's."

A man with down-home tastes, too. That was refreshing. "Okay, I haven't been to White Castle in a long time, and it does sound good. Let's go."

We drove to Seventy-ninth and Stoney Island and sat in the parking lot to eat. He ate four of their tiny double cheeseburgers, fries, and a drink. I could only manage two, but it felt good to let go and not be so concerned about my diet for a change. I had so much fun with Paul, he was like my long-lost friend. I was so relaxed with him and I could tell that he was relaxed with me. When we arrived at my house, he walked me to the door.

"Jasmine, it was truly a pleasure spending the only hours I will have off from work in the next few weeks with you. I hope it was as pleasurable for you as it was for me."

"Are you kidding me? I had a great time, Paul, and I'm looking forward to the next time."

"Okay, I'll call you and see if you're available. In the meantime, can I call you to talk?"

"My feelings would be hurt if you didn't."

He kissed me on the cheek before he left.

When I closed the door, I leaned against it and smiled. I liked Paul.

The next morning, when I saw Ashley at the dealership, she asked how the date had been.

"He was nice."

"Nice? That's all you can say?"

"Okay, Ashley, I liked him a lot. Okay?"

Tiffany walked up to us and said, "Who?"

"I had a date with one of Ashley's friends last night."

"You went on a blind date?"

"Yes, I guess you could call it that. I really liked him."

"I knew you would," Ashley said. "He really has his shit together. I'm so glad you two finally met. So where did you go, what did you do?"

I told Ashley about our evening and that we planned to see each other again. Tiffany was hanging on every word.

A few weeks after our first meeting, Paul and I had another date scheduled for the coming weekend. I really did look forward to seeing him. We had talked on the phone quite a few times since our first date, and I was really enjoying getting to know him. He was just as busy as he had warned, but that was okay, I had a lot on my plate, too, so it worked out.

Paul called early Sunday morning, and I asked him if we were still on for our date.

"Yes, we are. I'm looking forward to seeing you."

"I'm pretty excited, too, Paul. What are we doing?"

"Why don't we do some sightseeing?"

That took me by surprise.

"Let's visit the museum, the aquarium, and after that have dinner. We'll end the night at a club some-where."

"That sounds like an all-day affair. You have that much spare time?"

"I have the whole day off and I want to spend every minute of it with you."

"Okay, let me get ready, then. I guess this will be a two-part day. After we do the sightseeing thing,

I'll need to come home and change for dinner and clubbing."

He sounded like he hadn't considered that. "Yeah, you're right. Are you okay with that?"

"Sure, it sounds like fun. What time should I be ready?"

"It's eight forty-five now. How about eleven o'clock?"

"Okay, I'll be ready and waiting."

When I got off the phone, I was pretty excited about spending the whole day with Paul. I found a pair of jeans and a T-shirt to wear for sightseeing, and for dinner later I chose the blue dress that I'd worn to meet Sean's mother. I felt only a twinge of regret as I pulled the dress to the front of my closet.

Paul arrived promptly at eleven o'clock. We went to the Field Museum and the Shedd Aquarium, then had lunch at La Strada on Michigan Avenue.

At the aquarium, Paul was my tour guide. He was very knowledgeable and talked extensively about sea life. He knew the differences between saltwater fish and lake-water fish and which types of fish swam in each. I was impressed. He also knew quite a bit about technology, and I learned a lot from him while we were at the museum, too.

He dropped me off at my house at five thirty and told me he would be back by eight o'clock, so be ready.

I had a message from Dave asking me if I had changed my mind about anything since our last conversation. I erased his message. Something about that click of a button was very satisfying.

Paul rang my doorbell a few minutes before eight, and I was looking forward to having more fun with him. I had one kind of fun in particular in mind.

"I bet you're surprised that I'm ready, aren't you?"

He looked me over. "Yes, and you look great, Jasmine."

"Thank you."

In the car, he said, "I stumbled onto this restaurant about a month ago. I stopped in one night after work and I felt so out of place. It's very intimate. Ever since, I've wanted to go there with someone special."

"I'm sure I'll love it."

Glow was the name of the restaurant, and it was very intimate. The overhead lighting was low and each table was candlelit. Most of the tables were small, just enough space for two. Once we were seated, Paul ordered a bottle of wine.

"I'm really enjoying my day with you," Paul said. "I feel like I've known you forever. I can be myself and I don't feel like I have to put on a show to impress you. This is great."

He was blunt and straightforward. I liked a man who wasn't so complicated. "I feel the same way. I'm so relaxed with you. I'm always looking forward to talking to you and spending time with you. I'm very happy that Ashley introduced us."

"So am I."

"How are you enjoying your new condo?"

"I love it. I have a fantastic view of the city and the lakefront. It's not very far from here, if you'd like to see it."

That had been my idea all along. "I would love to. I've seen all of the construction down in this area. I thought about looking at something new, myself."

"You have a beautiful home. Why would you consider moving?"

"I'm just curious. I don't think I really want to move, I just want to see what those condos look like inside." I gave him a devilish smile.

"Okay, we'll stop by on our way to the club."

We ordered our entrees and made small talk while we ate.

After dinner, we went to Paul's condo. He lived in one of the building's penthouses.

When we stepped inside, I said, "This is beautiful, Paul. The view is spectacular." He explained some of the artwork as he gave me the grand tour. When we stepped onto the balcony, I turned to him and said, "Can we stay here?"

"Sure, why don't you relax? I'll put on some music and fix you a drink."

I leaned against the railing, admiring the beautiful view of the lakefront. I could see the Ferris wheel at Navy Pier and boats docked at the Yacht Club.

Sade sang in the distance. Paul joined me on the balcony a short time later.

"This is perfect, Paul."

"I sit out here for hours sometimes. I love to watch the sunrise from my bed in the morning."

I wanted to say that I would love to see it, too, but I didn't want to insinuate anything. I ended up saying, "I'm sure the view is beautiful."

"Would you like to dance?" he asked.

"Yes."

He took my hand and pulled me to him. We were so close that I could feel his heart beating. He leaned down and kissed me lightly on my lips. "Jasmine." He went silent for a moment. "Jasmine. I'm happy to be with you right now."

I kissed him with a little more pressure and said, "I'm happy to be here."

"Will you spend the night with me?"

"Yes." *I'll get to see that sunrise, after all.*

After a few songs, he whispered while kissing my ear, "You're making me weak, Jasmine."

"How am I doing that?"

"Just being this close to you. You turn me on, baby. I want you so bad."

That's what I had wanted to hear. "I'm here to give you what you want, Paul. Are you ready to go inside?"

He took my hand, kissed me on my lips, and we walked inside to Paul's bedroom.

It had been a while since I'd had sex, at least four months, and I was more than ready for Paul.

In the end, he gave me what I needed. No fireworks

went off, but he didn't disappoint. He kept working away. He was steady. *That's what I need*, I told myself, *a man who's steady.*

The next morning, while Paul and I lay in his bed watching the sunrise, he told me that he had to be at the hospital at seven o'clock.

"I'm sorry that I have to leave so early and won't be able to take you home. If you don't mind taking my car, it will give me an excuse to see you again when I come by to pick it up."

"I'll hold your ride hostage and you'll be forced to see me again," I teased.

"Forced. No, I look forward to seeing you again, Jasmine."

I smiled and he kissed me. "I really had a good time yesterday and last night. I can't remember the last time I enjoyed anyone's company as much as yours."

"I had a great time, too, Paul."

"If I'm not able to get to your house for the car today, I'll try again tomorrow."

He gave me the keys to his Benz. He also had a Nissan Maxima, which he usually drove to work. He showed me how to lock up and where to find toiletries.

"Okay, Jasmine. I've got to go. There is food in the refrigerator if you want breakfast, just help yourself."

After he left, I did fix something to eat. I was starving. I cleaned up the stuff from last night. Then I took a walk-through. His condo was truly beautiful. It was professionally decorated with state-of-the-art everything. I was impressed.

I was accustomed to driving Lexuses and hadn't realized how nice the Mercedes drove. I really liked his car, too.

So why couldn't I fight off this shadow of disappointment?

19

I needed to get away from everything, so I headed to Detroit to spend time with my mother. While I was driving, I thought about how everything was going. I was happy with my professional life. I was living the life I'd dreamed about. I took care of my mama and Aunt Frances, and they were happy. I had every material thing I could dream of and more. I had more money than I could ever spend, and the opportunities to make more were endless. I had multiple houses, women throwing themselves at me, but I was lonely. Everyone kept telling me that I needed to find someone to settle down with.

My mama and Aunt Frances were sitting on the porch when I pulled up.

Before I could even get out of the car, my mama said, "I was wondering when you were gonna show up. I was expecting you hours ago."

"It's just one o'clock, Mama."

I hugged them both before sitting on the porch.

"What are you two out here talking about?"

"You."

"What about me?"

She bowed her head like I'd seen so many times. "You don't want to know, Sean."

I didn't want to know, but they would tell me anyway. "I hope it was good."

"Well, Sean, you know your mama and I just want you to settle down with one nice girl and stop seeing all of these women that ain't right for you."

"I'm not dating, Aunt Frances."

"Why not? You're a great catch. What do you kids say, you got it going on."

Hearing the phrase come out of her mouth made us all laugh.

"If I had it going on, I wouldn't be single."

My mama said, "Are you saying that you don't want to be single anymore?"

"That's what I've been thinking lately. Most of my friends are married now, and they have all of these parties and stuff for couples and I feel out of place sometimes. I guess I'm tired of these go-nowhere relationships."

"What about Jasmine?"

A flash of temper entered my voice. "Ma, didn't I tell you that was a dead issue?"

"What happened this time?"

I shifted in my seat. I needed to talk about this, but I was apprehensive. "It's her ex all the time. I rushed to Chicago from New York to see her because she called and told me that she was still in love with me, and when I got there, her ex was sleeping on her sofa."

Both of them were startled by that news. "Did she explain why he was there?" Aunt Frances asked.

I sighed. "Yes, but I don't know if I believe her. Besides her ex always being in the picture, she has too much mouth. She doesn't listen to anything I tell her. Every time I say something, she has an answer."

"What is wrong with you, Sean? What, do you want an airhead? You want someone that's submissive, don't you?"

"There's that word again," I said. "You sound like Jasmine now."

"Sean, baby, you know I love you and I want to see you happy and in a good and loving relationship, but you don't know how to compromise," my mama said. "You want everything your way. You've got to learn to give some."

"Yeah. All right." I was mad because she had said the same things that Jasmine had, and I didn't want to talk about it any longer.

"Enough about me, how have you two been?"

Aunt Frances paused, like she wasn't quite ready to quit. But then she said, "We are great. I went to that new spa over by your studio and it was wonderful. I'm taking your mama there when we go back to Chicago."

"You're going to Chicago, Ma?"

"Yeah, I told Frances I would go home with her for a couple of days. You want something to eat?"

"Yeah, what you got?"

"We got some chicken and stuff left over from dinner last night. Go on in there and fix yourself a plate."

I called a childhood friend, Lester. Lester, Ray, Jimmy, and I went way back. When Jimmy and I left for L.A., Lester hadn't been willing to step out on faith with us. He stayed home and has been working for General Motors for the past fourteen years.

He was still single, and, just as I'd hoped, he knew all the hot spots. He took me to a new club named Fahrenheit, and hot-looking women were everywhere. Lester obviously spent a lot of time here, because everyone knew him.

While Lester was talking to some friends, I took a seat at the bar and ordered a drink. Soon I saw Lester approaching, but I couldn't see who was with him. Whoever she was, she was turning heads as they moved through the crowd. I got an instant hard-on when she came into full view. I didn't have to worry about memories of Jasmine.

"Sean, this is Monìque," he said with a huge smile. "I told her about you, and she wanted to meet you."

I stood up, hoping I could keep myself under control. "Monique, how are you?"

"I'm fine. Lester told me you was here from California."

I looked at Lester. "Yeah, I am."

"What you do out there?" She had this melodic, soft voice. "You in movies or something?"

"Naw, I'm a music producer."

She was impressed. "Really? Anybody we know?"

"Yeah, I'm sure. I've worked with a lot of people, including Ray Cash."

"That's really cool, Sean."

I stepped aside and offered her my seat.

She slid her sexy body past me, and I couldn't help but stare as she wiggled herself into the seat. In most cases, my staring would have been disrespectful, but I had a feeling that Monique was accustomed to men lusting after her.

"Please excuse my manners. Would you like a drink?"

"Yes, thank you."

I tried not to stare, but the skin-tight minidress she wore was begging for attention. She was voluptuous. Just looking at her kept my dick hard.

She woke me out of my stupor when she asked me to dance.

While on the dance floor, men and women were staring at her, none harder than me. She was dancing like a professional stripper and I wanted a private dance.

On our way back to the table, dudes were asking her to dance like I wasn't even there. But, lucky for me, she turned them all down.

Once we were seated, I moved close. "You look great in that dress," I said. I couldn't keep my eyes off her and she didn't seem to mind. As a matter of fact, she encouraged my behavior.

"Thank you, Sean. I wasn't sure if it looked right on me."

My eyes were glued to her cleavage. "It's perfect."

She smiled, happy to have my rapt attention.

"Hey, Sean, would you like to get out of here? It's crowded, and all of this smoke is getting in my hair."

I couldn't believe how my luck was playing out.

As we were leaving, I told Lester that I would be back to get him. He told me not to worry about it, he'd get a ride home from someone.

When I got outside with Monique, I asked, "Is your car here?"

"Yeah."

"Why don't you leave it? I'll bring you back to pick it up later."

We headed for a Holiday Inn that I had frequented when I was a teenager.

"You don't mind if we get a room, do you? I'm staying at my mom's while in town, and I don't want to disturb her so late at night."

"Sure, Sean, we can get a room."

I stopped by the liquor store and picked up a bottle of Rémy and some condoms before heading to the hotel. When I got back into the car, Monique put her hand on my thigh, leaned toward me, and smiled. I couldn't wait to get in the room and get her out of her clothes.

We didn't talk much and I didn't have to do much.

She was just as ready as I was. I was happy to see that she had a beautiful body under her dress.

She grabbed my dick and said, "You want this pussy bad, don't you?"

"Can't you tell?"

She giggled and said, "Yeah." She dropped to her knees in front of me, ran her tongue across her lips, and looked up into my eyes.

I hurried out of my pants and sat on the edge of the bed. As she crawled to me, her titties were bouncing and all of that big juicy ass was up in the air. I was gonna hit that from behind for sure.

Monique felt as good as she looked. I made sure to get her number so that I could see her the next time I was in town. I hadn't planned to stay all night, but we talked and I found her to be pretty cool. We stayed until the sun came up the next morning.

While I waited for her to get her things together, I flipped through the TV channels. My cell phone rang and I saw that it was Ray. I thought about not answering his call, but I never knew with him. It might be an emergency.

"What's up, Ray?" I said.

"Sean, man, where you at?"

"I'm in Detroit, visiting with my moms. What's up with you calling me before noon?"

"I wanted to get together for lunch because I need to talk to you about something, but if you're in Detroit you obviously can't."

"Are you in Chicago or L.A.?"

"Chicago."

"What do you need to talk to me about?"

"Listen, Sean. I saw your girl Jasmine last night at a club. We talked and danced and shit, and I really like her, man. I know y'all broke up and it looks like you're not interested in her at all anymore, so is it okay if I holla at her?"

I quickly said, "Naw, I wouldn't be comfortable with that."

"Why not? Y'all ain't together. Come on, Sean, you're standing in my way. She told me that she can't go any further with me because of you."

"NO! I mean it. She's off-limits!"

"All right, Sean. I wouldn't disrespect your wishes."

Ray was pissed—I could hear it in his voice—but I couldn't stand the thought of him being with Jasmine. I was getting pissed myself thinking about it. Did she slow dance with him? Did she let him touch her? He'd had the courage to ask me if he could date her, so they must have had a good time together. I wondered if she felt the same about him.

I thought about Jasmine during the entire drive to Chicago. Mom and Aunt Frances were in their own world, talking about the family reunion. All I could think about was Ray's hands roaming over Jasmine's body. I knew what he was like. He'd ask permission, and if he didn't get it, he'd go behind my back.

He would unless I stopped him.

20

Jasmine

When I got home, I went straight to my closet, looking for something sexy. Ashley and I had decided to party up north today. I wasn't in the mood for the regular Sisqo's crowd. I wanted new faces, different music and conversation. I wasn't looking for anyone to take home, but someone to flirt with. I picked out a short red dress that hugged every curve. When Ashley arrived, I felt better about my outfit. Her dress was as short and her heels were just as high. We were going to have some fun.

When Ashley got in the car and we looked at each other, we busted out laughing.

"Girl, you know damn well we are gonna cause trouble dressed like this."

"I need a little trouble tonight."

"Yeah, me too."

I took a serious look at her and asked, "Is everything all right with Joe?"

"Yeah, everything is wonderful with Joe." She gave my hand a pat. "Girl, he is a freak. I need to brush up on my fantasy shit."

I was surprised to hear that about Joe, but I already knew it about Ashley.

"I wonder how Paul would react if I let the freak out on him? He seems so reserved," I said, discouraged. "I need to be able to be me with a man."

She gave me a sideways look. "Missing Sean again?"

"I guess I got to thinking about him and the wild sex we used to have." I agreed. "Anyway, we're going out to have a good time, and I'm over Sean."

When we arrived, I left my car with the valet, and Ashley and I sashayed into the club. The music was thumping and I started bouncing to it immediately. Before I could get a good look around, Jamie Foxx's latest song played and the crowd exploded in cheers. Immediately, a guy asked me to dance.

I checked with Ashley and she said, "Go on and dance, girl. That's why you wanted to come here. I'm going to the bar."

I followed my dance partner to the floor. I found this place to be everything that I needed. The crowd was mixed and everyone was dancing. I felt sexy and free, and my dance partner was very touchy-feely. I didn't care. I was lost in the music, thinking about nothing but having a good time.

After twenty minutes, though, I was ready for a break. I shouted to my partner that I was leaving the dance floor. He looked disappointed, but he understood. He was sweating and I was about to start dripping sweat myself. The club had multiple bars, so it took me a minute to find Ashley. I stood behind her because all the bar stools were full.

She turned around and said, "Hey, did you have a good time?"

"Girl, yeah! I'm sure I lost five pounds already. I need to cool off and find me another somebody to dance with. You dancing?"

"Yep!"

She jumped off the bar stool and headed for the dance floor. I took her seat, ordered a drink, and declined numerous offers to dance. I wanted to finish my Moscato before dancing again.

A guy with his shirt unbuttoned to his waist walked up to me and stuck his hand out, and I accepted it. We quickly discovered that we were perfect dance partners. We never said anything to each other, but we were in sync. We danced through song after song, and I was in another world. I hadn't felt this good in a long time. Finally, my partner tapped me on the shoulder and said that he needed to cool off.

As I made my way off the dance floor, I ran into Ray, Sean's friend.

We stared at each other for a few seconds while he figured out how he knew me.

He pointed and said, "Jasmine, right?"

"Yes."

"Where's Sean?"

I shrugged. "I don't know. We don't talk anymore."

"Really." His head jerked at the loudness of the music. "Come on and join me for a few minutes. I can hardly hear what you're saying."

I followed him to another part of the club, where he offered me a seat and a drink.

"I'll have a glass of Moscato, please."

After he placed our order, he said, "I saw you out there dancing. You can move, girl!"

I flushed with pleasure. "Thanks. I needed to release some stress, and I feel great now. What are you doing in Chicago? Are you still working with Sean?"

"Naw, we finished that album." He gestured around us. "I like Chicago. There's lots and lots of really beautiful women here, and I like to be surrounded by beautiful women. Say, since you're not dating Sean anymore, would you like to go to dinner with me tomorrow?"

I thought about Sean telling me that Ray was off-limits. He'd been very serious when he'd said it, and I would continue to respect his wishes. I wasn't getting into another mess like I did with Nicco and Michael. I shook my head. "Although Sean and I aren't dating any longer, I wouldn't feel comfortable about going out with you."

He flashed a disbelieving smile. "Just dinner, we don't need to call it a date."

"Nah, I'll pass, but thank you for asking."

"Can I get a dance, at least?"

"Sure." I didn't see anything wrong with that.

We hit the floor, and it turned out Ray was a great dancer. We danced to a few fast songs, and when a ballad began, he pulled me close and we slow danced. When the music picked up again, I told Ray that I was going to find my friend and that I would return.

I found Ashley sitting at the bar.

"I saw you out there dancing with Ray Cash. People were taking pictures of y'all. You two dance well together."

"It was fun. He's saving seats for us in VIP. Come on."

Excited by the idea, Ashley grabbed her drink, slid off the bar stool, and followed me upstairs.

People stopped me along the way to say how much they had enjoyed watching me and Ray dance. I had to admit that it was really fun.

Ray was waiting for me to return, and we joined him at his table.

"Ray, this is a good friend and my business partner, Ashley. Ashley, meet Ray Cash."

"Ashley, it's an absolute pleasure to meet you. I see that birds of a feather flock together."

"What do you mean?" she said.

"Two beautiful women together."

"Thank you," she purred.

We ended up partying with Ray and his entourage for the remainder of the night.

Ashley and I left around two thirty. Ray tried to persuade me to spend the night with him, but there was no way that I was going to do that. If I got involved with Ray, that would definitely be the end of any chance that Sean and I might have. I didn't know why I was holding on to that.

In the car on the way home, Ashley asked me what was going on with Ray.

"He kept trying to get something started, but I'm not interested. I mean, he should be ashamed of himself by coming after me."

"Are you going to tell Sean?"

"No. We don't talk anymore, remember?"

"Have you thought about calling him?"

"No," I said, too fast. "I have a date with Paul on Sunday, and I'm really looking forward to it." That didn't sound convincing, even to me. Glumly I added, "I think I'm giving Sean too much power over me. I'm starting to act like Nicco. Well, I'm starting to think like him."

"What do you mean?"

"I may just want him because he doesn't want me." That thought annoyed me. I wasn't going to hang on. "I do just fine without Sean. When I hear about him or if I'm reminded of him, though, I want to be with him."

Ashley could only shake her head. "Face it, girl, you got it bad."

21

Jasmine

Sometimes just thinking about a person brings him closer, and that's what happened to me. The next day I was surprised by a message from Sean's aunt Frances. She asked me to call her because she wanted to make reservations at the spa to get the royal treatment one day this week for her and her sister. She left a number with a Michigan area code. I hoped she wasn't talking about Sean's mother. I guessed she would have said if she was bringing her.

After showering and changing clothes, I headed to the spa. It was pretty crowded. We had a large following on a regular basis, but we also had walk-ins every day. Business was booming.

I decided to call Aunt Frances before I forgot again.

"Good morning, Aunt Frances, this is Jasmine. I got your message. You want to come in one day this week?"

"Oh yes, Jasmine. My sister and I want to get a manicure, pedicure, body wrap, facial, and get our hair done. All of this will take all day, won't it?"

The way she spoke reminded me of Sean. "Yes, expect to spend the day being pampered. When would you like to come in?"

"How is tomorrow at eleven?"

"That's good. I'll see you and—what's your sister's name?"

"Vivian."

"I'll see you and Vivian at eleven. I'll make sure someone is available to get you started when you walk in."

Sean had never told me his mother's first name. He called her Ma. I wondered about that for a few minutes. I should have just asked.

I stopped at the dealership to take care of a few things and a short time later I went home. I slipped on a pair of sweats and a T-shirt after a warm bubble bath.

I had almost drifted off to sleep when Paul arrived around ten thirty. He came inside and we gave each other a brief kiss. He said, "I'm starving. I don't know if you've eaten anything, but I need to get something to eat. Come on and go for a ride with me."

"Do I need to change clothes?"

"No, you look great. Why don't we get something and bring it back here?"

"Okay. But you're going to make me fat, Paul."

"Let's get a pizza from Home Run Inn."

That was too tempting. "All right. I'm going to the gym tomorrow."

We got our pizza, came back to my place, ate, and started watching a movie. I persuaded Paul to stay the night with me. We climbed into bed around two o'clock. We didn't make love but cuddled all night. I think we were both too tired.

Paul promised to stop by the spa before heading to the hospital the next morning. When we woke up, we made love and it was real good. He was gentle and passionate. I didn't want it to end.

After breakfast, we got dressed and Paul followed me to the spa for a tour.

It was usually very busy during the morning hours and a few customers were waiting in the reception area. Paul and I were headed to my office when I heard someone call my name. I wasn't totally surprised to see Sean's mom standing next to Aunt Frances.

"Aunt Frances, Mrs. Williams, it's a pleasure to see you again."

Aunt Frances said, "I wanted to bring Vivian along."

Mrs. Williams was looking pointedly at Paul.

"Oh, I'm sorry. Aunt Frances, Mrs. Williams, this is a friend of mine, Dr. Paul Temple." I turned to Paul and said, "Paul, Aunt Frances and Mrs. Williams are the aunt and mother of an old friend of mine."

"Doctor?" Mrs. Williams said.

"Yes, ma'am. It's a pleasure meeting you ladies."

"You too, Dr. Temple," Aunt Frances said. Mrs. Williams didn't say anything.

"Jasmine, I need to get to the hospital. I'll get the rest of the tour later." He bent down and kissed me on the lips. "I had fun with you."

He turned to Aunt Frances and Mrs. Williams and said, "Ladies, it was nice meeting you both."

"I'll call you later, Paul."

After he left, I said too brightly, "Are you ladies ready to get started?"

Aunt Frances said, "Yes."

Mrs. Williams said, "So, Jasmine, you aren't seeing my son anymore?"

I blinked, startled by her directness. "No, we broke up a while back. How is he?"

"He's okay. He came to visit me earlier this week." She was looking around the spa. "I'm impressed with what I see so far."

"Let me get you started on some of your treatments so that you can decide for yourself if it's as wonderful as you've heard."

I started walking toward the reception desk.

"Sean is taking us to dinner this evening," Mrs. Williams called after me. "I was hoping you'd like to join us."

I stopped, feeling a tickle on my neck. "Sean wouldn't want to see me," I said, trying to let her down easy. Then I instantly changed back to professional mode and said, "Come on, let's get started."

Sean's mother didn't move. "Can we talk somewhere private, Jasmine?"

I wanted to decline, but instead I offered, "Follow me."

We went into my office. I sat behind my desk and said, "What's on your mind, Mrs. Williams?"

"You and Sean. What's going on?"

I couldn't believe that I was trapped into discussing

how I felt about Sean with his mom and aunt. I gathered my thoughts and finally said, "Sean is uncompromising. He's doesn't listen to me and he wants everything his way."

She looked surprised that I knew these things about her son. "You're right, Jasmine. Sean is spoiled, and he has always wanted things his way. He's been able to walk away from anything that he couldn't control until he met you. I know he pretends that he can be without you, but he can't. He's not happy, Jasmine."

I didn't say anything. I was surprised to find them here speaking on his behalf. I was positive that he knew nothing about this. It wasn't his style.

"You know, the only reason he had that studio built here was so that he could be near you," his mother said.

I don't know if I was buying that, but it was nice to hear.

Aunt Frances put in, "Jasmine, I know you love him and I also know that Sean is a handful to deal with, but you know better than anyone else, when it's good with him, it's the best. Do you want to settle with Dr. Paul or whomever else, or do you want to be with the man you truly love?"

My eyes watered. In a shaky voice I said, "I can't do this with him anymore. He doesn't trust me. He jumps to conclusions all the time. I don't know what he wants from me anymore."

I pulled a tissue from my drawer and dabbed at my

eyes. "I'm sorry. Sean and I had a horrible fight the last time I saw him, and I don't think there's a chance of us working things out. I appreciate your concern for us, but I think we're done."

"I'm sorry you feel this way, Jasmine."

Aunt Frances stood and said, "Come on, Vivian, let's go and let Jasmine get on with her day." She turned to me and said, "Come here, baby, and give me a hug."

During our embrace she said, "Don't mind us, Jasmine. If you and Sean are meant to be together, then you'll be together. I won't meddle in your business again."

Actually I was grateful that they had come. "It's okay. I needed to talk about it anyway."

I called Valerie, our receptionist, and asked her to escort Aunt Frances and Mrs. Williams to their first appointment.

I left for the dealership before Sean's mom and aunt were done. I didn't want to get questioned any more or find out things that I didn't need to know.

Ashley was on her way out on a date when I arrived. I was happy that things were working out so well for her and Joe. I hoped I could find that kind of happiness one day. Dr. Paul was a good start, I told myself.

22

I rushed home to dress for dinner with my mama and Aunt Frances. I made it to my aunt's house by seven o'clock, and they were ready to go.

"Wow, you ladies are looking good. I must be the luckiest man on earth."

My mother was pleased by her gentlemanly son. "Thank you, Sean. You're looking pretty handsome yourself."

I had found a restaurant out south named Bogart's. The food was good and I thought they would like it.

Once we arrived and were seated, my mama said, "I saw Jasmine today."

Aunt Frances looked at her like she was crazy, but she had my full attention. "You saw Jasmine where?"

"She owns that spa that Frances took me to today."

I turned to my aunt. "You knew that, Aunt Frances?"

"Yes." She looked at Mama and rolled her eyes.

I looked down, fidgeting with my hands, and asked, "So, how is she?"

"She looked good. We also met her boyfriend."

I looked up suddenly and said, "Boyfriend?"

"Yes, she's dating a doctor."

The waiter came over and I ordered a bottle of wine for the table and a shot of cognac for myself.

"She asked about you."

"Mama, let's not talk about it, okay?"

"All right, Sean. How is the studio coming along?"

I was preoccupied with thoughts of Jasmine and didn't hear my mother's question.

"Did you hear me? I asked you how the studio was coming along."

"It's coming," I said, trying to sound interested in the subject. "We should be up and running in about a month or so."

The waiter returned with our drinks.

After placing our dinner orders, we talked about our family, commenting on who was doing what and so forth and so on.

The mention of Jasmine's name had gotten me going. After I dropped my mother and Aunt Frances off, I went home, put on some music, and poured myself a drink. I had a message from Katie, the party planner we had hired to arrange a gathering for the studio opening. After calling her back, I sat on the patio and stared at the night lights of the city and thought about how to deal with my feelings for Jasmine.

I hadn't thought about a date for the event, but now I realized that I would love to have Jasmine on my arm for the night. This was her town and she should be with me for an important event like this. That idea made me feel better. I'd see what tomorrow would bring.

The next day, I told Jimmy about my plans to see Jasmine and work things out with her.

"I'm so happy to hear that, Sean. You haven't been right since you broke up with her."

"My mother told me she owns that spa by the studio. She also said that she saw Jasmine yesterday and she's dating a doctor."

Jimmy was impressed. "How does she know that?"

"My mom saw them together."

"Do you think it's too late?"

"If she really loves me, it won't be too late," I said confidently. "I was thinking about asking her if she would be my date for the party."

"Time is getting short, man. The party is coming up fast."

I knew I had to make a decision. I drove by the spa, but I didn't see Jasmine's car. I tried calling her cell phone, but she had changed her number. I was getting frustrated.

I hadn't heard from Ray since he'd called asking if he could date Jasmine. Ray wouldn't go behind my back, I was sure of that, but Jasmine . . . I wasn't so sure.

I called her house and got her answering machine. "Jasmine, it's Sean. I need to see you. I need to talk to you. Please call me on my cell phone and let me know when you're available. I'll be waiting to hear from you.

It's very important. I'm in Chicago, so if you can see me today, let me know, and I'll be wherever you say."

After I hung up, I knew I had sounded desperate, but I didn't care anymore. If she didn't call back, I'd go by the dealership.

I was drunk when I went to bed. I still hadn't received a call back from Jasmine.

23

Jasmine

When I got home and checked my machine, I found a message from Paul, saying that he was thinking about me and hoped that we could get together soon, and a message from Sean. I hadn't heard from him in a while and I was sure that either Ray, his mother, or Aunt Frances had told him that they had seen me.

I wasn't ready to talk to him.

The next morning I headed to the dealership. I was in my office, working on the books, when I saw Ray walk through the door. He asked something of one of the salesmen, and I saw him point to my office.

I watched Ray as he walked across the floor. He was dressed in jeans and gym shoes, a throwback Chicago Bulls jersey and matching cap.

Boy, was he sexy.

"Ray," I said when he walked into my office. "It's so good to see you again. What brings you in?"

With a sly grin he said, "I wanted to see you again."

I passed that off. "Have a seat. Are you here to see me or buy a hot new Lexus?"

"Well, let's see what you're selling, Jasmine."

"What are you driving?"

"I don't have a car here. I'm renting a Range Rover while I'm in town, but I guess I can buy something to drive back to Detroit."

"Come on. I have a beautiful convertible that you would look really good in."

"Really? You think I look good, Jasmine?" He was such a flirt.

"Ray, you know you look good."

"Then, why?"

I gave him a knowing look. "Sean. You remember your friend, right?"

"Yeah, but both of y'all said that you're not together anymore, so what's the problem?"

"No, Ray. Okay?"

He rose to his feet casually. "Okay, Jasmine. Well, for now."

"Come on."

I pointed to the SC10 on the showroom floor. "Now, can't you picture yourself in this hot sports car?"

"Yeah, actually I can."

I brought him over for a closer look. The car could almost sell itself. "Check this out. It has a power-retractable aluminum alloy roof, and it accelerates from zero to sixty in five-point-eight seconds. You look like you live in the fast lane, Ray. This car has everything a young handsome guy like you should have in his collection."

He was delighted by my sales pitch. "Look at you, girl. Sell it, baby."

"Let's take it out for a test-drive."

"Let's go!"

I grabbed the keys for the demo, and Ray and I headed out. I showed him the operating basics. He dropped the roof as we hit Lake Shore Drive. Ray had a lead foot, but he seemed to be a safe driver.

As we sat at the light at Fifty-seventh Street, Ray said, "Let's see about that zero to sixty in five-point what?"

"Five-point-eight seconds."

When the light changed, Ray took off and, just as promised, we were at just over sixty miles per hour within seconds.

"Whooooa!" he exclaimed. "This car is hot!" He looked at me and said, "And I've got to have it. Sold!"

When Ray and I pulled into the parking lot, I saw Sean getting out of his car. When he saw us, he stopped in his tracks and stared at us for a few seconds before turning around and getting right back in his car.

Ray didn't see him, and I didn't want a scene, so I didn't stop Sean. Besides, it took me a few moments to get my thoughts in order, and by that time he was gone. I needed to finish up with Ray. Then I would call Sean to find out what was going on.

Ray and I walked the lot, looking for the color he preferred. Of course he wanted it fully loaded, and we had exactly what he wanted.

I thought about Sean all the way back to my office. I was anxious to call him to see why he had come over.

"How can I get the Rover back to the rental place?" Ray asked.

I saw Tiffany in the distance and, just like that, a plan formed in my mind. Tiffany wanted a man with money, and Ray couldn't resist a good-looking woman. It would be a match made in heaven. "I can get someone on my staff to drive the Rover. You'll need to give her a ride back, though."

"Not a problem."

After we were done with the paperwork, I handed Ray the keys to his brand-new black SC10, with the eighteen-inch six-spoke wheels. Ray did look good in the car.

"Hold on a minute, Ray, and let me see if Tiffany is available to drive the Rover for you."

I hurried to Tiffany's office and was happy to find her at her desk.

"Tiffany, I need a huge favor from you."

She looked at me sideways and said, "Sure, Jasmine, how can I help you?"

I smiled at her and said, "Ray Cash is in my office—"

"Ray Cash?" She sat up.

"Yes. He's a friend. He came in and bought a car, but he needs to return the rental he's been driving and he needs someone to drive it. I was hoping you would be that someone."

"Really, Jasmine? You trust me to do this?"

I gave her a broad smile. "Yes. Make the best of this opportunity, Tiffany."

"Thank you."

"You ready?"

She looked confused. "Now?"

"Yes. He's in my office, waiting for you."

She opened her desk drawer, pulled out a mirror and her makeup bag, and started touching up everything. When she was done, she stood, straightened her tight dress, and said, "I'm ready."

I escorted her to my office.

When Ray saw us approach, he smiled at me and nodded.

"Ray, I'd like to introduce you to Tiffany Daniels. She will drive the Range Rover to the rental office for you, but remember, you'll need to bring her back, okay?"

He was pleased with this outcome. "Of course. Tiffany, is it?"

"Yes," she said, blushing.

He extended his hand and said, "It's an absolute pleasure meeting you, Tiffany."

I sat behind my desk and watched them walk out together, engaged in conversation. I was pleased.

As soon as they were out of sight, I called Sean's cell phone, but didn't get an answer. I was sure that, as usual, he had jumped to the wrong conclusion.

I left a message. "Hi, Sean, it's Jasmine. I saw you at the dealership today, but you didn't come in and talk to me. I wish I knew why you changed your mind. Please call me and let's talk."

I waited all day to hear from him, but he never called.

When I woke up the next morning, my first thoughts were about Sean. I had been thinking about him constantly since I'd seen his mother.

Surprisingly, he called me a few minutes later.

"How are you, Jasmine? I saw that you called. What's up?"

"I saw you yesterday, but you left without talking to me."

"I didn't want to interfere. You were busy with Ray."

"So you left because you saw me with Ray?"

"Yeah. I didn't want to be in the way, Jasmine. I know you're attracted to him, he's attracted to you. I guess I should have expected this from you."

I was offended. "What does that mean? You should have expected what?"

"To see you with Ray."

"He came to buy a car, Sean. If you had come in, you would have seen what was happening, not what you thought was happening. Ray and I are not dating."

"How did he know where to find you? And he didn't come there to buy a car, he came there to see you, and you sold him a car. I'm not stupid, Jasmine."

"Okay, well . . . I'm not interested in Ray, Sean. You told me no."

"Okay."

At least he hadn't hung up yet. "So, why were you coming to see me?"

"I don't like the way things ended with us. I miss your friendship. I was hoping that we could talk."

"When?"

"Today?"

I was nervous, but I did want to see him. We agreed to meet at my house at five o'clock.

Although my feelings were still hurt by some of the horrible things that were said the last time I'd seen Sean, I wanted to see him. I told myself that it was just to clear the air, but I was really more excited about being near him again. If we couldn't work it out, I wanted to be able to call him a friend.

Ashley was at the dealership when I arrived. Joe was in her office with her. I just waved as I walked by because my hands were full and I needed to put my bags down. Ashley popped up and followed me into my office. She sat in the chair across from me, but she didn't say anything.

"What's up, Ashley?"

"Do I look different?"

I examined all the different parts of her, but I didn't see anything different.

"No. What, are you pregnant or something?" I asked in a suspicious tone.

"No. Look again, what do you see? There is an addition."

This time I saw the huge rock on her ring finger. I was overjoyed. "You're engaged?"

"Yes! Joe asked me to marry him last night."

"Congratulations! I'm so happy for you." I waved Joe over.

I walked around my desk, and Ashley and I hugged. When Joe came into my office, I gave him a hug, too.

"Congratulations, Joe! I knew you two were meant for each other."

We talked about the engagement and some of their future plans. They were so happy chatting about their wedding plans that I felt a little left out. Why couldn't I meet a man who would accept me as I was?

After Ashley and Joe left, I tried to concentrate on the paperwork that had piled up on my desk. I didn't get much done because I was really nervous about seeing Sean. I went home way early, around three o'clock.

I didn't know how to receive him anymore. It used to be I didn't have any worries about Sean. I was so relaxed with him and he was relaxed with me. Now I was apprehensive at the thought of being in the same room with him.

I didn't know what to wear. I didn't want to look like I didn't care, nor did I want to look like I'd gone out of my way to look extra good for him. Finally,

I decided that no matter what happened with us, I wanted to leave a lasting impression. I'd put something on his mind. I wore a thin white cotton dress, simple but sexy. Since it was a halter, no bra was necessary. To avoid panty lines, I wore a thong. I knew what kind of reaction I would get out of him, and I didn't care how uncomfortable it made him. I wanted him to want me.

When the doorbell rang, though, I was a nervous wreck. I pulled myself together, took a deep breath, and opened the door.

When I looked into Sean's eyes, I fell in love all over again. Damn, did he look good. He was freshly shaven, and his haircut was crisp and perfect as usual, but it was his eyes that got me. Sean had sexy brown eyes with thick, wild eyelashes. His gaze was mesmerizing. I pulled my eyes away from his and said, "Sean. Come on in."

I started to walk away from the door. "Can I get you something?"

He was standing in the doorway drinking me in. I turned around and said, "Are you okay?"

"Yeah, I'm good."

He closed the door behind him. I felt closed in and nervous because I didn't understand his reaction to seeing me. I didn't know if he liked what he saw or if he regretted coming here.

"I see you let your hair grow out," he said.

"Yeah. I had been wearing it short for so long, and I wanted to see if I like it long again."

He quickly said, "You look great. I hope you decide to keep it."

I blushed and said, "Yeah, I like it for now." I gave him a questioning look. "A drink?"

"Yeah. You got any beer?"

"Have a seat and I'll get it for you." He grabbed the remote and changed the channel from the news I was watching to MTV.

While I was in the kitchen getting his beer, I heard his phone ring, but he quickly muted the ringer. I returned and handed him a Corona. "So, Sean, what do you need to talk to me about?"

"I wanted to apologize for some of the things I said to you." He sounded like he had practiced before he came over. "I don't know anything about what you're doing or who you're doing it with, and if you say that nothing is going on with you and Ray, then I have to believe that. I'm just sorry that things didn't work out for us, and I was hoping that we could remain friends."

Damn! No getting back together. I was hurt, but I could deal with it.

In a sincere tone I said, "You and I have been good friends for a long time, and I don't want to lose that either, Sean. I would never disrespect you. I knew Ray was off-limits."

My phone rang, and I saw Paul's name and number pop up on my TV screen. Sean saw it, too. I didn't know what to do.

"Go on and get your call, Jasmine. I'll wait."

I went into the kitchen so that I wasn't talking to Paul in Sean's face. I tried to talk low.

"Hey, baby, thank you for the flowers. They are beautiful."

I saw Sean get up and walk to the window.

"Listen, Paul, I was on the other line with my brother. Can you call me back when you get another break?"

"All right, I'll talk to you later."

Sean came back and sat on the couch.

When I walked into the room, he said, "Things sound pretty serious with you and the doctor."

I smiled and said, "We're just friends."

"You calling him baby, he's sending you flowers and shit." He was acting all light and easy. "What's up, Jasmine? You can tell me."

I was surprised at his reaction. Where was the control freak? "Nothing is up, Sean. It's just like I said, we're having fun getting to know each other."

"You don't want to get serious with him?"

I shook my head rapidly. "No, I'm not trying to get serious with anyone."

He had an edge in his voice when he said, "Does he want to get serious with you? Does he know you see other men?"

I was puzzled by that remark. "I'm not seeing anyone else."

He flashed a hard smile. "How do you think your

man would feel if he knew you were standing in front of me half naked? Don't think I didn't notice."

"Notice what?"

"I can see straight through your dress, Jasmine. I can see all of you. I can see your nipples and the thong you're wearing. Do you think the good doctor would approve of your behavior?"

I promptly sat down, feeling exposed. My demeanor changed instantly. "I don't answer to anyone, Sean. That includes Paul and you. I can dress how I want to, and if you don't like the way I look, don't look at me."

He smirked and said, "Don't sit down now, I was enjoying the view. I never said I didn't like the way you look. As a matter of fact, I miss looking at you. What I asked was, how do you think your boyfriend would feel if he knew you were standing in front of another man half naked? Do you think that's the kind of behavior your doctor friend would like to see from his woman?"

I didn't think what Paul thought was any of his business. "Fuck you, Sean. You are not going to get to me today. How I dress and who I sleep with is no concern of yours." The more I sat there, the more steamed I got. "Why did you come over here with that shit anyway? You said you wanted to clear the air, bring some closure to this so that we can be friends. This is not the way to become friends again. Plus, you didn't want me anyway. You dumped me, remember?"

He jumped up and said, "I can't believe you,

Jasmine. You put that shit on to show me what I couldn't have, didn't you? Why didn't you just open the door completely naked? It would have had the same damn effect."

"You see, Sean, that's your problem," I fired back. "You always think everything is about you. I didn't wear this dress for you. I put it on because it's what I wanted to wear today."

"Do you dress like this for the doctor?"

"As a matter of fact, I do. Can we stop talking about Paul?"

"I don't like him getting what's mine," he growled.

I was appalled. "I'm not yours, Sean. You are so damn arrogant. You don't own me, and you can't have me whenever you want me."

"Are you sure about that, Jasmine?"

"Yes, I'm sure."

He crossed his arms over his chest, stared at me, and said, "Come here."

"No, Sean."

"Wasn't it your intention to give me some pussy today?"

I shook my head, though I was starting to under-stand. He was so attracted to me, the dress was driving him wild. "No. Why would you think that?"

He practically shouted, "Because of the way you're dressed. What am I supposed to think? You stand in front of me half naked, get me all excited. What's the point?"

I didn't have an answer. "There is no point."

"Come here."

I stood, unable to help my attraction to him. He pulled me close and kissed me. I didn't fight him.

He said softly, "You need to get rid of the doctor."

"No, Sean."

"No? Listen, baby, there can't be an us if you continue seeing him, and I want you, so get rid of him, Jasmine."

He started kissing me on my neck and untied my dress.

I wasn't strong enough to stop him. I pleaded, "Sean, please don't do this."

"You don't want me, Jasmine?" He fondled my breasts.

My dress hit the floor.

"I'm scared."

He kissed me deeply for a few minutes. When our kiss broke, he continued to plant kisses on my face and neck. "Don't be scared, baby, I'll take care of you. You know, the only way we'll have a chance at being together is if you get rid of him. Do you understand?"

I was under his spell. "Yes," I said in a dreamy voice. After a few seconds, I gained my composure and pulled away. "Sean, no."

"No? You can't have us both, baby. Why can't you let him go?"

I stepped away from him and put my dress back on. I was starting to recover. "I can let him go if I want to, but I don't like you directing my life. You can't just walk in here and tell me to change my life to accommodate you, Sean. Paul is my friend and I like him."

He looked completely frustrated. "What the fuck is this shit, Jasmine? You gonna let another man come between us?"

"I like him," I informed him. "If you want to be with me, you need to work your way back into my life. Just because I love you doesn't give you permission to take me for granted." I hoped I was being clear. "I love you, but if I can't be with you, then I won't, Sean."

Sean couldn't see beyond either-or, though. "It looks like you're getting serious with him. Before, when we were doing our thing, you didn't have a regular boyfriend, or at least I didn't think so. Now this dude comes along and you can't let him go. Jasmine, I want you to stop seeing him."

"Why should I? Do you want to be in a relationship with me?"

He didn't go that far. "I want to work toward that. I'm not saying that you can't have male friends, just this one. He's getting too close."

"Are you jealous of him?"

"Hell no!" He was outraged that I thought he would ever be jealous. "You know what? Fuck it. I see that I'm not important enough for you to do this one thing for."

"You are important to me, Sean."

He waved his hand at me. "Naw, not important enough. You shouldn't question me on something like this. He's a man, a man that you're fucking, and I guess you care about him more than you care about me."

He stepped away from me, straightened his clothes. He adopted a more businesslike tone. "I guess I was out of line here. We're supposed to put the mess in the past. Why don't we do that?"

I was totally confused. "Fine, why don't we?"

"Listen, I just wanted to tell you that I was sorry for the things I said to you before and that I was out of line today. I hoped that we could work at being together again, but I see that you don't want that, so I'll leave you alone. Remember, if you ever need me for anything, you know where to find me. You take care of yourself, Jasmine."

We stared at each other for a few seconds before I said, "I do love you."

"Yeah, I can tell."

He walked out the door.

24

After I left Jasmine's, I was pissed. I needed to get out of Chicago as soon as possible. I called my pilot, got on my jet, and headed home. I couldn't believe that she wouldn't let him go for me. I'm through, I decided. I won't try with her again.

While in transit, I called Brenda.

When I arrived home, Brenda was waiting in my driveway. She had a key card for the gate but no key to the house. Otherwise, she would have already moved herself in. When I saw her, I wished I hadn't called her, but after being with Jasmine, I needed to release some tension. When I got out of the car, she came running over.

"Sean, I'm so happy you called me. I've missed you."

I didn't say anything. I just kept walking.

Brenda had sensed my mood, and when we made it inside the house, she fixed me a drink. She always took care of everything she thought I needed. I never asked for anything, but she did whatever it took to please me. I should have wanted that, but instead I was all pissed off over a woman who wouldn't do what I ask. How messed up was that?

I sat on the couch and turned on the TV. Brenda handed me my drink.

"You want to go to the bedroom and watch TV or stay in here?"

"We can stay in here," I grumbled.

"What's wrong, Sean? You seem so distant."

I didn't want to tell her the truth, so I gave a standard excuse. "I'm just thinking about everything at the new studio."

"Let me give you a massage. Maybe you'll feel better after that."

She took my shirt off and started rubbing and massaging my chest and back. After she took off her clothes, I didn't get excited like I usually did, but a picture of Jasmine standing in front of me got my dick hard, and I was able to get the pleasure I was seeking from Brenda. I fucked her on the couch. No foreplay, nothing. Brenda never said a word, just took what she could get. After I finished, I took a shower and came back and sat on the couch. She showered in the other room and got in the bed after her shower. I couldn't deal with the idea of sleeping with her. I stayed on the couch, watching TV, until almost sunrise before I finally went to bed.

The next morning, I went into the studio to begin editing. I couldn't concentrate, though. I tried to stay away from everyone because I could hardly stand myself, so I knew they couldn't stand me.

When my phone rang, I was gruff. "Hello."

"Hey, Sean, it's Jimmy. Where did you run off to yesterday?"

"I went to see Jasmine."

"How did it go?"

"It's worse now," I had to admit. "I just can't control my damn mouth sometimes. I get so mad about these other men she sees, and I end up saying shit that I know is gonna hurt her feelings. I know it's over now, though."

"Why?"

"I told her I didn't want her to see the doctor anymore and she refused."

Jimmy was patient, as always. "What were you offering her? Did you tell her that you didn't want to see anyone but her?"

"No. I had planned to, but I got mad because she refused to stop seeing him." I tried to explain how it was. "He called her while I was there. She was all baby this and baby that. I was so pissed off, but I kept my cool."

"Man, don't get all upset again. I bet you're over there snapping on people in the studio. Everybody's been talking about how they wish you would get your love life in order and stop taking your frustrations out on them." A warning note entered his voice. "And if you say anything about this to any of them, I'm gonna kick your ass, Sean. I'm just telling you, man, people are sick of your ass. Go and get laid or something."

"I did. It didn't help."

I hear him sigh. "You know what, Sean, I can't help you. All I can tell you to do is try to work things out with Jasmine. Stop demanding that she does what you say. And stop getting all bent up because she won't follow your commands. I can just imagine what you said to her. You have a foul mouth when you don't get your way." He paused for a beat, then added his clincher. "It looks to me like you finally met your match and don't know how to handle it. Am I right?"

"I'm gonna let you go, Jimmy."

We both chuckled. He knew me too well.

"When are you coming back?"

"Soon. Nobody's gonna keep me here, that's for sure."

"All right, keep me posted. Oh yeah, before I forget, Lola and Carmen's get-together is Saturday, so make sure you're back by then."

25

After Sean left, I poured myself a glass of rum. I sat on the couch, going over what had gone wrong. After my first drink, I grabbed the bottle and continued to pour.

I couldn't believe him. I knew we didn't have a chance at being together after I'd told him that I wouldn't stop seeing Paul. I liked Paul a lot, but I was not in love with him. If Sean had asked me to stop seeing Paul because he wanted a monogamous relationship, I would have agreed. But he didn't want that with me—he just didn't want me to see Paul anymore. He could be so mean sometimes, and his offensive words had taken away any chance that we had to work things out.

I needed to finish what Sean had started, so I called Paul. He asked me to meet him around ten o'clock at the Westin and said a key would be waiting at the registration desk.

I showered, changed into the red wrap dress that I'd worn for Michael. A thong and a Barely There bra was all I wore underneath.

When I arrived at the hotel, I retrieved the key and

headed to the room. I was on a mission to make the kind of love that would obliterate all thoughts of Sean. When I opened the door, Paul was lying across the bed, but quickly jumped up and met me at the door.

"Jasmine, I'm so happy that you called."

At least someone was. "I'm so happy you were available."

"Would you like something to drink?" he said.

I really didn't need another drink after all the rum I had drunk before I arrived. "What you got?"

"There's some stuff on the bar here, or we can go downstairs to the hotel bar, if you want."

"Let's go down to the bar."

He grabbed his jacket and we headed downstairs. All the way I could feel his eyes on my ass. My dress fit like a glove and my breasts were bouncing like jumping beans, but I didn't care. I needed to drown my sorrows. I knew what I was doing was wrong, but I couldn't help myself. This was therapy. I needed to make myself feel better, and I always felt better when a man was lusting over me, which is exactly what Paul was doing.

When we made it to the bar, men and women gawked at me and I knew why. I looked like the whore I was acting like. When I sat on the bar stool, I let the wraparound dress fall open, exposing my legs.

Paul pulled me close and said, "Are you all right, Jasmine? You really don't seem like yourself tonight."

Little did he know. "Yes, I'm fine. I'm a little tipsy and very horny, but besides that, I'm good."

"You are looking so good. I can't wait to get you alone."

"In time, baby, and then you can have all of me."

When our drinks arrived, I drank mine in a few minutes and asked for another.

We engaged in small talk for a little while before Paul excused himself to go to the restroom. The minute he was out of sight, a man from the bar approached and asked if he could buy me a drink.

"I'm here with someone."

He flashed a smile. "How can we lose him and get you to spend some time with me?"

"We can't."

"Oh, all right then. Well, I wanted to tell you how sexy you look in that dress, but I'm sure you already know that."

He looked me over once more and smiled. "Damn, baby, you're gonna cause some trouble in here." He handed me his card and said, "Here, just in case you change your mind."

I took his card and smiled.

Paul saw the guy walking away as he returned. "Who was that?"

"I don't know, some man trying to get with me."

"I can see why. You are looking too sexy."

I leaned over and whispered in his ear, "Paul, did your dick get hard when you saw me?"

He was shocked to hear that kind of talk from me. He had never seen my wild side, and I believe he was turned on. He grabbed my hand and said, "Come on, I can't take it anymore. Let's go upstairs."

I was very relaxed and ready to do whatever he wanted.

When we entered the room, he was all over me instantly. He untied my dress, pushed it off my shoulders, and watched it fall. While he removed his jacket, I took off my thong and bra. I walked over to the bed and sat on the edge with my legs open. He removed his tie and shirt and walked up to me. I unbuckled his belt, unbuttoned and unzipped his pants. When I slid my hand inside his underwear, his dick was hard.

Whenever I closed my eyes, I heard Sean telling me that he didn't want me. Well, Paul did want me, and I would give him all the loving that Sean didn't want.

He removed his underwear, leaned over me, and pushed me back on the bed. He sucked and kissed all over my body. I wished he were Sean, I pretended he was Sean, but he wasn't.

Paul took full control of our lovemaking. I was happy about that. I gave myself to him completely. He knew that something was wrong with me, but I wasn't telling and he didn't pressure me for answers. Finally, I turned around so that he could take me from behind. I didn't want Paul to see the tears as I cried while I thought about Sean.

I didn't stay long after he fell asleep. I made it home shortly before the sun rose.

The next morning, I told Ashley what had been

going on with me and Sean. I hadn't said anything before because I didn't want to whine about my problems while she was so happy about her engagement.

"I think it's over for real this time. I mean, I guess it was over before, but I still had hope." I dropped my head into my hands. "I can't keep doing this with him. I don't know what he wants from me. He hasn't made a commitment to me, and it didn't sound like he was trying to. I feel so stupid sometimes."

"Why?"

"Because I almost had sex with him. And I would have, if I hadn't pulled myself together and broken the trance. I was talking all tough, but when he touched me I was helpless. I stood in front of him naked on the inside and outside. I gave myself to him and he didn't want me. I think he just needed to prove to himself that he could have me if he wanted me, and he made his point."

Ashley was silent for a few moments. "This has been an interesting year for you, Jasmine. At least you finally got rid of Nicco."

"Yeah, he must have met somebody, because I haven't heard from him since the day you and I went out to that club."

I had never told Ashley what had happened in New York between me, Michael, and Nicco. I was too ashamed. The only good thing was, I hadn't heard from Nicco.

"What day are we going to New York?"

"Tuesday. I really don't feel like going. I could just go home, get in bed, and stay there forever. I'm tired of dealing with all my problems, or rather, men problems. I'm getting to the point where I don't want to be bothered with anyone."

She gave me a funny look. I'd always had one man or another.

"Hey, have you and Joe set a wedding date?"

"No." That reminded her of something. "I wanted to take you to dinner and ask you this, but I can't wait. Will you be my maid of honor?"

I was thrilled. "Of course, Ashley. It's an honor for me. When will you set a date?"

"We plan to talk about it this weekend. As soon as I know, I'll let you know."

"Okay." The moment of shared happiness passed, and I started to think about the work day. "I'm going to the spa to do some paperwork. Are you coming over later?"

"No, I'm going home. I'm tired."

"Okay, Ashley, I'll see you tomorrow—after court."

"Court? For what?"

"Remember Tyrone?"

"Yes," she said, mystified.

"It didn't just go away. I have a court date tomorrow."

She looked pained that I had to go through it. "Why didn't you say anything about this before now?"

"I had too much other shit going on. I tried not to

think about it. My attorney said the case will probably get thrown out."

"If not?"

"I don't want to think about if not."

She was growing worried. "What did he say were the possibilities?"

"Since I don't have a record, probably probation or community service," I said, annoyed. "I'm counting on it being thrown out."

"Do you need me to go with you?"

I patted her arm lightly. "No, I should be fine. You know that I'll call if I need you."

"Yeah, you will. All right, later."

I was so tired from everything that was going on. After stopping at the spa, I headed home to a bubble bath and bed. I wasn't looking forward to going to court, but I knew I had to deal with this situation.

When I arrived at the Criminal Courts Building at Twenty-sixth and California, I saw Tyrone and his wife sitting outside the courtroom. If looks could kill, I would have dropped dead on the spot. I wore an off-white Ellen Tracy suit with a short, form-fitting skirt. The jacket was tapered and it hit every curve. I wore a pair of off-white Chanel alligator and lambskin pumps that I had picked up the last time Sean and I had stayed at the Wynn in Vegas.

I don't think the wife recognized me, because I wasn't dressed when they had come to my house.

Tyrone saw me, though. He started fidgeting the moment he laid eyes on me.

I was in a bitchy mood because I had to appear, plus I was dealing with emotional turmoil. Tyrone wasn't man enough to handle his wife and it pissed me off. As I walked past them, I said, "Hello, Tyrone. You're looking even better than I remember."

He had to hold his wife down because she leaped up off the bench to get to me. I just kept walking, swinging my hips, and smiled as I walked into the courtroom.

Tyrone and his wife followed with the prosecutor, discussing the assault charges. When I made eye contact with the prosecutor, I smiled at him. When our case was called, I saw the look of surprise on the prosecutor's face when I stood up and made my way to the front of the room. While standing in front of the judge, my attorney explained the circumstances surrounding the incident. As I'd expected, the case was dismissed.

Tyrone's wife was livid. She was almost locked up because of her courtroom behavior. When we got outside, she followed close behind me and said, "You got lucky this time, bitch, but your shit is gonna catch up with your nasty ass. You better hope and pray I never see you on the street."

I was walking to the exit but I stopped and turned to her. "Listen, sweetie, your husband has been all over me, trying to get with me every chance he gets. Don't think that he hasn't called me since that incident. If you think he's not still chasing me, you are a damn fool. He's married to you, not me. He cheated on you, not me. You need to get your priorities straight and start talking to him, not me, about what's wrong in your marriage."

26

I didn't rush back to Chicago. I needed to forget about Jasmine. I called Sophia, a model I'd met during a video shoot a couple of months earlier, and asked her to accompany me to the studio opening.

I flew Sophia in for the weekend. We had spent a little time together about a month earlier. I'd taken her to dinner, we'd partied at a club for a little while, and she had stayed the night with me. I'd talked to her a few times since, but nothing serious. I liked that about her.

Our party planner rented a limo to drive me around for the night. She made sure the media would cover the event.

I was at the airport when Sophia arrived. After Derrick brought the jet to a stop, I parked my car close-by and waited. Sonja, our flight attendant, was the first to get off the plane, looking sexy as hell. A few seconds later Sophia appeared, looking even sexier.

"Damn, I'm a lucky-ass man," I said to no one in particular.

Sophia wore a short black dress and high-heel sandals. Damn, was she hot. She put on her sunglasses and began walking down the stairs. I had been leaning against my car, but walked to the steps to greet her. I took her hand as she reached the bottom and gave her a hug. Sonja was coming downstairs behind Sophia, and I was mesmerized by the sway of her hips as she approached me. We smiled at each other as I pulled away from Sophia.

"How was your flight?" I asked Sophia.

"It was really nice, Sean. Thanks for sending your jet for me."

"Good afternoon, Mr. Williams."

"Sonja. It's good to see you. Are you staying overnight?" I could never keep my eyes off her ass.

"Yes. I'm visiting a friend. Are you returning with us tomorrow?"

"I'm not sure. I'll let Derrick know. Enjoy your stay."

"Thank you."

Sonja got into an Escalade that was idling nearby, and they disappeared down the road.

I turned to Sophia and said, "You ready?"

"Yeah."

I opened the car door and helped her inside. Meanwhile, Derrick brought her bags to the car and helped me place them in the trunk. I talked to Derrick for a short while before Sophia and I headed to my condo.

When we arrived there, I showed Sophia around. "I've got a lot going on today, Sophia. I hope you don't mind that I can't hang around here with you."

"No, Sean, don't worry about it. You already told me what to expect, so go."

"I'll send the car back to pick you up at five o'clock?"

"You're not coming back before the event?"

"No. I'm taking my things with me—I don't have time to come back," I lied. "I'll have the limo pick me up from around back, and we'll make an entrance together, okay?"

"That sounds good."

I went to the studio to see how things were going. I didn't really need to be there. The truth was, I didn't want to spend a lot of time with Sophia today. I needed a date, and that's the only reason she was here.

At the studio, I did some mixing before it was time to get ready. I had a full bathroom in my office and I dressed in there. I was ready when the limo driver called to let me know that he was waiting out back.

The door was opened and I saw Sophia's legs stretched out in front of her. I climbed in and was met by her beautiful smile. At that moment, I wished I had spent the afternoon with her. She was sweet and wanted to please me. I slid next to her with my eyes on her breasts, which were on display for the night. I decided to move in for a kiss.

As I got closer, my dick got harder. I buried my head in her neck, kissed her along her neckline, and said, "You smell as good as you look."

She blushed and said, "Thank you."

I pulled away. "I can't wait to see all of you. You ready for this?"

"Yeah, I'm ready."

When Sophia and I stepped out of the limo, camera bulbs were flashing and microphones were shoved in my face. Sophia and I posed for lots of pictures, and I answered questions for the journalists.

The turnout was great, and Sophia and I had a good time together. She was very attentive and looked good on my arm. That was what I needed, I told myself. No ties, no burdens.

When we returned to the condo in the wee hours, I couldn't wait to be alone with Sophia.

She sat on the couch and kicked her shoes off while I put on some music and fixed drinks for both of us. I soon joined her and we talked about her upcoming photo shoot.

Out of the blue, she said, "Do you mind if I take this dress off? I need to relax."

"Sure, please do." I thought she was going into the bedroom to change, but she stood in front of me and slipped out of her dress. She wore a black-lace set underneath. Instantly attracted, I stood and pulled her close and kissed her hungrily. She took my hand and led me to the bedroom.

Sophia was exactly what I needed. She was sexy and knew it, and she knew how to work her body. Still, I couldn't help but think of Jasmine. I caressed her, kissed her, and let her see my gentle side—something no one besides Jasmine had ever seen—and Sophia ate it up.

I didn't want her to get the wrong idea, so I finally got my emotions back in check.

I was up early the next morning while Sophia slept. I woke her so that she could prepare for her flight. Derrick had said to be at the airport by nine thirty.

Sophia's photo shoot was at two o'clock, so she needed to be in L.A. as soon as she could. I waved goodbye, happy that she hadn't read more into our night than what it was. No ties, no burdens, that's what I needed.

After dropping Sophia off at the airport, I headed to the studio. I was proud of our accomplishment. The studio was state-of-the-art. We hadn't cut any corners with materials or equipment, and, best of all, we'd come in under budget. Yet I still wasn't satisfied.

All morning I thought about Jasmine. I should have taken her to the opening. I needed to talk to someone about my feelings for her. It seemed that no matter what I did, I couldn't shake her loose. Jimmy was a good listener, but I decided against that. I had been edgy and snapping on people, so I finished editing the track that I was working on and went home.

I called Jasmine at work, just to talk. Since we had said we were friends, I was placing a friendly call. Jasmine wasn't there, though, and my call was routed to Ashley.

"Hey, Ashley," I said. "I was trying to reach Jasmine and I got you somehow."

"Sean?" she said, surprised. "What's up?"

"Listen, Ashley, I had a grand opening party at the studio yesterday and lots of pictures were taken. I wanted to talk to Jasmine about them—I don't want her to be under the wrong impression."

"Pictures of what?"

"Me with a model friend of mine. She was my date for the event and I didn't want Jasmine to think that I was dating someone else. You know how these tabloids tell their own story."

"I thought you and Jasmine broke up, Sean."

"We did break up. I don't want her to see the pictures and think the wrong thing." When I said that, I realized it didn't make much sense, but she didn't comment.

"She's not here yet, but I'll be sure to warn her about them. Okay?"

27

Jasmine

When I walked into the dealership, I was surprised to see Ashley in her office. She was usually running the spa these days.

"Hey, girl, what's up?"

"Come here. I need to show you something." She looked deadly serious.

"What is it, Ashley?"

She handed me the entertainment section of the newspaper. My mouth dropped open and I sat down hard in the chair. My eyes began to tear up as I stared at the picture of Sean and some woman on the cover.

"Who is this woman?"

"Some model."

"He looks happy with her. Wow. This is real, Ashley. He's done with me."

She handed me a tissue and I wiped my eyes. "He called a little while ago."

I turned sharply. "He called you?"

"He called looking for you, but got me. He wanted

to warn you about the pictures he knew would hit the newsstands today."

"Why?"

"He wanted you to know that the model was just a date and not someone he's going out with."

I couldn't understand why he'd call to say that. "Do you see why I'm always confused about the way he feels about me, Ashley? Why does he do shit like this?"

She just looked at me in pity.

I pulled myself together and pretended to be all right. "Oh well, life goes on. Thanks for warning me. I'm sure there are other pictures that I won't be able to avoid."

Ashley headed over to the spa, and I went into my office and tried to concentrate on work, but I couldn't. Sean was all I thought about. Here I was feeling guilty for thinking about Sean while I was having sex with Paul, and all the while he'd been with another woman. I wondered if he had thought about me while he was having sex with her.

Later in the day, I saw Ray on the showroom floor, talking to Richard. I hoped that nothing was wrong with his car, so I went out to greet him.

"Good evening, Ray. Is everything all right?"

He turned and looked at me lustfully. "Jasmine!" he said and opened his arms for a hug. Just as I walked into his arms, I saw Tiffany come from around the corner. We parted easily.

"I'm here to pick Tiffany up for lunch. Thanks for the hookup."

"You're welcome, Ray. I thought I was right on with this one."

"You were."

28

Sean

The next morning, my mom called from my grandmother's house in Mississippi and asked if I was coming to the family reunion. At first I told her that I wouldn't be able to make it. After a little thought, though, I called my mom back and told her I would be there the next day. I hadn't seen a lot of my family in a while, and I needed a change of scenery.

We arrived in Jackson, Mississippi, early the next morning. Derrick didn't hang around, returning to L.A. as soon as he could. I rented a car and arrived at my grandmother's house in Greenwood by eleven o'clock. The picnic wasn't scheduled to start until noon. I had missed the dinner the night before, but would be able to participate in the remaining weekend activities.

My grandmother was sitting on the porch when I pulled up in front of her house. When I stepped out of the car, she said, "Sean, boy, is that you?"

"Yeah, Grandma, it's me." I came up the stairs and gave her a hug and a kiss. My uncle Leroy was sitting with her, and I gave him a hug also.

"I thought you wasn't gonna make it, Sean. Your mama said you had some business to take care of. I'm so glad to see you. I miss you, baby."

"I miss you, too, Grandma, and I promise, I will visit more often. Why don't you come out to California and visit me for a while?"

She drew back her hand in horror. "Them folks is crazy out there. I don't know, Sean. Let me think about it for a while, okay?"

Laughing, I said, "Okay, Grandma."

"Yo mama 'n 'em in the house. Why don't you gone in there and say hey to everybody?"

I went through the house, chatting with different relatives. Before I could finish my rounds, I heard someone call my name from the front of the house.

"Sean, bring your tail out here, boy. I know you back there."

When I came up front, my cousin Larry was smiling at me. We hugged like brothers, and I knew it was gonna be a good time from that point on. Whenever me and Larry got together, it was on.

He said, "Come on, take a ride with me."

After talking to my mama, I followed Larry to his car. "So, what's been up, Mr. Music Producer?"

"Little bit of everything, man."

"If you didn't show up this year, I was headed to L.A. I thought you forgot about yo folks."

"Nah, man, it ain't like that. It's just always something

going on. You know how it is. This year, though, I knew I needed to get down here and see y'all."

My cousin Larry was a big, thick country boy. He was a solid 260 pounds, six foot two, with chocolate-brown skin and a bright smile, which he flashed on me. "Well, I'm glad you got your priorities straight. You came by yourself?"

"Yeah."

"Man, when are you gonna get married?"

"I don't know. I ain't as lucky as you. You and Stacy been together since high school. That doesn't happen for everybody."

"You ain't got no girlfriend or nothing?"

"Nah, not right now."

"Damn, man, all those fine-ass women in L.A. and you're single?"

"Sometimes it's better to be single. You don't have to answer to anyone."

He laid a hand on my shoulder. "You know we getting older, Sean. It's time for you to settle down."

I shook off his hand and laughed. "Man, you sound like my mama and Aunt Frances. Get off me."

"I'm just saying. Maybe I can hook you up with one of these good ol' southern girls."

"Man, let me be single and enjoy it. You just want me to be tied down like you. How many kids you and Stacy got now?"

"Six, and I think she's pregnant again." He groaned. "She ain't said nothing yet, but I can always tell."

I couldn't believe it. "How many kids y'all gonna have?"

"Shit, when you gonna have any?"

I chuckled and said, "I'm gonna, okay?"

I had a great time hanging out with Larry. I had invited him and his family to visit me in L.A., and I really wanted them to come. My grandmother was the only other person I had extended the invitation to. Not like I didn't love my family, but Larry was my closest cousin and I wanted to spend more time with him.

I was up early the next morning. My thoughts got stuck on Jasmine, as usual, but I quickly put her out of my mind. When I stepped out into the summer sun, I knew it would be another scorcher. Yesterday had been hot and overcast, but today the sun was shining hot and bright.

My mother and Aunt Frances were waiting for me at Grandma's house. Grandma had already gone with Uncle Leroy and his family. The family was gathering at a park in nearby Grenada.

Once we were on the road, my mama said, "Just warning you, Sean. Mama is gonna be talking to you about yourself."

I knew they had been talking about me, they always did. "What about me?" I said defensively.

Aunt Frances said, "Ain't it about time you settle down, Sean?"

I was getting it all over again. "I'll get married

one day, okay? Mama, you'll get your grandkids, and, Aunt Frances, you'll get your nieces or nephews, okay, ladies?"

Mama said, "I'm just saying, Sean, I'm not getting any younger, and neither are you. My mama wants to see you settled down."

"I hear you, Ma." I quickly changed the subject. "Hey, did y'all see that young dude with Aunt Kiki?"

"You know we did."

They started talking about Aunt Kiki, and that let me off the hook. I knew this wasn't the end of the conversation, but at least I got a temporary reprieve.

When we arrived at the park, I saw more people that I hadn't seen in years. After talking it up in the sun for hours, I felt burned up and tired. I found a seat under a huge tree and dozed off.

Larry invited me to their house after we returned from the picnic to play cards and just hang out with him and his boys. I hadn't been able to relax like that in a long time. I knew that Jimmy was handling our business, and I refused to worry about anything.

We sat in Larry's garage and played bid whist, drank beer, and talked shit. They asked me a lot of questions about the music industry and the Hollywood scene. I told them some stories that got them roaring.

I had a good time. When I found my way back to the hotel, it was after midnight.

The next day, Larry suggested to me and some of

the other guys that we go to Biloxi in the evening to gamble.

My cousin Rick had an Escalade, which five guys rode in, and I rode with Larry in his van, which sat eight.

It must have been my night because I hit almost everything I bet on. I won twenty-nine hundred dollars at the blackjack table. Since we were all drunk, we decided to rent a couple of rooms and stay the night. Larry told us that he'd call Grandma's house and let everyone know that we would be back in the morning. We bought liquor, picked up six or seven girls, and headed to our suite.

We had the radio tuned to WJMI, a hip-hop station in Jackson. Some of the guys were dancing with the girls and a few drifted off into the bedrooms. I drank and played cards and had a great time. I hadn't thought about Jasmine once until I finally crashed.

I woke up to my phone vibrating on the nightstand. It was Stacy. Apparently, Larry had forgotten to call to let everyone know where we were. Luckily, one of the other guys did call and check in with his wife, and the word got around. The word didn't reach Stacy's ear, though, and Larry was in big trouble.

Someone started banging on the door. Larry got up and opened it.

"What, man?" he said groggily to Mike, our little cousin.

"You better check your phone, man, and call your wife. You're in trouble, Larry."

Larry opened his phone and said, "Damn! Fourteen missed calls." He turned the ringer on and the phone rang.

"Hello—" From that point on, Larry struggled to get a word in. Stacy was hollering nonstop, and I busted out laughing. He gave me a serious look and put his finger up to his mouth.

I couldn't stop laughing. He never got a word in after "hello."

When he finally got off the phone, he said, "What the fuck you laughing at, Sean?"

"You! Stacy wants to kick yo ass, man, and you trying to talk me into getting married. Fuck that!"

"Man, shut up! I'm going to wake up these other knuckleheads so we can be on our way."

"All right." I knew his pride was bruised, so I didn't say anything more about Stacy cussing him out.

I cleaned myself up and was ready to go within the hour.

During the ride, Larry talked about being married and raising six kids. He complained about the lack of sex in his life, but we teased him that he must be getting some, or some of those kids ain't his. Pretty soon he was in his original good mood. Although his marriage sounded like a lot of work, Larry and Stacy were happy, and they did everything together. They clearly loved each other.

We didn't make it back to Greenwood until noon. We had a lot of explaining to do. My mom wouldn't have worried if everyone else hadn't begun to worry. Unfortunately, everyone thought that all the people at home knew where we were.

After getting everything cleared up, some of us went to the farm where my mama and her brothers and sisters grew up. I needed to get away from the drama, so I followed that group. After church the next day, I'd be on my way home.

I had a terrible hangover and wanted to find a quiet spot to sleep. Uncle Leroy showed a few of us a spot out in the field, where we chilled. I told them about Jasmine and I admitted that I needed some guidance. These guys were my age and all of them were married with children. For the first time, I admitted that I was afraid of being locked into a relationship.

After talking about Jasmine, I grew quiet, thinking about her while my cousin Jeffrey talked about issues in his relationship. I knew I needed to compromise with Jasmine, and I was willing to do that. It seemed that everyone thought Jasmine was the one for me and encouraged me to go and get my girl.

We returned to the house late for dinner. My mother told me that my grandmother had been looking for me earlier. I found her sitting on the back porch, looking out into the corn field.

"Hi, Grandma."

"Sean, come on and sit down with me."

I was glad to comply. I missed sitting with my grandmother. We would sit for hours while I was a kid, sometimes talking, sometimes not saying anything, just enjoying each other's company. When I was growing up, my grandmother had predicted that I would be successful. She said that I was blessed.

"You know, Sean, I thought out of all of my grandbabies, that you would be married first. You always had girls falling all over themselves for you." She looked at me. "You're so busy with your career, it seems like you would want someone to come home to regularly. You have so much to offer a nice young lady, Sean. Are you seeing anybody special?

"I ain't getting no younger and you my first grandbaby. I want to be around for your wedding and get to hold your babies. Don't you want some babies?"

"Yeah I do, Grandma."

"How old are you?"

"Thirty-four." I could feel the pressure of her grip and she wasn't letting go.

"You ain't having no trouble meeting gals, are you?"

"No, that ain't the problem, Grandma." I glanced around, feeling uncomfortable. "I actually met the girl. It just seems like we can't work it out so that we can be together."

She suddenly released my wrist and leaned back. "You know I loved yo' granddaddy, but when we first met, I wouldn't go out with him because he was bossy and always tried to tell me what I couldn't do." She gave me a knowing look. "Back then, women were passive, but not me. I spoke my mind and did what I wanted to do. After yo' granddaddy saw that I wasn't gonna mind him the way he wanted me to, he let me be—and things changed." A distant smile appeared on her lined face. "There was nothing I wouldn't do for him and he knew that, but he also knew to let me make my own decisions."

She leaned forward and looked me in the eye. "I know you have some of his traits, Sean, I've seen them in you from the beginning. If you trying to make this gal do what you say and she won't mind you, you're making a big mistake, baby. Let the girl be. Ain't that what made you fall in love with her?"

"Yeah," I agreed. "But I'm the man, Grandma, and she's supposed to do what I say."

"Boy, hush. You act like this is the last century. Let her be and you'll see that things will work out for the best."

"Okay, Grandma."

"I want to meet her soon, Sean."

"Okay, Grandma."

When I finally returned to my hotel room, I thought about what Grandma had said. I decided to start listening to what Jasmine was saying and stop telling her what to do. I couldn't let the doctor have her, and I needed to work on getting her back. When I went to L.A. the next day, I would wrap up what I was working on and go back to Chicago and get my girl. I finally had a peaceful night's sleep.

29

Jasmine

Tuesday morning Ashley and I met with Kendall and her staff in New York to discuss our latest venture. Creating a new partnership was a big step for us.

Ashley and I were very excited about the possibility of opening another spa in L.A., the biggest Secrets location to date. We told Kendall that we would get back to her with our decision by the end of next week.

After our meeting, Ashley and I had dinner. She talked excitedly about her wedding, and I listened and added suggestions about some of the details. Talking about the wedding really made me think about Sean, and it took everything in me to contain my emotions. I didn't want Ashley to feel sorry for me, and I didn't want to bring her down. She was always so happy when she spoke of Joe.

When I returned to my room, I started crying. I was in love with Sean, and I couldn't stand not being with him any longer. I decided to tell him that I would do whatever it took for us to be together. I called his cell phone but got his voice mail. I didn't leave a message. What I had to say, I wanted to tell him directly.

The moment my eyes opened the next morning, I thought about Sean again. I was happy that I hadn't gotten through to him the night before, because I might have said some things that I didn't want him to know. I knew that I was being too emotional and that I needed to get myself under control.

I opened the desk drawer, took out a pad of paper and a pen, and started a list of some of the changes I had to make.

1. Stop sleeping around. ☺ (That will be hard to do.)

2. Tell Paul that I can't see him anymore. He is a great guy, I like him a lot, but I am in love with Sean and I need to start doing whatever it takes to make a life with him.

3. Go to Sean and tell him how I feel.

I was confident that I could do the first two things. I know Paul liked me a lot, but he wasn't in love with me, so he would understand when I told him what was going on. The hard part would be telling Sean that I wanted to be with him. Not because it was hard to tell him I loved him, but because I was afraid that he would reject me again.

During our flight back to Chicago, I told Ashley how I felt about Sean and what my plans were. She thought it was a good idea for me to let him know how I felt, but she was cautious about how Sean would receive me.

"You know, Ashley, what scares me the most is revealing myself to him again. I remember how easily he dismissed me. I'm so afraid that he'll just laugh at me and tell me we could never be together."

"Isn't it different this time, Jasmine? This time you'll tell him what he wants to hear. And you have to make it clear that he can't date, either. Right?"

I answered with some force. "Of course that would have to be a part of it. That was our problem initially. We didn't say what we expected from each other. Hopefully he still cares about me enough to listen to what I have to say."

"I'm sure he does, Jasmine." She smiled at me. "I think you two were meant to be together, but you're going the long way around to get there."

I stopped at the spa for a massage and to grab some paperwork to take home. I wanted to call Sean, but I needed to get my affairs in order before I did that. I laughed at my unconscious choice of words.

I called Paul and asked him if he had time for dinner that evening during his break or if he had any time off in the next few days. He said that he would be available for lunch the next day.

I made us a reservation at Ben Pao. I was very nervous about what I had to say to him, but I didn't want to do it over the phone. I wanted him to see my eyes when I told him. I also wanted him to know that what we'd had was real, had been fun, but I couldn't get over the true love of my life and had to pursue that relationship. I hoped with all my heart that he would understand.

I went to the dealership to catch up on some of the paperwork there. Kendall called and said that she was going to L.A. on Monday to look at some sites and suggested that Ashley and I come along. She would be staying at the Bonaventure in downtown L.A., so Ashley and I made reservations there, and booked our flight for Monday morning.

I kept looking at the clock. My lunch date with Paul was at one o'clock, and it was already after noon. I knew traffic would be a mess, so I started my trek up north a little early.

When I arrived at the restaurant at twelve fifty-five, Paul was waiting. He greeted me with a kiss. Luckily, we were seated right away.

Paul grabbed my hands and said, "I missed you, Jasmine. You look great."

"Thank you, Paul." I pulled my hands away, not wanting to go there.

"How was your trip?"

"It was very productive. Ashley and I decided to join the partnership, and we're going to open a spa in L.A. We're really excited about being a part of this expansion."

"It sounds great. You guys are doing a great job with the spa here."

"Thank you, Paul."

"Is there something wrong, Jasmine? You seem distant."

I took a deep breath, gathered my thoughts, and said, "The reason I wanted to see you today, Paul, is to tell you that I won't be able to spend time with you anymore."

He sat back in his chair and said, "Really? Why not?"

"I'm still in love with my ex, and I don't think it's fair of me to keep seeing you when my heart is somewhere else." I looked down at the table because I couldn't look him in the eye any longer.

He didn't make me suffer for long. He reached for my face and lifted my chin. "I know you still love him, Jasmine. I knew I never had you, although it was great spending time with you. If Sean is the man that makes you happy, then you should be with him. I won't say that I'm not disappointed, because I am. I wanted a more permanent relationship with you, but I understand."

He was so nice, which was part of the problem.

We ordered lunch, but I didn't have much of an appetite and Paul picked over his food, too. Afterward, Paul walked me to my car, gave me a soft kiss on my lips, and said, "I hope Sean realizes what he has."

With mixed feelings, I watched Paul walk away. I would miss him.

•   •   •

I headed to the spa after lunch. Business was bustling and I had lots of work to catch up on, but I didn't get much done. I hung around the office for a couple of hours before going home.

I was nervous but excited at the same time. If things went the way I hoped, we'd be back together and I wouldn't let him get away again.

First, I wanted to get comfortable before talking to him. Sean was the man I wanted to spend the rest of my life with, so I needed to give him what he wanted. I need to stop fighting him and submit.

After kicking my shoes off at the door, I dropped my bags on the couch and headed to the kitchen. I needed to feel wine flowing through me. I wanted to be as relaxed and confident as possible when I told Sean how much I loved him and that I was willing to do what it took to make it work. I didn't want to talk myself out of calling, so I carried my glass into the living room and sat in my favorite spot on the couch. I took a few sips of wine before setting the glass on a coaster. I closed my eyes and took a deep breath before picking up the phone and dialing Sean's cell phone number.

I exhaled when my call went straight to voice mail. I ended the call. I was both relieved and disappointed. I was afraid that he'd seen my number and decided to divert the call. I should have left a voice mail, but decided to call his number in L.A. instead. This time I left a message.

"Hi, Sean, it's Jasmine. I don't know if you are in Chicago or L.A. I tried calling your cell phone, but I didn't get an answer. I would like to see you—that's if you have time for me. Our last meeting didn't go the way I hoped, and I would like another chance to get our friendship where it should be."

I decided to cut the shit and get to it. After a short silence I said, "I miss you, Sean. Tell me what you want. Tell me what it will take for us to build a relationship together, and let's work on making it happen." I couldn't help adding, "Don't you miss me, baby? How can you stay away from me like this? You make me feel like I didn't mean anything to you, and it hurts, Sean. Don't you love me? Please call me at home. I'll be waiting to hear from you."

After I hung up the phone, I felt better than I had in a long time. I would make myself completely available to Sean if he wanted me. All he had to do was call.

30

Jasmine

I waited all weekend to hear from Sean. When Sunday night rolled around and I hadn't heard from him, I knew that he was done with me. I felt like a damn fool, again. I was totally deflated. I loved him, but even I'd learned where to draw the line.

I lay awake, thinking about my life, wallowing in self-pity. I didn't think things could get any worse.

My doorbell rang at one fifteen in the morning. I thought it might be Sean, so I ran to the window to see who was parked in my driveway. I was shocked to see Ray's car. I didn't recall giving him my address.

I was afraid that something had happened to Sean, so I threw on some sweats and hurried downstairs to answer the door.

He smiled woozily and said, "Jasmine, I wanted to talk to you."

I raised my eyebrows in surprise. "At one thirty in the morning, Ray?"

"Yeah. I was thinking about you right now and thought we could finally have that talk that we never seem to be able to have."

He was drunk. I didn't move from the foyer. "What talk?"

"About us."

"Tiffany seems pretty happy these days. I thought things were going well with the two of you."

"She's cool. And by the way, I like how you threw in a substitute for yourself." He wiggled a finger at me, like that wasn't fair. "I still want the original, Jasmine."

I couldn't help smiling. "Ray, you can't stand rejection, can you?"

"Are you rejecting me, Jasmine?"

"It's the challenge, isn't it?"

He moved close to me and said, "It's my attraction to you, Jasmine."

I stepped back and we stared at each other. My brow furrowed when the doorbell rang.

"You expecting someone?"

"I wasn't expecting you."

I was shocked to see Sean on my porch. I couldn't believe my eyes.

"Shit."

"What? Who is it?"

"Sean."

"Yeah. Shit."

I reached for the door.

"No. Don't open it."

"What? I have to, Ray." He walked to the couch and sat down.

I wanted to smile when I saw him, but I knew I had some explaining to do before we'd be smiling about anything.

Sean was disappointed to see his friend. He finally said, "I got your message, Jasmine, but I didn't expect to see Ray when I got here."

Ray stood and said, "What's up, Sean. I've been here—what, Jasmine?—five minutes?"

I nodded my head.

"Sean, Jasmine hooked me up with Ashley's sister, Tiffany, and I wanted to talk to her about it."

"At one thirty in the morning, Ray? Didn't I tell you to stay away from Jasmine?"

He put his head down in shame. "Yeah, man, you did."

"Then why do I see you every time I see her?"

He turned to me and said, "Are you calling him, Jasmine?"

"No, I haven't called him," I said coolly. "I don't even know his phone number."

"Look, Ray. Whatever is going on between you and Tiffany will have to stay between you and Tiffany. Jasmine isn't available to play mediator."

Sean was acting no-nonsense and Ray was no fool. "All right. Look, I'm gone, y'all have a good night."

Ray walked out.

Sean turned to me, eyes ablaze. "Did you let him touch you?"

"No." I expected him to go off again, but instead his face cleared.

"Okay." He looked behind him and said, "You're not expecting anyone else tonight, are you?"

"No." I wanted to get past this and said, "So, you got my message?"

"Yes."

"I called you three days ago, Sean. You didn't respond."

"I was at our family reunion in Mississippi, and I didn't get your call until I returned to L.A.," he explained. "If you'd left that message on my cell phone, I would have gotten it sooner."

He did seem genuinely apologetic, so I took that as a good sign. "Sean, please. Can we start from right now? Can we?"

He was hesitant. "Okay, Jasmine. First and foremost, I don't ever want you to be with another man. Under no circumstances will it be acceptable, none. Do you understand?"

"I want the same from you, Sean. Did you make some phone calls and have conversations before you came to see me?"

He waved his hand, absolutely not. "I had already taken care of my personal life before you called. Jasmine, it wasn't your phone call that brought me here. I'm ready to settle down and get serious with you."

I blushed. "I'm ready, too."

I led him by the hand to the couch, and we talked for a few hours. I was sleepy, knowing I had to be up early, but I didn't want our time to end. It was after four o'clock when I fell asleep in Sean's arms on the sofa. I had to be up by six to get to the airport.

I woke up close to six thirty, and I woke Sean up, too. "Sean, I need to get to the airport. Me and Ashley have a meeting in L.A. at two o'clock this afternoon."

"Derrick can take you."

"No. We already have everything scheduled."

He took my hands. "When will you be back?"

I moved close to him, kissed his lips, and said, "Tomorrow. We're only staying overnight. Can we make plans for an intimate dinner tomorrow night?"

He kissed me tenderly on the cheek. "Yes. I look forward to it." He stood and said, "Go on and get ready. I'll drive you to the airport."

We headed upstairs. He lay across my bed, watching TV, while I showered and dressed. I couldn't believe it. We were together.

Our flight to L.A. was scheduled for seven fifty. After Sean dropped me off at the airport, I couldn't hold back my excitement when I saw Ashley.

"What's up, Jasmine?" she said with a big smile on her face. I guess my happiness was contagious.

"I got my man back."

She hugged me and said, "I'm so happy for both of y'all. Everything cool with everybody else?"

"Yeah, everything is cool. Being together is what we both want."

As we waited to board the plane, I told Ashley what had happened. But I left out the part about Ray. Finally, I had learned to keep my mouth shut about some things.

When we reached our hotel, I ran up to my room and called Sean.

"Hey, baby," he said. "Everything all right?"

"Yes, everything is perfect." I was giddy. I didn't know what to say.

He said, "I guess I can get your cell phone number now."

"Of course you can. You have total access to me." We exchanged all our current phone numbers.

"What do you have planned once you leave L.A.?"

"Back to work."

"Can you take a trip with me for a few days?"

I was excited. "Where are we going?"

"I need to schedule a consultation with a ship maker in Gulfport, Mississippi. I'm thinking about purchasing a yacht. Can you go with me?"

A yacht? "I'm sure I can work it out."

"Road trip okay with you?"

"Yes. That will be nice."

We got caught up on some things. There was electricity in our words.

"Jasmine. This is it, baby."

"I know."

"All right. Are you free this evening?"

"Ashley and I planned to have dinner at a Mexican grill that Kendall and her friends were talking about. They made it sound like the best Mexican food in the world, so we wanted to go."

"I'll take you and Ashley."

"Are you on your way back?"

"I should be there by dinnertime. I'll pick you ladies up at eight o'clock."

Kendall liked the first site, a nice building in Hollywood. It had once been a retail store and needed a lot of conversion work. The buildings in New York, New Jersey, D.C., and Chicago were all designed alike. We wanted something different out here.

Kendall was so taken with this building that she wasn't interested in seeing the other locations. Ashley and I told her, though, that we weren't sold on this location.

When we arrived at the next site, everyone was in awe. It was a beautifully restored 1920s Victorian mansion in Beverly Hills. The place was spectacular, and the property had been recently rezoned for commercial use. We decided immediately that this would be the next Secrets Spa location. It had beautiful views from every window, views of the ocean, the city, and the hills. I could see myself living here. Seriously, I wanted this house for myself. We all started throwing out ideas on decorating, what each room would be used for, where our offices would be located.

I said, "Excuse me, ladies, but what are we talking

about, our offices? Ashley and I live in Chicago, and, Kendall, I know you're not about to leave New York. Someone else will be enjoying this view."

"I guess I got caught up in the moment," Kendall said. "But damn, Jasmine, couldn't you see yourself sitting at your desk in front of this window, looking out at the ocean, relaxing and enjoying life?"

"Girl, you know I could, but I have a life in Chicago and I can't just pick up and leave like that."

"Why not? Your man lives here," Ashley said.

That sounded like a great idea, but I wasn't showing it. "It's not that simple, Ashley, and you know it."

After we toured the outside of the property, we all agreed that this was the best location. Kendall scheduled a meeting with the bank for nine o'clock the next morning.

As we headed back to the hotel, Ashley asked about our dinner plans, and I told her that Sean was on his way to take us to dinner.

"Didn't you say he was in Chicago?"

"He has a private jet, Ashley. He'll be here."

"Well, it's still early, I need a snack. Pull into that Carl's Jr. What time is Sean picking us up?"

"Eight o'clock. He said he hadn't heard of La Salsa Grill and I'm surprised. Sean eats dinner out almost every night."

She leaned across the seat toward me. "It sounds like he needs a woman to take care of him."

"And now he has one."

"I'm happy that you two are working things out," she said, starting to laugh. "The only time you seem happy is when you're with him."

When eight o'clock rolled around, Ashley and I were waiting in the hotel lobby. I saw Sean as he pulled into the entrance. He was driving an M35 Infiniti, and he looked good in it, as he did in all his cars. The valet opened the doors, and Ashley and I climbed inside. I leaned over and said, "I love you, Sean, and I don't ever want to be without you again."

"I love you, too, baby. I'm just happy that we have this opportunity to try again." We kissed, a little long in the presence of company, but we couldn't help it.

Sean turned around as Ashley climbed into the backseat. "Ashley, what's up, girl?"

"Hey, Sean. It's so good to see you again."

He chuckled. "Yeah, here we are again." He pointed a finger at me. "It's for good this time, right, baby?"

I folded his finger inside my hand. "Yes."

The restaurant was everything that Kendall had said it would be. We had a few drinks and a really good time. Sean and I kept stealing glances at each other. I started to get excited at the thought of being alone with him.

When we got back to the hotel, Sean grabbed his overnight bag out of the trunk of his car.

"We'll see you in the morning, Ashley."

"Yes, let's have breakfast."

Sean had our room upgraded to a suite. "When did you do this?" I asked.

"All it takes is a phone call. Only the best for you."

Our suite had a sitting area with a spectacular view of the city. Once we were seated, Sean opened the chilled bottle of champagne. He handed me a glass. "Jasmine, today is the first day of the rest of our lives." He pulled me close. "I'm sorry about all the bullshit we went through. I love you more than I was willing to admit, but I can admit it now, and I'll show you."

"I love you, too, Sean. I'll do whatever it takes to make this work."

A little too casually he said, "By the way, my grandmother wants me to bring you down South to meet her."

That rocked me for a second. "You told her about me?"

"She said that she wants to meet my wife and children before she dies."

"Your wife and children?"

Sean nodded slowly.

I didn't say anything. I stood up and walked over to the window. Sean came up behind me and put his arms around my waist and started kissing my neck.

"Mmmm . . ."

"I've missed you."

He turned me around and we kissed, long and hard.

"Listen, baby, I know I'm saying some things to you

that you probably thought you would never hear from me, and I hope I'm not scaring you, although it's a little scary to me. I want you to know how I feel."

"It is a little scary, Sean. I knew I had to tell you the truth about how much I love you. I didn't know that you would do the same. I don't ever want you to doubt my love for you."

"I won't, and I don't want you to doubt my love for you, either. We'll stop in Greenwood to see my grandma when we go to Gulfport next week, okay?"

I could see that it was important to him. "Okay. How long, did you say?"

"Just a few days. We can leave Sunday and come back Tuesday. I just want you to meet my family."

"Okay," I said, warming up to the idea. "I'd love to meet your family."

He picked me up and carried me to the bedroom. He put me down at the entrance, where rose petals in a variety of colors were scattered over the floor and on the bed.

My breath caught in my throat. I turned to Sean with tears in my eyes. "It's beautiful, Sean. You surprise me with something beautiful every time I see you. I love you."

He took my hand and led me to the bed. He unzipped my dress and helped me step out of it.

I wore a black-and-white lace thong and bra set. Sean looked me over and said, "I love you, Jasmine, and I'll give you the world, if you'll let me."

When we made love, it felt like it was our first time. We lay awake for hours, talking and caressing. Once we settled down to sleep, we held each other tight. I didn't want to let him go.

The next morning, we met Ashley for breakfast before our meeting. Sean told us to meet him at the airport at three o'clock.

Everything went smoothly with the real estate agent, and we signed a contract to purchase the Beverly Hills property. Kendall scheduled a meeting in New York for the end of the following week with our attorneys to discuss all the legal documentation. Ashley and I told her that we would be there.

When we met Sean at the airport, we told him all about the spas. We talked about the dealership, too. Sean told us that he was opening a new studio and some of the clients that were already scheduled to record.

When we arrived in Chicago, Ashley headed to her car, and Sean took me to the spa. He came in with me and I introduced him to everyone. After a quick tour, I saw that everything was running well. From there we headed to his studio. Jimmy was in the engineer's booth when we walked in.

He busted out laughing when he saw us together.

"What's so funny?"

"The two of you. I hope this is for real this time, Jasmine, because I'm gonna have to kick his ass if it ain't."

"Man, shut up!" Sean said, but he wasn't mad. "What's going on around here?"

"Everything is cool. I'm waiting for Ray to get here and record this final track. You're gonna do the editing, right?"

"Yeah, I already told y'all that I would."

"I'm just asking, since you're with Jasmine and all. I just didn't know if you would have time."

Sean looked at Jimmy and shook his head.

"Oh, by the way, Sean, I'm outta here in the morning, and I'll see you in two weeks."

"Two weeks?"

"Yeah. There's nothing left for me to do this week and I'm going to Cancun next week, so this week and next week is basically two weeks."

"All right, Jimmy."

We turned toward the door when we heard Ray enter, with Tiffany in tow.

"Sean, when did you roll into town? Jimmy didn't know when you were coming back!" He stopped when he saw me at the end of the mixing board. "Ah, I see now, you were with Ms. Jasmine."

Ray came over to me, grabbed my hands, and said, "What's up, baby? You're looking as fly as ever! You gonna give Sean another chance?"

"Yeah, Ray, we're trying to work things out."

"So that's it, huh?"

We laughed. "Yeah, Ray, that's it."

"All right. Y'all ready to get started on this last track?"

While Sean and Ray talked about the taping, I walked over to Tiffany, who sat in a chair by the door.

"Hey, Tiffany. It's been a while since I've seen you."

"Yeah, you're always gone somewhere."

I smiled while thinking about my current accomplishments. "I've been busy lately. So how are things going with you and Ray?"

"I'm sure better now that he sees you with Sean. He had been asking me questions about you, but seeing y'all together should help him focus on me."

"Well, good luck with him, Tiffany."

"Yeah, thanks."

Sean walked up to us and said, "You ready, baby?"

"Yeah. You remember Tiffany, right?"

"Yes. It's good to see you again."

She smiled and said, "You, too, Sean." For once, she had something nice to say. "You two look good together."

31

We were all set. I was taking her to Greenwood the following week to meet Grandma. Once I got the okay, I'd ask her to marry me. I didn't want to wait any longer. I wanted the world to know that she was my wife, and when I put that ring on her finger, she and everyone else would know that my feelings for her were real.

First I had to get the ring. I was going to Michigan while she was in New York at the end of the week. I'd ask my mama to help me pick one out.

My mother would be happy that I'd worked things out with Jasmine. She had always wanted me to have what I wanted, and I wanted Jasmine to be my wife.

I woke up early Friday morning, talked to Jasmine before her flight, and hit the road to Detroit. My mama was cooking when I came in. I gave her a hug.

"Sean! What a pleasant surprise this is. Why didn't you tell me you were coming?"

"I wanted to surprise you. I woke up this morning thinking about you, and here I am."

She was pleased. "It's good to see you. You want something to eat?"

"No, I'm good."

"Are you okay? I mean, you always have so much work to do."

"Nothing is wrong. I think everything is finally right. Jasmine and I are back on track, and I'm going to ask her to marry me."

She almost dropped the pan. "Marriage. Are you sure, Sean?"

"Yes, Mama. I love her and I can't deny it. I realized that the only time I'm happy is when I'm with her."

She came over to give me a hug, a nice long one. "Congratulations, son. I knew you two would eventually come to your senses. I've been waiting a long time to hear you tell me that you were in love and getting married. Maybe I can get some grandchildren soon."

I wanted to put in a note of caution. "Don't rush it, Mama, I haven't asked her yet."

"You don't see a problem, do you?"

"No. I believe she will say yes. We talked about a lot of stuff, and we both know that we're not happy apart. We want to be together."

"When will you ask her?"

"I'm taking her to Greenwood to meet Grandma on Sunday, and I'll probably ask her while we are down there."

"Do you already have the ring?"

"No. I was hoping you would go with me to pick one out."

That sounded like the best idea she'd heard all year.

We headed to a jeweler in Auburn Hills that I used quite often. My mother was more excited than I was, and she peppered me with questions as I drove.

"Do you know what size ring she wears?"

"Yes. I've bought her jewelry before."

"Gold, platinum, do you have any ideas about what you're looking for?"

"No. I think I'll know it when I see it."

When we arrived, Mama was all over the place, all at once.

"My son would like to see engagement rings, please."

Edward said, "Sean is getting married?" He looked at me questioningly.

"I'm going to try. What you got for me?"

"Come on over here and have a seat." Edward pulled out a tray with six different rings. "These are a few of our latest designs in engagement rings. I can design something for Jasmine or you can submit your own design."

I smiled and said, "Did I mention Jasmine?"

"This is for Jasmine, right?"

"Yeah."

"I'm glad to hear it, man. You've talked about her so much, I knew it had to be. Congratulations."

We shook hands. "I have a couple of other rings that I think you would like."

Edward came back with two trays. I knew which ring I wanted the moment I saw it. Multicarat, princess cut, platinum, it was perfect.

"Mama, come and look at this."

She inhaled, covered her mouth with her hand, and said, "Sean, it's beautiful. I think it's the one."

"So do I."

I was proud. It was a big step for me. My life was about to change dramatically, and man, I was ready.

32

Jasmine

Friday morning, Ashley and I were on our way to New York to finalize our plans for the spa in L.A. I couldn't concentrate on it the way I should have because I kept thinking about Sean. I was nervous about meeting his grandmother. That was a serious step, especially since she had told him that she wanted to meet his wife. But I didn't read anything into it. I'd learned not to read into what Sean says. I just would wait to see what happened.

Our meeting was productive, and Kendall volunteered to oversee most of the construction. Ashley and I would take turns visiting L.A. in the coming months.

I was ready to get back home and spend time with Sean. He had invited me to his condo for the weekend. When I got home from New York, I packed enough for the weekend and for our trip down South. Sean was at my house at nine o'clock to pick me up.

As soon as I saw him, I got butterflies in my belly. He kissed me and said, "I've missed you. How was your trip?"

I liked the idea of being missed and I smiled. "It

was good. I'll be spending more time in L.A. while we try to get this thing off the ground."

"That's good for me."

"Not if you'll be here. How long will you be here, anyway?"

"Well, I'm not really sure. We have a lot of projects already lined up. I don't necessarily have to be here for all of them, though."

"We'll just take it one day at a time. I'm glad you're here now. I'm sure we'll make the best of our time together."

He carried my bags to his car and we headed for his condo. During our ride his phone rang. It was synced with his car. A voice came over the speaker.

"Sean. Hey, baby, this is Brenda."

He glanced at me—not to worry. "Hey, Brenda, what's up?"

I looked out the window.

"I was calling to see when you were coming home. You know I can come to Chicago and take care of you."

He took the phone off speaker and picked it up. Even so, I could still hear her.

"I won't be there for a while. I need to talk to you about something."

"What's up, Sean?"

"I can't see you anymore."

"I thought we talked about this. I told you I won't pressure you. I just want to be with you sometimes."

"I know we talked about it, but the situation has changed. I'm in a committed relationship now."

"With who, Jasmine?"

"Yeah, Jasmine. I want to make this work. You understand, don't you?"

"No, I don't understand. When did you decide this? I just want to spend time with you every now and then. Can't we do that? I'll do all the things you like me to do for you."

"That's okay, Brenda. I'm good. I've got to go, you take care of yourself."

He hung up the phone.

"I'm sorry about that, Jasmine. I guess I forgot to make a few more phone calls."

When we got to his house and went inside, I said, "This is a beautiful place, Sean. A little light on furniture, but it's really nice. Why didn't you decorate?"

He shrugged. "I bought this place so that I'd have a place to stay while the studio was under construction. I recently decided that I would keep it. It's a good investment."

"Well, I love it. I'm gonna take a shower and slip on something comfortable."

I didn't know how many women Sean had calling him, but his phone continued to ring nearly nonstop. He gave them all the same "I'm off the market" speech. I guess I could understand how he'd forgotten a few, but I wouldn't understand too much longer.

33

We arrived in Greenwood around two in the morning and I was dead tired from the drive. Jasmine offered to help drive, but I told her that I could handle it. We checked into our motel, and I was asleep within minutes.

We were up early the next morning because Grandma was expecting us for breakfast. I could tell that Jasmine was nervous, but I assured her that my grandmother would love her.

"I don't know what to wear, Sean," she fretted as she searched through the pile of clothes spread out on the bed.

"It's not that serious. Whatever you wear will be fine."

"No, it won't," she said forcefully.

I gave up. I just sat in the chair and watched her change clothes over and over. I didn't realize that she had brought so many. I saw at least six different outfits, and we were only here for a few days.

"Jasmine, why don't you just wear those shorts you just had on?"

"Shorts? Is that respectable for meeting someone's grandmother?"

"Yes. It's hot."

She didn't think so. "I'll wear this sundress." She changed into it, stood in front of me, and asked, "How does this look?"

She looked delectable. "It looks great. Can we go now?"

"Sean, that's all you can say?"

"Jasmine, please," I said, laying on some charm. "Everything you tried on looked good to me. I think you're worrying too much about your appearance. She will love you no matter what you are wearing."

At last the worry dropped off her face. "Okay, Sean. I'm sorry that I'm being so paranoid. Let's just go."

Grandma was sitting on her porch when we pulled up. I had called her a few days earlier to let her know that I was bringing Jasmine to meet her. I also told her that I planned to ask Jasmine to marry me while we were there, and asked her to keep my secret.

I helped Jasmine out of the car. We held hands as we climbed the stairs.

"Grandma, this is Jasmine Taylor. Jasmine, this is my grandma, Mrs. Sara Ward."

"Come here, baby, and give me a hug. I'm so happy to meet you, Jasmine. You call me Grandma, okay?"

"Okay, Grandma. I'm very happy to meet you, too."

"Y'all come on in the house and get something to eat."

Grandma had cooked all kinds of food. Maybe she was a little nervous, too.

"So, Jasmine, you know you the first girl Sean has brought down here for me to meet, don't you?"

"Yes, ma'am." Jasmine looked at me and added, "I hope I'll be the last."

My grandmother eyed me sternly. "You must be awfully special, baby, 'cause Sean keep all his business to hisself. He don't let nobody know what's going on with him. So to show up with you, this is serious."

"Grandma, please."

"Okay, Sean. I'm sorry, baby, but you know it's the truth. Larry and Stacy will be by here in a little while. I thought they'd be here by now. You know his wife is pregnant again?"

"Yeah, Larry told me."

She trained her sights on Jasmine. "You want children?"

"Yes, ma'am."

"Well, neither one of y'all is getting any younger. That's all I've got to say about that right now."

"Anybody home? Grandma, where y'all at?" Larry shouted through the house.

"That boy is so loud," she said to us. "We back here eating. Y'all is late," she called.

Me and Jasmine smiled at each other.

Larry came into the kitchen and kissed Grandma.

"I'm sorry for being late. Stacy is the slowest person alive. Hey, Sean, I see you made it."

I stood up and we hugged. "What's up Larry, Stacy?"

"Hey, Sean."

I said, "Jasmine, this is my cousin Larry and his wife, Stacy."

She stood and extended her hand, but Larry pulled her close. "Girl, come here and give me a hug." She and Stacy hugged, too. "It's nice meeting y'all," she said.

Larry had his eyes popped open at the sight of her. "It's really nice meeting you, Jasmine. We was starting to wonder if Sean was having trouble getting a girlfriend."

"Sean ain't never had a problem getting a girlfriend," Jasmine said, and we all laughed.

Grandma said, "Y'all come and sit down and eat this food."

After everyone was seated, Stacy asked, "So, Jasmine, do you work with Sean?"

"No. I own a car dealership and a day spa in Chicago."

"How long y'all been knowing each other?"

"Almost three years."

I could see that Stacy was set to interrogate her. "Hey, cool it with the questions. She's here now, she's with me, and that's enough."

"All right, Sean, relax. We ain't gonna find out nothing you don't want us to know."

I turned to Larry. "Come go out to the car with me for a minute. I want to show you something."

The spell Jasmine had cast over Larry was finally broken.

When me and Larry stepped outside I said, "So, what you think?"

"I'm trying to see why you hesitated one single minute."

I shoved my hands into my pockets and looked down. "Stupid. I was just stupid, trying to convince myself that I wasn't ready for commitment."

"Are you ready now?"

"I bought a ring."

He looked stunned. "A ring? Damn, Sean. Man, you're serious. Did you ask her yet?"

"No, but I will today."

"Well, good luck, man. I'm sure you don't need it. I can already see that she's in love with you." He licked his lips. "She sure is pretty, Sean."

"Yeah, she's that and so much more."

"Do you have the ring with you?"

I pulled it out of my pocket and showed it to him.

"Damn, Sean. This is a major rock."

I smiled and admired the beautiful ring. "Yeah, I hope she likes it."

When me and Larry came back into the kitchen, I overheard Stacy and Jasmine talking about me.

"Hey, are you harassing my woman?"

"No, we're just getting to know each other."

"Jasmine, Larry, and Stacy invited us to their house for dinner this evening."

She turned to Stacy and said, "Thank you, guys. I look forward to spending more time with y'all."

Larry and Stacy did some serious husband-and-wife jujitsu with their eyes, and then Larry announced, "We need to get back home and start cooking and stuff. We'll see y'all later. Bye, Grandma," he called out.

Jasmine went into the living room to watch TV. I excused myself to my grandmother's room to show her the ring.

"So what do you think, Grandma?"

"I like her and I think she will make you very happy. She sure is pretty, Sean."

"Yeah, she is pretty, but that's not why I love her. I feel good and happy and relaxed whenever I'm with her."

I pulled out the ring and showed it to her.

"Here is the ring I'll give her when I ask her to marry me."

She took the ring box and said, "This is beautiful."

"It's for the most beautiful woman in the world. Do you think she'll like it?"

"Of course," she said flatly. "She would like it if it were a piece of wire. As long as she loves you, it won't matter. When are you going to give it to her?"

"This evening after we leave Larry and Stacy's."

"Come back by here tomorrow before you leave so that I can congratulate y'all."

"Okay, Grandma. We're about to go back to our motel. I'll see you later."

"Okay, Sean. I love you, baby, and good luck."

"Thanks, Grandma."

Jasmine was watching a game show. "Are you ready to go?"

"Yes, if you are. Let me say goodbye to Grandma. Where is she?"

"She's in the back bedroom." I showed her where Grandma's room was, then I sat in the dining room, looking at family portraits, while they talked.

I heard Jasmine say, "We will be back to see you before we leave. It was really good meeting you."

"It's good to meet you, too, Jasmine. I think you are just what Sean needs."

I started smiling when I heard that.

We headed back to the motel and napped for a few hours.

Later that evening, when we arrived at Larry and Stacy's, we found people everywhere.

Lots of my cousins had showed up, and I was happy to be able to show Jasmine off. We ate, drank, played cards, and talked about everything. Jasmine and I didn't make it back to our motel room until three thirty the next morning.

Without a thought, Jasmine pulled her dress over her head and walked past me in her underwear. Any other time I would have been all over her, but I was gripped with fear and couldn't move. That box felt like a boulder in my pocket.

She stopped prancing and said, "I had a good time, Sean. Your family is pretty cool."

"Yeah, they are," I said, my voice a croak. "Come here, Jasmine, I need to talk to you."

She looked uneasy. "What's wrong?"

"Nothing. I guess I was having so much fun that I lost track of time, but I don't want another day to pass before I ask you this."

I took her hand, got down on my knee, and said, "Jasmine, will you please marry me?"

She looked so shocked.

At last, she said, "Yes, Sean, I love you. Yes, I will marry you."

I slipped the ring onto her finger and she gasped when she saw it. I stood up, pulled her into my arms, and kissed her deeply. "This is the most beautiful ring in the world, Sean. I love you and I love this ring."

"I knew you would. I want to make you happy, baby."

"You already have."

"I don't want to be engaged forever, though. Do you think we can be married before the year is out?"

She pulled back a little. "It's already August. Can you wait until May or June?"

I was about to argue, but I remembered Grandma's words. "I really don't want to, but if that's what you want, that's what we will do." I thought about it for a second. "Can't we get married in November? You're pretty resourceful. Can't you pull something together before Thanksgiving?"

She smiled at my eagerness. "I probably can."

"Okay, let's get married the Saturday before Thanksgiving. Anything you need, let me know, and if I can't do it myself I will have someone take care of it."

"Why the big rush, Sean?"

"I'm ready to spend the rest of my life with you. I'm ready to start a family."

"You're ready for babies already?"

"As soon as possible, Jasmine. I want to see you all swollen up with my seed. Can't you see a little Sean running around the house?"

She liked this side of me, I could tell. "Yeah, I could. Okay, baby, we'll get married the Saturday before Thanksgiving. I don't ever want to be without you again."

"I want to have an engagement party next Saturday. We can do it at my condo. Let's start working on that as soon as we get back."

"Okay. You're really into this, aren't you?"

"I'm really into you, Jasmine. I just want the world to know how much I love you."

The next morning, when we arrived at Grandma's, she was smiling when she saw us.

"Why are you smiling like that, Grandma?"

"'Cause I saw that ring shining on Jasmine's finger

when y'all pulled up." She nodded, as though this was how it must be. "Y'all come here and give me a hug. Congratulations to both of you. Y'all done really made me happy. Welcome to the family, Jasmine."

"Thank you, Grandma."

"When is the big day?"

"Saturday before Thanksgiving."

"I'm glad to hear it ain't gonna be sometime next year. Let's do it and get me some more great-grand-babies."

Jasmine looked at me and we started laughing.

"Don't y'all be laughing at me. I can't wait until Sean has his own babies. He sure was a bullheaded little boy and I'm sure he's a bullheaded man. So I'm just gonna wait and see how he is gonna handle a child just like him."

"I ain't that bad, Grandma."

"I've got some business in Gulfport this afternoon."

Jasmine and I each gave Grandma a hug, then we were on our way.

34

When I arrived at the dealership, Ashley was already there. She came walking toward me saying, "Oh, my goodness, Jasmine."

"What?"

"I saw it when you were coming in the door."

"You saw what?"

"Your ring."

I lifted my hand to look at it. "Yeah, Ashley, he asked me to marry him."

She hugged me and we walked into her office.

"I'm so very happy for the two of you. I know this is what both of you want, and I'm happy to see you two together again."

"So am I, Ashley. We already set a date."

"When is it?"

"The Saturday before Thanksgiving."

"Wow, that's soon."

"He doesn't want to wait."

She gave me a quizzical look. "Are you pregnant?"

"No. We just want to be together and start a family."

"You're ready to have a baby?"

"Yeah, I am. Can you help me plan the wedding?"

"Of course I can. We can plan both of our weddings together."

"He wants to have an engagement party at his condo next Saturday. I need help with that, too."

"Saturday? Well, we'd better get started."

"He said he would fax me a list of the names and addresses of all of his friends that he wanted to invite."

My phone rang.

"Good morning, Mrs. Williams."

"Good morning, Mr. Williams. How are you today?"

"I'm wonderful now since you're going to be my wife. I was thinking about having our engagement party on a yacht. What do you think?"

"I think that's a great idea. You still want to do it next Saturday?"

"No, I know that isn't enough time to let everyone know. How about two weeks from Saturday? That should be enough time to get everything together. We can have the party in Marina del Rey. What do you think?"

"What about my friends that live here?"

"We can fly them out. We can take close friends on the jet and buy tickets for everyone else. I think two weeks is enough time. It's on the weekend, and most people will be off from work anyway. Are there a lot of people you want to invite?"

"Well, yes, I have a lot of friends that I would like to see there."

"Invite whoever you want to, baby, I'll take care of it. We can fly them out that afternoon, and they can return later that evening or the following morning. If they want to stay longer, they can make other arrangements. I'll take care of the yacht and the entertainment, and you take care of the food and other stuff."

"I love you, Sean."

"I love you, too. Will I see you this evening?"

"Yes. Can you come to my house? I'll fix you dinner."

"Okay, I'll see you when I'm done at the studio."

When I got off the phone, Ashley said, "What sounds like a good idea?"

"Sean wants to have our engagement party on a yacht in Marina del Rey."

Her eyes lit up. "In California?"

"Yeah. He said that I can bring my closest friends on his jet and that he would pay airfare for everyone else."

"Damn. Sean got it like that?"

"Girl, you know he does."

She was getting excited. "I'll expect to be on the jet."

"You will. Sean will take care of the yacht and the entertainment. We need to find a party planner. You feel like going to L.A.?"

"When are you talking about going?"

"Tomorrow or the next day. I'll make some phone calls, set up some meetings."

"Okay, let me know."

Tiffany walked into my office. "Welcome back, Jasmine. Ray told me that Sean took you to meet his family down South. I hope that went well."

I was surprised at the nice way Tiffany was talking to me.

"Thank you, Tiffany."

"Wow! Look at that rock on your hand. Are you and Sean engaged?"

I was beaming. "Yes, he asked me while we were in Mississippi."

"I wish you and Sean well, Jasmine."

"Thank you. How are things with you and Ray?"

"So far it's going well. He's fun, funny, kind, and he seems to adore me."

"That's perfect, isn't it?"

"Yes, it is!"

"All right, ladies, I've got lots of work, so if y'all will excuse me."

The third Saturday in August was a beautiful, sunny day in Southern California. Sean's jet was full with family and friends preparing for our engagement party. The jet sat ten comfortably. Everyone else from our area was coming out later on a commercial flight.

We arrived in L.A., and it was already nine thirty when we got to Sean's house in Malibu. The party was to start at four o'clock. I had an appointment for a facial and massage and to get my hair done starting at eleven. I was happy that I could have these services done at the house, because it saved a lot of time.

Sean pulled me into the bedroom and closed the door. "This party is going to take us one step closer to our wedding. I can't wait to have you here with me all the time."

"We really didn't discuss that, did we?"

"I know you don't want to move here, do you?"

I had already given this question some thought. "We can split our time between both locations. We both have business here and in Chicago, so we can plan to be at the same place at the same time. I just want to be with you, Sean."

He started undressing me and I let him. At first I felt awkward because I knew his mother and his aunt were nearby, but it got so good that I forgot about them totally and just let go. Sean had me moaning, not realizing that the window was open and his mother and aunt were on the patio below. I had thought we were going to make love, but he fucked me real good. After we showered and got ready for our massages, we joined Sean's mother and aunt on the patio.

Aunt Frances said innocently, "Did the masseuse arrive?"

"No, they aren't scheduled to be here until eleven," I said.

"Oh, I heard all of that moaning. I didn't know what that was."

I was so embarrassed, I just looked away. Sean started laughing.

"What's so funny, Sean?"

"Nothing, Mama, I just thought about something."

"Was that the doorbell?" I said, dying to escape. "Let me go and see."

The limousine arrived at three thirty, and Sean gave us a tour of the ship. There was a ballroom where the main event would be held and three bars. The decorations were beautiful. The weather was perfect at eighty degrees, and there was a sunny blue sky.

Our guests began to arrive at approximately four o'clock. Sean and I stood on deck to greet them as they arrived. He had invited some of the artists he worked with, a lot of people I'd met over time just being with him, and a lot of his friends that I hadn't met. Grandma, Larry, and Stacy came out from Greenwood, and his friend Lester and his date came out from Detroit. I was happy to see Ray and Tiffany when they arrived. They were still going strong.

Everyone kept asking to see my ring and telling me how lucky I was. I hoped they were telling Sean that he was lucky, too.

We took the yacht with our guests for a sunset cruise and partied offshore for hours.

Around midnight, I saw Sean staring at me from across the room and I smiled. A few minutes later, he whispered in my ear, "Take a walk with me, baby." He slipped his hand in mine and kissed me. "Come on. I have a surprise for you."

I followed Sean to the upper deck. Two chairs facing the shoreline awaited us. A bottle of Krug was chilling in an ice bucket.

"Have a seat, Jasmine."

Sean opened the champagne. I could hear everyone belowdecks having a great time. The music was good, the food was perfect, and I had never been happier in my life.

Sean handed me a glass. "Jasmine, I love you."

"I love you, too, Sean, and I promise to do everything I can to make you happy."

"You already have by saying you'll be my wife. I'll try to be the man you want me to be, Jasmine. I'm not perfect, and there will be times that you're mad at me, but please always remember that I love you and would never do anything intentionally to hurt you. I want to give you the world. Will you let me?"

"Yes, Sean, it's me and you now."

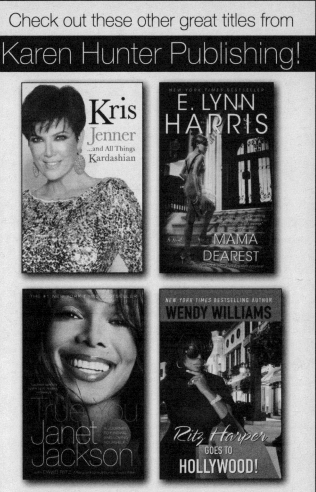